D0629241

HALFWAY HOME

HALFWAY HOME

Julia Coley Duncan

ST. MARTIN'S PRESS

New York

Manufactured in the United States of America

Library of Congress Catalog Card Number 78-19845

Library of Congress Cataloging in Publication Data

Duncan, Julia Coley.
Halfway home.
I. Title.
PZ4.D9117Ha [PS3554.U4638] 813'.5'4 78-19845
ISBN 0-312-35710-9

For my mother,
with love and respect.

ACKNOWLEDGEMENTS

To these special people for their love, encouragement, and support all through the writing of *Halfway Home:* to my children Julia and Kristin for their patience with my long hours at the typewriter; to my teacher and friend, Clif Warren, without whose guidance this book would have had only one reader; to my agent Freya Manston for her unfailing belief in *Halfway Home;* to my patient and talented editor, Marcia Markland; a most special thank you to my uncle, John Coley, for his perceptive editing and continual encouragement; and to Judy Bond, thanks for that rare and magical gift, a childhood friendship that has lasted a lifetime.

HALFWAY
HOME

CHAPTER 1

FAINTLY, from deep in the pasture behind the house, came the choppy yapping of a pair of blue tick hounds whose sleep had been disturbed. "That's Cookie just slipping away from her house," Annie thought. She had better hurry or Cookie would beat her, and half of the fun would be getting there first, crouching behind a dew-blackened log—ready to pounce. Annie dropped the last few feet from the crab apple tree beside her window to the ground. If she cut straight through the grassy side yard instead of going around by the sidewalk, she could still beat Cookie to the railroad tracks and be at Hank's place first. Gathering her nightgown under her arms and across her stomach, she ran, stepping high.

At the edge of the side yard, where the moon cast a shadow in front of the canebrake, Annie stopped and glanced back. No lights in any of the windows. No plaintive cries from Ruth-baby, her three-year-old sister and bedmate. Only her own dark footprints, streaked across the gleaming grass. Annie shivered in her white summer gown. "They're not going to catch me," she whispered to no one.

She and Cookie had made many other summer-night forays: back and forth to each others' houses, to the barn, even down by the creek once to wade in the warm water in the middle of the night. But they had never left Annie's father's property at night before. Now, as she stood at the edge of the yard, everything looked strange and threatening, wrapped in long, dark shadows.

Crossing the driveway that led back to the Petuses' house with its white fluted columns, Annie headed toward the railroad tracks. In Winton, the railroad tracks cut straight through town, then curved around the Petuses' bass pond and the scuppernong vine at the very back of the pasture owned by Annie's father Laurence Trammell and headed north.

Annie skirted the edge of the woods until she found the almost overgrown cowpath now kept passable only by wild children and Hank Ketchum, who lived—at the town's obscure pleasure—in a tar-paper and corrugated-tin shack that looked across the tracks toward the loading dock of the Coca-Cola Company. Hank was a thick-necked, barrel-chested man whose long arms usually swung loosely at his sides unless he was working. His broad face was always dirty and covered with a week-or-so's black stubble. Summer and winter he wore layer on layer of ragged, outlandish clothes. Though he kept mostly to himself, he would work all day at another man's job for a handful of change or a bottle of pop, no matter how heavy or dirty the work. To the children of Winton, Hank Ketchum was an important enigma. His strange clothes and fierce appearance struck terror in their hearts. Older boys sometimes taunted him or threw small stones at him from a safe distance. Yet everyone knew that, if you found a wounded animal or a bird with a broken wing, the best you could do for it was to take it to the edge of the clearing beside Hank Ketchum's shack and leave it there. This contradiction never bothered the children who shared the woods and fields of Winton with Hank; they were content to relish both his scariness and his gentle, healing touch.

Just as a low pine branch swacked Annie softly on the side of her face, the path deepened into a shallow trough, then pitched sharply downward toward the tracks. Annie felt the fall of the land too late. With gravel bruising her still winter-soft feet and Johnson grass cutting into her fingers, she slithered noisily into the frightening blackness behind Hank Ketchum's shack.

A collision with a long black log stretching across the path knocked the scream back down Annie's throat and stopped her over-eager rush toward the bottom of the bank. The "log" gave a low groan of protest as it sat up. In the dim light, Cookie's eyes shone, emphasizing the blackness of her skin.

"Cookie Holloway, you tripped me," Annie whispered.

"Tripped you? Is that all the thanks I get for saving your life—for the third time!"

Annie snorted. "Anybody that would call it lifesaving to lend me a pair of socks and underpants after they pushed me into Coosa Creek in the first place, well, they been eating too many snake berries."

As her eyes gradually adjusted to the shadows in the path's trough, Annie could see Cookie's white teeth (even where the front one had a small chip gone), the silhouette of one cheek, and the dull glow the moon raised from her dark forehead. The fierce scowls and squints she used to punctuate every sentence were invisible in the darkness, but Annie could see the whites of her eyes swiftly expanding and contracting—now almost round, now oval, now only two tiny slits, and she supplied the missing parts of every expression automatically.

Now Cookie shook her head. "I suppose you don't count the time I pushed you off the Green Mountain trestle where you stood glued to the crossties grinning like a Chessie cat at the Georgia Pacific coming down on you like a ton of bricks."

"I was just fixing to jump myself—only to the left where that mossy bank is. As it was, it was just one more time you found an excuse to throw me in Coosa Creek."

"Never mind," said Cookie, "with you, there's bound to be hundreds more lifesavings to come. You beat all I've ever seen for upsetting things."

"Are you ready to quit talking now and swear in?"

"Of course, I'm ready. Why else would I be out here traipsing around in my nightgown?" Cookie said.

But as Annie pushed herself to one knee, Cookie suddenly grabbed her arm and pulled her back down beside her.

"What are we going to do?" she whispered.

"What do you mean? Just like we planned. Reach in Hank's window, grab one of his big toes, and swear the summer in."

Annie started to push up, but Cookie held fast, and she bumped down again, this time with a muffled yelp, into the wet Johnson grass.

"What's the matter now?" Annie asked, rubbing her hip and peering into Cookie's face, which now plainly reflected her misgivings.

Cookie reached out to finger the small pin hanging

from a chain around Annie's neck. "Don't you guess it would be just as good to be blood sisters? We could draw blood with your Sunday school attendance pin."

Annie shook her head. "We've been sworn sisters for years. This summer is special. We got to start it off that way."

"What is so special about this summer?"

Annie paused, doubtful that she could put her feelings into words. All year there had been little signs: her daddy teasing her about being his late bloomer; her mother mumbling in despair over each skinned knee and torn hem. Even Mrs. Wheeler, her sixth-grade teacher, who never seemed to notice anything except noise, had kept making references to their "last" this and that at Matthew Carter Elementary. Whenever someone acted up, there were vague threats as to what "this kind of behavior will get you in junior high." Annie herself had seen sensible girls suddenly turn soft and giggly when they reached thirteen. Cookie even claimed girls started bleeding on the inside once every month in seventh grade. True, it sounded unbelievable, but Cookie was often right about the most unbelievable things, and it sounded just awful enough to satisfy Annie's sense of impending doom.

There was no way around it. Life—which had been barely tolerable except for summers—would soon become intolerable year round. In the middle of this bleak outlook lay one small jewel—one last summer, to be savored and, above all, protected from outside encroachments.

Despairing of an answer Cookie sighed, "Never mind, I don't guess Mama would have approved anyway, that being a Presbyterian pin and me being a deepwater

Baptist and all."

Annie got up, pulled Cookie to her feet, and pushed her lightly toward Hank Ketchum's dark shack. "Hey, Cookie," she whispered after her, "if you're my sister, is Rose my mother-in-law?"

Cookie shrugged her shoulders without looking around. "I don't know about that, but if Mama ever finds out what we been up to tonight, you can just take my place 'cause my time on this earth will be up."

Down the last few feet of the path to the small back window of the shack, they crept. The crude shutter was propped up like the raised eyebrow of a one-eyed man.

Standing on tiptoe, Annie could just make out Hank's shadowy bulk stretching from the door on the opposite side of the shack all the way across the small room. The only place for his feet was flat against the wall just under Cookie and Annie's heads, unless, of course, he wanted his head right in the draft from the window summer and winter.

Pinching their shoulders tightly together and bracing their toes on the bottom board, Cookie and Annie squeezed their arms and shoulders through the narrow window. Daintily, using only her thumb and forefinger, Annie raised one corner of a faded old crazy quilt that hid Hank's feet.

The bottoms of his feet were as red as the red clay of the bank behind them, and there seemed to be an inch-thick layer of calluses every place except his soft vulnerable-looking arches.

Annie leaned in. The small room smelled as if someone had made a stew of creosoted logs, car oil, and damp clay and left the pot to simmer while Hank slept.

Cookie gave Annie a nudge, and they each caught one warm toe, big as a walnut, and in hushed voices chanted softly together:

By all that's blue and green,
And all summer's colors inbetween,
I swear to make this summer mine,
Free of school, and shoes, and ladies fine.

Cookie's voice was a soft, clear soprano. Annie's voice was a little lower, not quite so true, but true enough to make Hank Ketchum declare at the loading dock the next morning that angels had come to him in a dream last night and sung him to the sweetest rest he'd had since his mama died.

Just as the last soft words were caught away in the sighing pines, a low groan from the other end of Hank Ketchum sent Annie and Cookie in dirt-spraying retreat back up the worn pathway.

In perfect step, their bare feet slapped softly on the pine-straw-covered path. Neither stopped nor looked back until they were in the thickest part of the canebrake just past the Petuses' driveway.

As the rustling canes quieted again, Cookie leaned over, her hands on her bent knees, trying to still her noisy breathing. Annie felt a wave of giggles stirring just above her stomach. Placing both her hands over her mouth, she coughed, rolling her eyes wildly. Cookie pounded her on the back until tears ran down both her cheeks.

"Boy, this summer's going to be different, all right," Cookie said. "I can feel it in my bones."

Annie felt a trickle of despair. Cookie did not

understand at all. "Not different," she explained. "The same. This summer is the last real summer we'll ever have, most likely. So the same is more special than different. Understand?"

Cookie's face suddenly sobered. "We're almost not kids anymore. Is that what you mean, Annie?" The thought held them both silent. Then, shaking herself to dispel her gloomy thoughts, Cookie spoke again, "But even if we was to grow up, we'd still be sisters. That won't ever change."

"Hush," Annie answered. "We're gonna have one rule for this summer, and that is everything the same. If anything at all is gonna be different, it can wait until next September."

Cookie nodded. "That'll be plenty soon for me. I got to get home now. Otis is a light sleeper. He might miss me pretty soon." Cookie always called her father Otis, like everybody else did. "See you in the morning."

Annie felt herself blushing and turned her face into the shadows of the canebrake. "I'd better not."

"What you mean, 'Better not?'"

"Got to go somewhere."

"Well, where then?" demanded Cookie, not to be put off.

"Up to the Petuses' house. She's having some sort of to-do."

Cookie's eyes widened in genuine shock. "She's only got boys. Is that what you call keeping things the same, Annie Trammell, going to a boy-girl party at silly Willy Petus's?"

"'Course not," blurted Annie in a burst of relief. "Miss Florence has got this niece from Fayetteville coming to visit, and she's having one of those coke parties for girls for her, so she can make some friends. It doesn't mean a thing. Why, I might even be out of there before you finish your chores. You head that way as soon as you finish. I'll meet you at the side door of their house, just by the statue of that naked boy."

"I thought you told me that wasn't naked, that was art," Cookie retorted, but she grinned as she turned toward home.

Cookie's long, thin arms moved as she ran, angled sharply at the waist. Her strides were long and eager, heedless of her long nightgown. At the barbed wire fence, her ghostly form bent, then disappeared into the pasture.

For a few minutes Annie stood nursing an unaccustomed feeling of loneliness. She longed to race after Cookie and finish the night curled up in her lumpy hideaway bed. Her mother would have a conniption fit. "There are some things, Annie, one just does not do," her mother said whenever Annie asked to stay the night at Cookie's.

Restlessly Annie turned to look at her own dark house and lifted her gown for the dash across the wet grass, when an excited giggle and the soft, hollow applause of the clapping canes froze her flight. Quickly she dropped to her hands and knees behind the thick leaves of a low sprout, her heart pounding in her chest. If whoever it was turned around and really looked her way, surely they would see her white gown, gleaming now as Cookie's had where the moon's rays pierced the canes.

"You do beat all," whispered a girl's voice she knew she had heard but couldn't place. "The idea of dragging a girl out this time of the night. You boys are all the same."

A hoarse answering whisper came. "You didn't have to come. Don't have to stay."

"Mr. Big Shot. And only fifteen, too!"

"I'm big enough to shut your mouth, Wadine Pratt!"

Annie gulped. It was only B.C., Cookie's brother, and Wadine Pratt, that dumb white girl that came to help out at the Petus house in the summertime. She started to call out, but for a moment her relief held her limply in her place.

A wild giggle, shivery and unnatural, sent a new wave of apprehension through her.

"Your hands are cold as ice."

"They'll get warmer," B.C.'s voice came back, taut now with an anxiety Annie had never heard in it before.

Annie rose to her knees, meaning to flee toward the safety of her own house, but the black and white scene before her cut into her unexpecting, unprepared brain.

B.C.'s long, black fingers jerked, trembling over a tangle of buttons on Wadine Pratt's white blouse. Her small, white brassiere rode up around her neck like a piece of ragged rope as B.C. half-pushed, half-lowered her backward against the rattling canes.

To Annie, the noise seemed deafening, but Wadine only shushed B.C. lightly and asked him did he plan to invite the whole neighborhood.

At last the blouse relented and hung open, puffed sleeves clinging like epaulettes to her shoulders. B.C. groaned and rocked back on his heels.

"Well?" Wadine demanded, arching her back against the canes so that her small, pale breasts caught the moon's light.

Silence, as cold and painful as fingers stuck to an ice

tray, held even the whispering canes still.

Annie's stomach heaved and bitterness filled her mouth. If B.C. sees me, if B.C. ever knows, he'll kill me, she thought. For the B.C. she knew was proud, a relentless tease with a hair-trigger temper. Her knees throbbed; she dug her fingers into the damp earth to hold them still.

B.C. continued to lean back on his heels, arms hanging limply by his sides, head bowed.

A harsh, shrill laugh sent a shudder down Annie's spine. "You don't *know!*" Wadine hissed. She struggled to raise herself on one elbow, her arms partially pinned by her twisted blouse.

"I do too know," protested B.C.

"Well, then?" Wadine said, impatiently waggling a plump knee.

On all fours, B.C. crept closer to Wadine, until he knelt almost between her knees. Matter of factly Wadine lifted her hips. With violently trembling fingers, B.C. began to tug awkwardly. At last, after a desperate jerk, Wadine's bright pink pants slid down her thighs, pulling her knees together.

"Oh God," moaned B.C., staring down at Wadine, who now looked like a roped calf.

"You hurry up," Wadine whispered loudly. "This ain't exactly no comforter I'm laying on."

B.C. lifted one hand. It waved in the air irresolutely, and he glanced nervously back toward the grassy field shimmering behind him. His voice seemed to jump out of him, a frog's ragged croak.

"Wadine, it's getting awful late."

"So what?"

"Maybe we should go now . . . We could always come back tomorrow night," he added in a low voice.

Wadine struggled to raise herself on one elbow, and something in her blouse gave with a thin, ripping sound.

"You got me climbing out windows, running around in the middle of the night, lying here on the bare ground freezing my behind off, and you don't even know."

"I do too," B.C. protested, "I . . . I just don't want to right now."

Wadine jerked furiously at her brassiere, then sat up and began buttoning her blouse.

"Well, don't worry," she blurted, "you didn't really think I'd have anything to do with a black boy, did you?"

Pulling at her pants, she tried to rise at the same time, furious at her slowness and her awkward position.

Finally getting to her feet, she stood stiffly over B.C.'s kneeling form. "If you ever come near me again, I'll . . ."

"Wadine," B.C. began.

Wadine tossed her head. "Don't you ever say my name again, you dirty-mouthed nigger." She gave a hitch on her skirt. "Mama says a girl can't be too careful of her reputation."

Annie saw B.C.'s fingers dig into the soft earth, but he said nothing.

A look of sly cunning appeared on Wadine's broad face. "Maybe I oughta just holler rape and have you hung right here and now."

With a jerk, B.C.'s head came up, and Annie saw a mixture of disbelief and fear struggle on his face. After one last satisfied toss of her head, Wadine wheeled and walked quickly toward the drive leading to the Petuses' house.

B.C. stared tight-lipped after her retreating figure. "God damn you, Wadine Pratt. God damn you," he whispered. Then he flung himself full-length on the ground and cried.

When at last B.C. left, cutting across the grass and ducking under the fence exactly where Cookie had, Annie sank to the ground, her forehead on cool, damp earth heavy with the smell of mushrooms and leaf mold.

A wave of shudders along her back and legs left Annie feeling weak, glad to be hugging the dark, crumbly earth. Refusing to think about what she had just seen, she kept her eyes shut tight and visualized the scene about her as it looked from her bedroom window—a silver lake bordered by familiar landmarks, its purity unbroken. After a long time she raised her head and, keeping her eyes resolutely on her house, she walked toward home.

As she climbed shakily back over her windowsill, she heard her mother's faraway, peevish cough. Ruth-baby had curled up tightly around Annie's pillow as if she were depending on it to float her until morning.

Annie quickly balled up her wet nightgown and poked it behind the radiator, shivered into a pair of jeans, then a T-shirt (no sense in dressing twice) and, giving Ruth-baby a push, reclaimed her side of the bed and her pillow.

As she huddled against Ruth-baby's warm back, the hall clock struck the hour (was that two or three strikes she'd counted?) and a short burst of staccato barking came from the pasture. Everyone was home again.

* * *

When Annie opened her eyes, the bed beside her was

empty and the sunlight had crept all the way across the room to the fireplace. She felt as if she had not slept at all. Wearily she closed her eyes again, but a vivid picture of B.C. and Wadine, their bodies intertwined awkwardly, made her open them immediately. Annie pressed a fist against her pounding heart and spoke to the silent room. "I'll tell Rose," she said, and the moment the words were spoken she knew she would not tell a soul, not even Cookie, what she had seen in the canebrake.

With an effort, she threw back the sheet, stood in the center of her bed, and made three walloping bounces, the way she did every morning. On the way down the last time, she heard her mother's voice calling from the breakfast room.

"Elizabeth Anne, stop that jumping and get yourself down here immediately. It's almost nine o'clock. And don't put on those awful blue jeans. Come down like you are."

Vaulting from the bed to the floor, Annie called back so her mother wouldn't send Rose up after her. "I'm coming, Mama."

Shoving her jeans and shirt into a drawer, she grabbed the by-now-dry nightgown from behind the radiator and raced for the stairs with the garment still coming down over her head.

Her mother sat at the far end of the table in a lavender robe that made a startling foil for her dark red hair. She was as small and well-knit as Annie's father was tall and lanky.

He sat at the near end of the table, his light brown hair so streaked with gray that it looked dusty as he bent over the morning paper. After a moment, he turned and pushed his glasses back against the bridge of his narrow nose. Annie paused at the doorway, her eyes on her father. She had often been told she was the spitting image of this tall, thin man with the pale, freckled skin.

"Annie, just look at your gown. What on earth were you wrestling last night?" her mother asked, not for an answer. "When will you learn just to lay there and sleep?"

"Now, Louise," her father spoke, "she can't very well help how she sleeps." For a moment he studied Annie with what seemed to be academic interest, then returned to his paper.

Louise Trammell tucked a strand of hair back into place and reached into her robe pocket for her handkerchief. "That's fine for you to say. How do you know that Ruth-baby's safe sleeping in the same bed with Annie?" She lifted her handkerchief to her mouth to cover a paroxysm of coughing that made her eyes look weak and unfocused and left a bright red circle on each cheek.

"Now, Louise," Laurence replied, "I didn't mean to start your cough again."

Louise called out toward the kitchen, "Rose, if you could just bring me two of those pink pills . . ."

"Yes'm, right away," came a rich, deep voice right back, as Rose Holloway, Cookie's mother, backed her broad hips through the swinging door to the kitchen and cautiously turned toward the table with a tray holding a bowl of steaming oatmeal for Annie.

Rose gave Annie's crumpled nightgown such a piercing glance that Annie ducked her head to stare at the bowl Rose plunked down noisily in front of her.

Rose stood her ground, the empty tray hanging from the hand on her hip. "Did you sleep well last night,

Annie?" she asked. Annie couldn't look up.

"My pills, Rose, my pills," Louise reminded her.

Rose wiped the back of her heavy arm across her damp forehead. "Yes'm," she said, backing through the door again, her eyes still keeping Annie pinned to her chair.

From behind his newspaper, Laurence Trammell made a noise. "It made the paper," he muttered. "I wouldn't have thought that it would."

Louise frowned. "What made the paper? Why must you always speak in riddles?"

Looking up as if surprised to find that someone had been listening, Laurence smiled. "It's only that yesterday there was a bit of a ruckus, right in front of the First National. Ben Reilly, one of the street sweepers, accidentally got Mel Decker's pants all dirty with his broom. Well, Mel got all hot under the collar, like he always does about everything, and demanded an apology and I don't know what all."

"I don't blame him one bit."

Laurence shrugged his shoulders. "Well, Ben, he was doing his dead-level best to apologize, but he couldn't get a word in edgewise. Then, bless pat, if that new, young colored pastor over at the Emanuel Methodist Church doesn't just step right up and say that it wasn't Ben's fault anyway, that Mel had not been looking where he was going, and he should be apologizing to Ben."

"Why, that's outrageous," Louise protested. "Something ought to be done."

As Annie watched, a flicker of humor touched her father's pale eyes. "Maybe enough was done. It set Mel Decker's blood pressure back about ten years and scared Ben Reilly half to death."

"You know that's not what I mean at all. Something ought to be done about that man who calls himself a preacher." Louise's gaze seemed to look out over their heads. "If my papa were alive . . . "

Carefully rolling his napkin and pulling it back into its silver ring, his face still and watchful, Laurence Trammell pushed his chair away from the table.

With a little shake of her head, Louise turned her attention back to Annie. "Laurence, don't you dare leave this house without speaking to Annie about her behavior."

Annie's oatmeal reversed itself in her throat. She smoothed her nightie across her chest as hard as she could with the palms of her hands; then, noticing her knuckles were still etched with red clay, she quickly sat on them.

"Now, Louise," her father began, "she's only a child. It doesn't seem as if it should be necessary at her age."

"If you didn't know it, ladies don't just happen. And besides, she is not just a child. This very morning, she is going up to Florence Petus's house to a party for her young niece from Fayetteville."

Her father stood behind his chair, straight as a poker, his hands resting lightly on the chairback. "I hear the poor child's mother is fighting a morphine addiction at that place in South Carolina."

"Laurence, talk to Annie!"

Anxiously Annie waited, wondering which sin she had been caught at, if not her trip last night, and what pleasure she and Cookie would have to forego for the next week.

Tentatively her father touched his tongue to his lips. "Annie, your mother and I feel that it is time for you to change your . . . that is, to polish up your manners a bit . . .

I think that is how you women put it." He stopped, looking down at Annie with a puzzled frown. "After all, Annie, you'll soon be a woman, just like your mother here, and you need to start meeting other young ladies your own age."

Out of the corner of her eye, Annie saw her mother nod.

"There, Louise, dear. Everything's all set. Annie can spend the next several weeks getting to know little . . .?"

"Mary Ellen."

"Whatever, they'll both be the richer for it, I'm sure," her father answered as he turned to walk down the long hall toward the living room.

Her mother pushed her plate carefully away from her and leaned back, a rare light in her eyes.

Leaning disconsolately on her elbows, Annie glanced at her mother and could almost see the young planter's daughter her father had described bringing to this house for the first time sixteen years ago. After that triumphant arrival, the story became unclear, at least to Annie. They had married late in life and childbirth, which had come even later, had broken her mother's health. Now she rarely bothered with the day-to-day job of running the household and rearing two daughters. All this she left to Rose. Her thoughts seemed preoccupied by memories of her happy, pampered childhood.

"Rose," she called now, staring at Annie's face as if she were looking for mealy bugs on a camellia bush, "Elizabeth Anne is due at a coke party at Miss Florence's house at ten o'clock. Will you see to it—before you do anything else today—that she is clean from one end to the other? I mean, you better go up with her yourself. I swear I don't think she knows the ins and outs of her own ears yet.

And that pale green dotted swiss with the velvet sash should be just right. If it still fits. It wouldn't be the first time she's outgrown a dress before I ever got it on her."

"Mama," Annie ventured, without much real hope, "I don't want to go to the party."

Her mother frowned. "Hush, dear, of course you do."

Annie shook her head with determination, and her mother's eyes widened. "Not want to go to a party? Why, at your age I'd been to a dozen parties." For a moment a smile touched her lips, but it was chased by another attack of coughing that left her breathless.

Rose stuck her broad, black face through the swinging door that led to the kitchen. "Don't you worry, Miss Louise. She'll be ready and shiny as a new tin roof," she said, wiping her wet hands on her apron.

Annie rose and moved slowly along the wall to the other swinging door leading into the hall.

"—and don't you move one other muscle, Miss Annie, not one, if you and that shouting-to-be-heard nightie know what's good for you," she finished, shouldering her way back into the kitchen without even bothering to see if Annie was again in her place at the table.

A short while later, Annie's painfully amplified screams reverberated in the small, upstairs tile bathroom. She had backed against the lavatory, her eyes shut tight and both hands clamped protectively over her ears.

"You've broken my ear. It was my best ear, and it'll never hear again."

No response. The bathroom was completely quiet except for the drippy faucet. Annie opened one eye. Rose smiled and tugged at the kerchief tied around her short grizzled hair. She had leaned her broad bottom against the bathroom door, cutting off Annie's only avenue of escape.

"Well, then," Rose answered complacently, "my only sorrow is that you don't do your walking on that ear. Don't think I don't know that you and Cookie were out juning around last night till all hours while decent folks were sleeping. Fell in the creek again in your nightgown, didn't you? Now how do you think your mama's going to cotton to that?"

Annie held rigidly still. Rose had an absolute gift for making you think she was going down one track, when all the time she was circling around behind you, laying the way smooth as cream for you to talk yourself out of two weeks' dessert.

Deciding that right now was not the time for a discussion, Annie mutely offered her other ear. Rose was so taken aback that she washed it as gently as Annie had seen her dry new baby chickens: She even agreed to let Annie tuck her new jackknife in her pocket under her handkerchief "for safety's sake." For, as Annie put it to her, "Your life isn't worth a hot popsicle at William Petus's house unless he knows you aren't just another simpering girl."

By a quarter till ten, Annie was ready. As Rose jerked and poked a few last times at some sort of bow she'd tied right on top of Annie's head, Annie took a quick, furtive, downward look at herself. She could just see the fronts of new, white patent shoes. They were perfect crescent moons. Her pale-green, white-flecked skirt reminded Annie of a strange, wonderful creature she had found last year in Coosa Creek, hugging the sandy bottom under the footbridge. She felt an unaccustomed warmth in her arms and neck, as if she'd just had one of Rose's hugs.

"There, that's the best I can do," muttered Rose, stepping back. "Child, you sure are growing, aren't you? Never mind, it happens to the best of us," she said, giving Annie a brusque hug. "Now, I'm going to take off this here apron. Your mama said I'm to deliver you like a quart of milk right into Miss Florence's waiting arms. In one minute, you get yourself downstairs and nowhere else, you hear? We're going the front way, on the sidewalk. You're a lady today, or my name is gonna be Black Rose for sure."

Rose began her slow rolling walk toward the stairs. At the top step, she called back up again. "Now you come straight on down, Annie Trammell. There's no time for lollygagging this morning."

"I'm coming, I'm coming," Annie answered, but she didn't get the tone just like she meant to. Passing up and down at the foot of the bed, she contemplated just throwing herself spread-eagle across it and howling until her mama was sure to know that she had finally pushed her too far; but reluctantly, almost with shame, she found herself wondering what it would do to the stiffly starched dotted swiss and her velvet sash, soft as pussy-willow buds between her fingers.

Tears of indecision filled her eyes. Maybe her mama was right. Maybe parties and such things were important. She felt so sad and lovely standing there, her arms resting lightly on her skirt. With a rare twinge of curiosity, Annie turned slowly toward the free-standing mirror in the corner. She had thrown her T-shirt over the top of the mirror, so her face wasn't visible. But below the T-shirt, before her horrified eyes, Truth mocked her flirtation with Beauty. Her elbows and wrists were so prominent they made her arms look disjointed. And her arms! They hung down, down, down—a good three inches below her indecent dress. The dress looked like it should be on short, fat Ruth-baby. The full skirt made her legs look thinner than ever; her shinbones reflected the light like Grampa Trammell's cavalry sword. The green velvet ribbon rode high up on her stomach so that it seemed as if her legs must be attached just under her armpits. Her mirror told her plainly, without any double talk: She wasn't just ugly, she had seen that in her mother's eyes long ago—she was deformed! Well, she didn't have to have her nose rubbed in it. And she certainly didn't have to be exhibit number one at any coke party.

Her fists clenched, Annie bolted for the stairs. Not even bothering with the smooth, mahogany banisters for a change, she launched herself outward from the top of the stair, landing blindly, her feet pumping wildly, ready to deliver her from wherever she landed to the farthest place she could find from mirrors, dotted swiss, and coke parties.

With some vague instinct for survival she realized and was grateful that something soft and resilient had broken her fall. But still blind with anger and the fear of being stopped, she never quit pumping her legs, though a vise seemed to be clamped across her shoulders.

"And just where you off to?" bellowed Rose, her arm flung across Annie's chest. "It's a miracle you didn't break every bone in my body." She swayed uncertainly to her knees, pushing with her free hand against the bottom step. "The Lord knows I never thought I'd see the day I'd be offering up a prayer for Miss Florence Petus, but I do believe I could manage a sincere one this morning, if I kept it short."

Suddenly Annie burst into tears. Rose collapsed sideways onto the stair tread and took her onto her lap for the first time in almost a year. "Now, what on earth's making you fuss so? All dressed up, going to a fancy party—that's nothing to cry over, child."

"Do I have to go, Rose? Really have to?"

"As I see it, I reckon you do," Rose answered gruffly. "It won't last long, honey. You might even like that little girl. Anyway I bet she's lonesome up there with only Willy and Joe-Joe Petus for company. She'll be much obliged to you for coming." She pulled Annie's arms slowly from around her neck. "Now, you go show your mama how sweet you look, and we'll start out. No more tricks, now, I'm getting too old to keep up with you rascals."

As Annie reluctantly pushed open the door to her mother's dimly lit room, she was surprised to see her still up, sitting in her Boston rocker, which she had drawn up close beside the window.

Without being asked, her mother offered, "Can't stay up much longer, but I did want to get a good look at you all dressed up before I have to tuck myself back in that old bed again. Hand me that bottle of whitish medicine as you come, will you, dear? I've got a terrible stomach this morning. And I've been good as gold about not eating anything at all that's interesting."

Carrying the bottle in front of her, Annie stopped just close enough to put it in her mother's outstretched hand.

"Well, now, let's see you," her mother said, and Annie turned around slowly, holding her arms stiffly at her sides.

"Why, Annie, you look lovely," her mother said, but her smile seemed to be directed to someone far away. "When I was thirteen, I had a dress not too different from that one. It was pale yellow with tucks across the bodice. I counted those tucks—there were sixty-three of them. Imagine my remembering that! It was Papa who taught me the importance of good grooming. I will never understand how your father can be so oblivious to . . . to the niceties of life."

Through the down-tilted venetian blind, Annie could see only one narrow slot of world. It was like standing with your head bowed in church. A mangy bantam rooster that must have strayed from Rose's house wrestled halfheartedly with a worm under a Peace rose, then wandered out of Annie's view with a single, haughty step.

Her mother smoothed her skirt over her knees. "When I was a little girl, I had everything a little girl dreams of. I slept in a big canopied bed with more dolls than I could count—the very one you and Ruth-baby sleep in now." Her mother's narrow nostrils quivered and Annie twisted her sash, anxious to be gone. She had heard all this before, and it made her feel more hopeless than ever.

"In the afternoons there were tea parties and croquet on the lawn. All the little girls in town used to love to come to my house because I had a little pony and a cart. I wore a gold locket . . ." Her mother's voice faded, and she began biting on her lip. Then, with a look of resigned determination, she turned her gaze on Annie. Annie fought an impulse to cry out for Rose.

"Can you imagine what my papa would have said about torn hems and lost sashes and, heaven help us, blue jeans?"

Annie dropped the corner of her twisted sash, praying her mother would not notice it.

"The Fairbaults lived in the Delta for five generations, and not a one of them would have dreamed of living any place else or doing anything else except running The Place."

From previous encounters with her mother, Annie understood that The Place was something that was more, much more, than a farm, more like a plantation. But her mother felt that "plantation" sounded the least bit too . . . something . . . so it was better just to say "The Place" with a little emphasis in your voice that left everybody wondering how many acres in a Place.

Her mother's mouth drooped. "Not one of them ever worked so much as a day in a store, though that's a fine thing to do, I'm sure. It's just that the Fairbaults never did . . ." Again her voice trailed away, and Annie felt Rose, standing just behind her, draw herself up and deliberately pull in a deep breath. Something in Rose's manner seemed to make her mother uncomfortable, for she twisted her hands in her lap and dropped her gaze. Annie could only think how lucky she was that all the Fairbaults were dead. They would have hated her on sight.

"I'm only telling you these things, Annie," her mother said with a quick, petulant glance at Rose, "so that you'll know who you are. 'Blood will tell,' Papa used to always say."

With a tiny shiver, her mother pulled a shawl closer about her shoulders and, forgetting Annie, turned to stare out the window.

Standing in the doorway, Rose beckoned cautiously to Annie, her hand down low. "Miss Louise," she said, "you better get some rest now. And don't you worry, I'll deliver

Annie to her party, an unblemished lamb." As she turned, she added under her breath, "the Lord willing."

But Louise Trammell did not answer. The old memories seemed to have had a disturbing effect on her. She began to rock back and forth in her chair, tapping the smooth arms of her rocker. To Annie she looked as if she were struggling with some unspoken urge, a positive itch. The strange inner struggle went on until Annie felt an answering tingle in her own scalp.

For a few moments, she leaned closer to her mother, dispassionately studying her puzzling behavior. Then as a new thought struck her, she jerked suddenly backward into the venetian blind and it fell to the floor with a crash. "Rose," she whispered hoarsely, "I think maybe Mama's having a fit."

Either the falling blind or the accusation seemed to wrench her mother from her far-off battlefield. She narrowed her eyes against the glare and glanced down indignantly at the venetian blind splayed out across her feet. "It's no more than I deserve," she said, glancing at Annie.

Annie wondered what it was her mother deserved—the venetian blind or Annie herself. Her mother's pronouncements always seemed to have two meanings.

"But it's not too late. After all, with the good bloodlines ..."

Reluctantly Annie ruled out the venetian blinds.

"It's just a matter of time and dedication . . ."

Annie took a couple of mincing, backward steps toward the door.

". . . and we have the whole summer ahead of us. Why, it will be fun. Parties, pretty dresses." Louise Trammell smiled vaguely toward the spot where Annie had been standing. "She just needs a mother's finishing touch."

Once she was safely in the hall, Annie looked back even though she meant not to. The room was flooded with unaccustomed light; and her mother pushed her rocker gently to and fro, keeping time with her words, the venetian blind still caught on her foot. Opening and closing like a child's dissonant accordion, it came in on each downbeat of the rocker.

Turning from the glare back toward the cool and shadowy front hall, Annie bumped blindly into Rose's soft stomach.

"The door's that way, sugar," Rose said softly, giving Annie's shoulders half a turn.

At the hall closet, Annie paused. "I feel chilly."

"No, it's the first day of June," said Rose, as if that settled that.

"Well, I'm cold. Maybe I'm coming down with something. Maybe I've even got a fever."

"You coming down the street with me to Miss Florence's is all you coming down with," said Rose firmly, placing a precautionary hand on Annie's shoulders.

Two white patent leather boats, long and ugly, swam through heavy mists. Annie blinked. "Rose, can't I at least wear my raincoat?"

Rose's round face seemed to pinch in on itself, like one of Cookie's scowls. It occurred to Annie that she and her mother were blood relatives, just as kin as Rose and Cookie were, and a hard shiver shook her.

"Please, Rose?"

"All right, then. Quick, get it on, and let's go. If you're any later, there probably won't even be any coke left at this everlasting coke party of yours."

Annie buttoned every button on her Sherlock Holmes raincoat, even the small one under her collar, then she pulled the belt as tight as she could around her waist. The morning seemed to have put Rose in a black mood. Annie thought she heard her mutter something about the Delta Fairbaults and her hind left leg, but she couldn't be sure; and she certainly knew better than to ask. Instead she practiced cracking her knuckles, stepping over the cracks in the sidewalk as she went.

CHAPTER 2

As THEY TURNED into the Petuses' long driveway, the sun beat a tattoo on Annie's shoulder blades. The June sunshine was ripening every leaf and bud so fast, a subliminal green haze seemed to hang in the air. Annie turned up her collar, jammed her hands into her pockets, and practiced walking with a slow roll like Hank Ketchum. She'd have that Mary Ellen Parker dreaming about going home to Fayetteville before lunch.

The Petus mansion rose before them over the tall boxwoods lining the driveway that curved around in front of the house to the side-yard turnaround. The house was only two stories high, but they were the two tallest stories in town. Everything inside and out was oversized. You couldn't just walk up the front steps. You had to put one foot on each over-long step then bring your other foot up to the same step before being able to reach the next higher one. So you felt awkward and jerky all the way to the red tile veranda that stretched the length of the house. It took both hands to turn the gleaming brass doorknob whether you were a grown-up or a child. The large rectangular brass plate behind the knob threw back at the already delicately jarred visitor a bleary, fun-house mirror image of himself that usually included a sheepish grin.

Such subtleties were lost on Annie. She strode grimly

up the grassy bank beside the steps, gazing wistfully toward the leaning rock chimney top just visible behind her own house's rooftop. That chimney belonged to Cookie's house. On the veranda, the front door was open wide; and Miss Florence Petus herself stood waiting for Annie with outstretched arms.

"Well, here comes our little cow's tail—and a pessimist to boot. Don't tell me that you think it's going to rain on Mary Ellen's first day in Winton?" Miss Florence crooned at Annie; and Rose faded quietly back down the spine-jarring steps.

"Daddy said she came in last night, on the nine-fifteen. Said she had four suitcases."

"Well, Laurence always was a stickler for details," Miss Florence said, a tiny frown creasing her broad forehead. Then she brightened. "But a visit doesn't really begin until you've had your first welcoming party, does it now?"

A skirmish began over the raincoat. As fast as Miss Florence undid one button and moved to the next, Annie buttoned the first one back again. As Annie's fingers were more agile than Miss Florence's, she had time to look around a little while waiting for Miss Florence to finish unbuttoning the next one. After the second unbuttoning and rebuttoning, Miss Florence gave Annie a long, baleful stare.

"I've got a chill," Annie explained. "It's probably catching."

When Miss Florence didn't comment, Annie drew a long breath and strode toward the living room where four girls she knew from school and a stranger who had to be Mary Ellen were sitting primly erect, hands in their laps. The four girls Annie knew sat elbow to elbow on a long, curving sofa covered in pale yellow silk, the color of new pecan tassels. Mary Ellen sat on a matching chair at the far end of the sofa. All around the room there were figurines of birds and flowers that looked real enough to confuse cats and bees. Gold damask drapes hung in long slender columns on either side of double-hung windows that reached from the floor almost to the ceiling.

Except for Racine Craig's titter, no one made a sound as they all took in Annie's Sherlock Holmes raincoat and her oversized green bow and watched her walk to the opposite end of the living room to sit on a straight-backed side chair.

"I'm Mary Ellen Parker from Fayetteville," said the stranger, her speech noticeably slow and soft though, thought Annie, Fayetteville must be at least thirty miles *north* of Winton. Before Annie had a reply to such an obvious remark, Mary Ellen gave a small gasp. "Whatever happened to your legs?"

Annie looked down curiously. Her legs from her knees to her white sock tops were covered with dozens of bright red scratches from the briar bushes in the pasture; at least half a dozen black, blue, or purple bruises from swinging on the wisteria vine; and one long strip of grazed flesh down the side of her left leg from sliding down the bank behind Hank Ketchum's shack.

She raised her head and gave Mary Ellen a blank stare. "Oh, those. I got those catching freight trains down to the Green Mountain trestle."

Four gasps simultaneously came from the direction of the sofa. Mary Ellen withheld judgment and, instead, called out loudly to her Aunt Florence that they were ready for their cokes now. Grudgingly Annie sensed that

her schoolmates were more impressed with how
unimpressed Mary Ellen was than with the notorious
Annie Trammell.

Two-Time Harris came in, wearing his short white
starched jacket and carrying six coke bottles on a tray
and a small, silver dish mounded with fudge brownies
made by his wife 'Lilly' the cook. Two-Time Harris
("Two-Time" because he was two times bigger than he
needed to be) was Cookie's uncle by marriage and a
longtime accomplice in Cookie's and Annie's more
elaborate schemes. His plump, light-brown wife Lilly,
Rose's sister, took care of cooking, cleaning, and the
general patrolling of William and Joe-Joe Petus.

Now, without taking a step, just pivoting a little at the
waist, he served each girl on the sofa and then Mary Ellen
a coke, a tiny napkin, and a fudge brownie. Only Winkie
Tomlin was fast enough to get two. His long, scooped-
out face looked so sorrowful that each girl in turn gave
him her most radiant smile and her most cheerful "Thank
you so much, Harris." All to no avail, for this was Two-
Time Harris's customary house face, and even his wife
Lilly got no different, until he stepped over the threshold
onto the back steps.

Off-duty, Two-Time had a laugh that could rattle the
windows of his small house and, on occasion, a volatile
temper that seemed to erupt for no reason at all and
resulted in broken chairs, bent forks, and once, a smashed
door. When Two-Time was angry, Lilly fluttered about
him like a kite caught in a downdraft, and her very
nervousness seemed to calm him until he would pull her
clumsily onto his knee and hold her until they both could
smile and turn again to other things.

Turning his doleful face now to Annie, Two-Time came the length of the long, narrow living room in three strides and held out the tray toward Annie as if he had never laid eyes on her before in his life.

Sitting stiffly on the edge of her chair, her face a lugubrious reflection of her comrade-in-arms' face, Annie reached out for coke. Then her hand stopped in midair.

"Two-Time, my coke's got a sock on it!" she said in amazement, staring at the knitted tubular coaster that had been pulled on over the bottom half of her coke bottle.

A laugh as cool and sweet as strawberry pie filled the room. "Why, she's never seen a coaster," said a silvery voice, and four nervous giggles, too long stifled, followed in relief.

"Have a fudge brownie, miss," Two-Time said in his saddest voice. "They're Lilly's speciality."

But that sweet laugh of Mary Ellen Parker's seemed to have glued Annie's arms to her sides. She stared up into Two-Time's red-rimmed eyes. Two-Time eased a brownie onto a tiny napkin and placed it on Annie's knee. She heard a faraway voice say, "Thank you so much, Harris," and she wondered whether she or Mary Ellen had spoken.

Mary Ellen Parker had curly hair, the gold-tinged-with-brown color of spoon bread hot from the oven. In fact, everything about her looked delicious, like something you might need to taste to fully appreciate. Three charms dangling from a gold chain on her small wrist tinkled constantly as she punctuated her words with small punches of her right forefinger. With her left hand she had effortlessly managed to balance a napkin, a brownie, and a coke on her knees. In Fayetteville, she told them, she had a pony, two sweethearts named Alton and Tom, and was secretary of her Sunday school class for the third straight year.

"Annie, why don't you take off that dumb coat before you burn up?" Racine Craig asked, eager to make some sort of contribution to such an elegant occasion.

"Yes," said Luanne Allen, "unless you think it might cloud up and rain in here."

"It wouldn't dare," said Winkie, shocked at the very idea.

Mary Ellen chimed in with her eiderdown laugh, "Well, it just might. Aunt Florence just had a sprinkler system installed." Six heads lifted to look at the white pipes running unobtrusively around the edges of the ceiling.

"I still think Annie is going to burn up in that raincoat," said Racine, not to be diverted.

As if he had been summoned, Two-Time stepped softly into the room. He nodded solemnly toward Annie and, moving behind her chair, raised a double-hung window as far as it would go, well above Annie's head. At the protesting screech of the seldom-used window, all the heads at the other end of the room turned quickly toward Annie but saw only mournful Two-Time Harris going around again with another plateful of fudge brownies.

After the discussion of the weather, there was a decided lull in the conversation. To fill the silence, Winkie kept reaching out to the coffee table and stuffing another brownie in her mouth. Annie had just stood to thank her hostess for a great time when Mary Ellen plunked her still untouched plate and coke on a tiny table beside her chair, folded her hands neatly in her lap, and asked casually,

"Would anyone care to see an alligator?"

Winkie pushed hurriedly back on the sofa as if to get her feet farther from the floor.

"An alligator!" came a mixed chorus of voices ranging from excitement to incredulity.

"Hah," said Annie, backing toward the door, the polite comment about the great time forgotten. "There are no alligators around here. Certainly not in Mr. Petus's old fish pond."

Mary Ellen rose daintily from her chair. "I didn't say in the pond. He's upstairs, in William's bathtub."

"Oh, you mean one of those little baby gators you bring back from Tampa. That's against the law, you know. You could get in lots of trouble if Sheriff Coggins finds out."

"When I say 'alligator,' I mean 'alligator,'" said Mary Ellen, walking out of the room and up the broad, curving front hall staircase.

At the end of the upstairs hallway, Mary Ellen paused, then slowly pushed open the door on her left and stood back. Her five guests peered in at once. In the semidarkness, two unblinking eyes reflected the eerie green light that filtered through the new leaves of the huge cottonwood shading William Petus's bathroom window.

"It might be a stuffed one!" Annie offered.

"Yes, it might be," allowed Mary Ellen sweetly. "Why don't you see for us, Annie?"

The other girls moved quickly aside, and Annie stepped into the dim bathroom. Half submerged, with only its nostrils and the bumpy ridge of its backbone out of the water, the alligator filled the tub end to end, give or take six inches. Annie sat on one edge of the tub and gave a halfhearted "Boo." The creature didn't even blink. She leaned lower, and shouted again, "Boo!"

A skinny fifth-grader named Frances Renfro said she bet it was almost lunchtime because she smelled fried chicken.

Feeling a strange surge of affection for the beast, Annie became as anxious as Mary Ellen to prove that the indifferent monster sulking in the tub below her was real. Bracing her hands on the opposite side of the tub, she leaned over until her mouth was almost touching what she supposed was an alligator ear. She smelled the swamp he must be pining for. "My mother wears alligator shoes!" she screamed.

Her voice bounced around the tiny room. "Alligators must be deaf," she said to the silent group of girls behind her. As she started to straighten up, the end of her raincoat belt dragged across the scaly nose. It wasn't a dragonfly or a brown toad or a crawdad, but at that moment Annie's belt seemed to give William Petus's alligator a reason for living.

Annie did not see the gator as it opened its pink maw and closed it again with a soft snap. She only saw five girlish mouths open wide—just like five baby gators following their mother through Lesson One of How to Catch Lunch. Then they thought to scream.

Hastily they backed toward the door and the gator's tail sent a plume of water after them. His powerful jaws tugged at Annie's belt as she tried to keep herself from being pulled into the churning water on top of him.

The heavy thuds on the stairway undoubtedly meant Lilly was on her way, and Annie desperately held on to the hot and cold water faucets, urging Lilly on as loudly as she could from her twisted, bent-over position. The other five girls continued their nonstop screaming from the hallway.

Just as her elbows began buckling, there was a loud tearing sound.

Winkie wailed, "She's gone. Eaten alive by an alligator."

Lilly's thunderous approach quickened noticeably, and she came heaving into the doorway.

"Annie Trammell!" she shouted loud enough to scare anything living or dead, except maybe an alligator.

Annie was sitting motionless on the floor in two inches of water, her head leaning against the tub. She and the alligator both had their eyes shut, both dreaming they were some place far away.

Lilly paused to decide where to begin and lost her chance to begin at all. For just then—with no sound of thunder, no darkening of the air, no hint of a breeze—it began to rain. Not just a nice, gentle, summer rain, but a real downpour, the kind that can last for days.

Lilly grabbed the doorknob, as if to check on where she was. Her mouth pulled slowly into a huge oval, and her eyes glazed over.

"My chicken! Oh, my Lord . . . there go the sprinklers!" Lilly's thunderous steps faded in uneven waves down the hall as she rushed headlong toward the kitchen. The five screaming girls bumped and turned around in small circles, caught in the backwash of Lilly's broad wake. Annie walked quietly through them and headed down the hall after Lilly.

Mary Ellen spoke first. "Stop screaming, you nitwits." Silence fell immediately. Then in a cool, practical voice she added. "It's raining in here. We've got to get outside."

Luanne Allen clung to Frances Renfro's neck so tightly she threatened to cut off her air. "Those sprinklers mean there is a fire," she shrieked. This idea seemed to give Frances all the courage she needed. Coming down on Luanne's foot with her long narrow one, she made a fast break toward the stairs. All five girls pushed past Annie on the staircase. The huge front door seemed too much for them in their frenzied state; and, sighting the open window in the living room, they raced through without even needing to duck their heads. From there it was only a few easy steps for most of them through Miss Florence's prize azalea bed to the lawn. It took Winkie a little longer, for she fell full-length twice before she cleared the low, spreading azalea bushes.

From the front entry, Annie watched their exit sadly. After wiping both her wet palms on the sides of her raincoat, she grasped the huge doorknob, opened the front door, and, unnoticed, walked the length of the veranda in the opposite direction. Maybe Cookie would still be waiting.

In Miss Florence's formal rose garden with its knee-high brick walls, narrow walks covered with pine-straw cut plots of spindly rosebushes into pie-shaped wedges and converged at the center on a small, cast-iron statue of a naked boy with a watering pitcher held listlessly against one shiny hip. Annie only half-expected to see Cookie. Her stomach told her noon had already come and gone. But when she stepped into the little roofless room, she saw Cookie first thing. She was sitting on the pedestal of the statue in the center of the rose garden.

Cookie and the small naked boy sat back to back, as if they had quarrelled and weren't speaking, despite the fact that the precocious boy held one arm toward heaven in supplication. Coming closer, Annie realized that Cookie was sound asleep, the back of her head resting comfortably on the boy's flat buttocks.

Without its usual parade of scowls, frowns, grins, and squints, Cookie's still face was a different thing altogether. Her soft lips were slightly parted in an undecided smile over small, even, white teeth. Her drooping lids looked almost purple in the unfiltered sunlight. A thin film of perspiration made her skin gleam, black shot with flashes of blue, just like the boy behind her.

The drone of bees intensified the feeling that the whole world must be napping. Annie swept a small bee sideways as it prepared to settle on Cookie's glistening forehead. Then, slapping her hand loudly against her raincoat, she gave a loud moan. As Cookie's head snapped forward, Annie moaned again. "Could thou not watch one hour?" she asked, pointing an accusing finger down at the still dazed Cookie.

Her eyes shaded with one hand, Cookie's stare went from Annie's wet hair to her water-darkened raincoat, then stopped, fascinated, on the shredded end of the belt which still dangled from the buckle in front.

"What on earth you been doing at that coke party of yours?"

"Wrestling alligators," Annie answered, leaning against the boy's hot metal shoulder.

Cookie cocked her head, and both girls listened to the quavery wail of the siren on the town's only fire truck. It seemed to be getting nearer and nearer. Faint screams, as long and continuous as miniature sirens, seemed to be coming from somewhere up at the Petus house.

"Lordy! Is there a fire?" Cookie leaped up hopefully.

"No, but I think we better put about fifty miles between me and Miss Florence Petus," Annie said, tugging at Cookie's sleeve.

"And miss the fire truck?!"

"It might not be the fire truck. It might be Harold Coggins coming after me!"

"The police?!" Now Cookie was really impressed and very reluctant to leave the scene of the crime or fire or whatever.

As the siren grew steadily stronger, in spite of her better judgment and sense of propriety, Annie became curious too. Perhaps it really was Harold Coggins, she thought. "Wonder what the charge will be?" she muttered and looked nervously toward the corner of the house.

"What?"

"Nothing. I just was wondering where we could watch without getting in the way," Annie said. "I hate crowds."

"Me, too," nodded Cookie emphatically. "Hey, what about William's old tree house?"

"That thing is rotten. We'll fall right through the bottom."

"Maybe it only looks rotten," suggested Cookie with a tempting grin. "A few soft boards shouldn't scare an alligator wrestler."

Annie sighed. "We better go around the back of the house and come up on it from the other side. I really *do* hate crowds."

Originally, the qualifications for entry to the Petus

boys' tree house were so stringent that Annie and Cookie
were effectively grounded. To insure privacy during
meetings, William and Joe-Joe dispensed with the usual
wooden boards nailed at intervals up the trunk of the tree.
The only access was a thick rope knotted every foot or so,
which they pulled up behind them during club meetings.

But now, the tree house was in a state of near collapse.
All the boards were spongy and green; there were gaping
holes in the floor; and the rope had snapped about
halfway up and dangled just out of Cookie's reach.

"Hurry," urged Annie, "it sounds like they're coming
around this way."

"It's no use. It's too high. We better hightail it."

"Wait a minute, Cookie. I'll give you a hand up. Lean
against the tree. Now, up on my shoulders . . . my
shoulders, I said. Can you reach the rope yet?"

"Got it," Cookie called back.

After peering into the cobwebby, tilting, little room,
Cookie appeared to be ready to come back down.

"They're coming," screeched Annie.

Cookie bolted over the doorsill and out of sight. In a
moment, she had loosened the rope from the crossbeam
where it was anchored and lowered it until Annie could
grasp the knotted end with both hands; then she retied it
and Annie scrambled up.

At the same moment, Miss Florence Petus came
around the southeast corner. The fire truck had long since
arrived and cut off its siren, but Miss Florence had kept
her smaller one going steadily. Her careful hairdo had
frizzed into a huge auburn halo, after having been
thoroughly sprinkled, then steamed dry again in the
noontime June sun. Tilting her slight body forward from

the waist as she ran, she zigzagged back and forth from one edge of the walk to the other. She looked like a tiny bull looking for something to charge.

"Better let the rope hang," whispered Cookie. "She might notice if you pulled it in now."

Suddenly Miss Florence saw what she seemed to have been looking for—a man in a red mackintosh that hung almost to his ankles came around the southwest corner of the house carrying a long fireman's hook.

Miss Florence snorted and stamped her small foot on the ground. "Get away from those camellia bushes," she cried as she charged forward.

Heedlessly the fireman pushed through the tall shrubbery next to the house and smashed the corner den window.

"Just checking, ma'am," he called out. "Can't be too careful."

"There is no fire, I tell you," Miss Florence yelled, shaking her clenched fist in the air.

"The board at the station sure lit up. You can't fool that board, ma'am," the fireman called back, kicking in another pane of glass. Pushing a large red hat back from his freckled face, he turned and squinted at Miss Florence's quivering hairdo and her damp dress. "Sprinklers appear to be working fine," he said. Then he glanced down and shuffled his heavy boots, as if he was embarrassed to see Mrs. Henry Petus in such a sad state.

"It was only a small grease fire on the kitchen stove, and Lilly put that out herself with a handful of flour. You, on the other hand, seem determined to kick my entire house down. If you'd really like to be of some help, why don't you and your men go upstairs and capture William's alligator?"

Miss Florence shuddered and covered her eyes as if to block out a terrible vision. "He attacked little Annie Trammell. The poor child must have been terrified. How on earth am I ever going to explain this to Louise Trammell?"

Cookie, just four feet above Miss Florence's head, rocked back and forth on her heels in silent laughter and gave Annie's belt an understanding tug.

Annie only sighed as Miss Florence and the red-coated fireman moved on around the corner, still arguing about the role he was to play in solving Miss Florence's problems.

"If you hurry with a couple of good howls," Cookie urged, "you might end up the heroine of this coke party."

Annie shook her head emphatically; she didn't feel up to any more activity of any kind. Then, as much to Annie's surprise as Cookie's, she began sobbing softly into her hands. Crouching on her knees in the cool, dank shadows of the rotting tree house in her wet raincoat, Annie felt old and stiff. She thought of her mother always warding off drafts and chills with shawls and stoles, and of the bedside table covered with medicine. Cookie sat quietly beside her until her sobs tapered off into quiet hiccups.

"Cookie, you know what I wish?" Annie finally asked, lifting her head.

Cookie shook her head. "I can think of an even dozen wishes you might have right about now."

"More than anything in the world, I wish Rose was my

mama as well as yours."

Cookie was silent for a minute. "Well, we're already sisters," she said, placing a comforting arm around Annie's shivering shoulders.

"I know, but looks like that isn't going to be enough to keep me from growing up white, and I just don't think I've got the makings for it."

Cookie nodded. "You'll make it, Annie," she said, then added softly, "I reckon."

Annie straightened up and gave her belt a determined jerk. "Let's go down to your house and read comics."

"For the millionth time?"

"I know. Let's go anyway."

CHAPTER 3

ANNIE PAUSED only long enough to remove her mud-stained shoes and clammy socks and stuff them in her raincoat pockets. Then she and Cookie cut across the backyard past the rose garden, skirted the bass pond, and climbed through the barbed-wire fence that marked the edge of Laurence Trammell's pasture.

Cookie's house stood in the middle of a small meadow covered with broomstraw that grew as high as Annie's waist. Waves of straw lapped gently against an invisible dike that preserved the oval of bare, packed yard that surrounded a small weatherbeaten cabin.

From this clearing, a steep path climbed up a rocky hill to the barn, and then crossed the backyard to the kitchen door of the Trammell house. To the west of the cabin were the hound pens and a small creek that cut through the bottom of the meadow toward the Petuses' property. Beyond the creek was another two acres of dense pine woods. The back line of the whole property was not a mile from Main Street.

The cabin had one big front room and one small one at the back with a low, slanting roof, where Rose and Otis slept. The small room used to be the back porch before Annie's father closed it in after B.C. and Cookie were born. A small outhouse sat fifty feet farther back.

Rose and Otis's cabin was the only one left in the Trammell pasture, though there were two other crumbling rock chimneys just across the creek.

Across the barbed-wire fence, there were still three cabins in the Petus section of the meadow. One of them belonged to Lilly and Two-Time Harris; the other two were now used to store things. A hard-packed clay path joined Rose's and her sister Lilly's houses.

Annie and Cookie followed this narrow path now through the warm, waist-high broomstraw to Cookie's house. Both girls had broken pieces of straw and pushed them between their two front teeth. They trotted as easily and steadily as dogs in a pack, slapping the soft straw tops with the palms of their hands.

Cookie's big brother B.C. was working on an old flexi-racer frame in the bare front yard. Three bantam hens scattered as the girls sank silently onto the front steps of the porch. B.C. gave no sign that he had seen or heard them come.

"What you doing?" Annie finally asked.

"He's making another old soapbox," supplied Cookie, her voice derisive. She took pride in the fact that her older brother had no idea she adored him.

"I can see that, but why? He's already got the fastest one on Mount Airy!"

"Mama says everybody on earth has got a talent. Well, collecting junk and putting it on wheels is B.C.'s talent. You should see what all he's got stashed behind that outhouse—as if there wasn't already enough junk around here."

The steadily mounting character assassination finally

prodded B.C. into speech, as usual.

"This is not a soapbox. It was a flexi-racer, and it's going to be one again. It's not for me. It's the main craving of Goober Lambert, for which I get his six-bladed pocket knife."

"You know Mama won't 'low you to carry no knife."

"For which," B.C. continued testily, "I mean to get Simp's bike frame."

"Is that what you call trading *up*? That tireless piece of trash hasn't seen a flake of paint since his brother Walter had it before him."

"That's your whole problem, Cookie," B.C. shot back, "you never can see the big picture."

"I swear," Cookie said, "the older you get, the crabbier you get, and you were born next to impossible."

Suddenly B.C. swung around, a wrench in one hand. "Get! Both of you, get!" he yelled.

Taken aback, Annie and Cookie retreated into the cabin.

Cookie pulled up a straight chair and propped her feet on the edge of the sofa while Annie stretched out. "Sometimes I hate B.C.," she said softly.

"Ah, Cookie. He doesn't mean anything."

"He's been meaner than a cornered cottonmouth all week. He doesn't have time for anybody."

The memory of B.C. sobbing in the canebrake made Annie stir uneasily on the sofa. She knew he had been shamed and scared, too. She had seen it in his face. But somehow his anger seemed too large and explosive even for what she had witnessed in the canebrake. Something else was eating on B.C., but she couldn't imagine what. Or maybe that was wrong. Slowly Annie rose, not listening to Cookie's indolent words behind her. Walking to the door, she looked out at B.C., his back bent over the dismembered racer, just as he had leaned forward over the taunting Wadine, and a strange quiver ran through the center of her body. Searching for distraction, she turned back to the room behind her.

If Annie had to be indoors at all, she was happier in Rose's front room than any other room she had ever been in. It was the living room and kitchen and the bedroom for B.C. and Cookie.

The floor, covered with cracked beige linoleum, sloped so sharply toward the back room that when Cookie and Annie played jacks, they always had to lean sideways and reach out to catch the ball as it bounced out of the circle toward the back wall. The rough brown sofa was pulled out at night to make Cookie's bed.

Across the corner past the sofa, Otis had hung a curtain made from an old chenille bedspread. Here Cookie dressed and kept her clothes, a few treasures, and a big picture of Mona Freeman. She and Annie had both saved the tops off twenty-five Dixie ice cream cups and sent them in for a picture of their favorite star. Annie had gotten Jennifer Jones.

The other side of the room had a gray fieldstone chimney in the middle and B.C.'s foldaway cot in one corner. In the corner opposite Cookie's makeshift closet were the sink, refrigerator, and an oilcloth-covered table with five unmatched chairs. The wobbly ladder-backed one was Annie's.

The wall behind the sofa and on each side of the fireplace was papered with pages of the Sunday funnies. As a page got worn, Rose overlapped it with another page, so you could only see part of most strips. This bothered B.C. no end, but Rose was adamant about nobody bothering her wall. She said it lent color, and, besides, it kept the drafts out. Annie liked to read what she could see, then supply the missing parts herself. The middle of things was the safest part to read anyway, it seemed to her.

Now she lay on her back on the sofa, her head propped on her hands, reading a section of "Mary Worth" that hung just above the back of the sofa.

Cookie followed Annie's gaze to the right spot on the wall. "Mary Worth! She reminds me of B.C. She collects people like he collects junk. She fixes them up, plays with them a little while, then trades up or trades down, depending on which way you looking at it."

"That's not so," Annie said, defending her heroine. "She just takes care of them until they find their right place. She seems more like Rose to me," she added, reluctant to admit this favorite idea.

"Yeah," Cookie said with a giggle, "junk collecting sort of runs in the family, that's a fact. I can hear your stomach growling from here. Let's get us some cold chicken."

As they leaned against the open refrigerator, the screen door swung outward and banged hard against the porch wall. In the doorway, blocking most of the light, stood Rose, both thumbs tucked under the waistband of her apron, her back arched tightly.

Slowly she nodded her head up and down. "Well, one thing I like about you girls, you both mighty dependable. If you are anywhere at all, you are leaning against a refrigerator door. Don't it never occur to you children to sit and eat some of the stuff I keep ladling out in two houses, three times a day?"

Big smiles spread across both Annie's and Cookie's faces. To be fussed at by Rose was like roughhousing on the floor with Two-Time. Sometimes you got hurt, sometimes even bad enough to cry; but you always came back craving more.

Rose pointed a finger at Annie. "You, miss, are supposed to be at a Coca-Cola party. It's almost one o'clock, and you aren't home, properly speaking, yet."

Annie watched Rose warily, her chicken leg held in midair, trying to decide if Rose knew about the ill-fated coke party.

"Mama said go, and I did. She didn't say anything about coming home."

"Two-Time came to the back door a while back," Rose said pointedly.

"Oh," Annie said as soon as she could get a large bite of chicken swallowed. "What did Mama say?"

Rose leaned even farther back, her hands pressing in at her waist. "After her stressful morning getting you off to the party, she had a little lunch in her room. Then Miss Elvira Cotton came up from the beauty shop to fix her hair for her. I haven't laid eyes on your mama since noon. Once you set foot in that house, though, she's bound to want to know all about that party."

"*All* about it?" asked Annie delicately. Rose was very sensitive about being truthful.

Rose groaned and rolled her eyes toward the ceiling. "I don't suppose she would be especially interested in an alligator, being as wary of animals as she is."

"She's not crazy about fires either," Annie reminded her.

"What! Two-Time didn't say nothing about no fire!"

"There wasn't any fire," Annie hastily corrected herself, "only fire engines. A false alarm. No sense in alarming Mama about a false alarm."

Cookie tried a little "Ha, ha," to help things along.

Suddenly Rose seemed really angry. As she drew herself up to her full height, Annie and Cookie instinctively came to attention in front of her.

"Honor thy father and thy mother: that thy days may be long upon the land which the Lord thy God giveth thee. *Exodus* 20:12."

"I'm sorry, Rose," Annie mumbled, still a little uncertain about her offense; but a Bible verse from Rose was always a serious matter.

"I guess your mama and daddy better get the same story with their meal that everybody else in this town will be getting with theirs." Rose looked sternly out the window toward the back woods.

"But Mama's cough," Annie pleaded.

"Mr. Laurence will be there to help her bear up."

"Everything?"

"Beginning, middle, and end."

Rose stepped back into the doorway, one hand on the screen door, the other on her hip.

In the temporary twilight, Cookie suddenly asked in her walking-on-eggshells voice, "Which version, Mama?"

There was an ominous silence. "I reckon I'll settle for the real version, if it's all the same to you."

"Mama, this morning, while me and Annie watched from the tree house, wondering how Annie had managed to cause so much commotion in such a short time, Miss Florence followed the fire chief around the house telling him all about the party and how William's alligator attacked one of the poor, dear children of her good friend and neighbor. Then the cook almost set the house afire, and her new sprinkler system nearly drowned the rest of her guests. She was mighty worried about how she was going to explain it all, but it looked like she aimed to try."

Rose stood motionless, her chest still puffed out. Both girls were well aware that Rose disliked Miss Florence Petus intensely, though she never said so in so many words, and the reasons were not clear to either girl. It seemed to have something to do with how she treated Lilly and Two-Time, or maybe her voice just got on Rose's nerves. It always sounded like hail on a tin roof.

Cookie finished in a rush of words. "Mama, maybe we should just leave all the explaining to Miss Florence." Then she and Annie waited, bracing themselves stiff-legged against the refrigerator.

A faint smile, or something like one, appeared in one corner of Rose's mouth. "After your mama and daddy hear from Miss Florence, they still going to have lots of questions."

"I won't say a thing but the truth, Rose," Annie promised eagerly. "I swear I won't. Please, let's wait for Miss Florence."

"I'll be in the kitchen as usual tonight, Annie Trammell. If I hear any monkey business, I'll do some story telling myself."

Cookie and Annie shouted in unison: "Thank you, Mama!"

"Thank you, Rose!"

Each of them grabbed one of Rose's thick upper arms and pulled her in a heavy dance around the cracked linoleum floor until she was gasping for air.

Rose retrieved her arms and laid them across her heaving breasts. "Leave me alone, you rascals. I got supper to get on the table. See that you come soon as you hear that bell, Annie. For once, I'd like you to beat your father to the table."

Rose about-faced soundlessly on the worn felt house shoes that she wore every day except Sunday; and in a minute, through the screen, the girls could see her lumbering past B.C. and on up the steep path, cutting obliquely uphill toward the barn.

CHAPTER 4

B.C. ROSE STIFFLY from his metallic skeleton and came
to sit on the top step of the porch, his close-shaved black
head pulled halfway down into his faded plaid shirt
collar. Without looking at either of them, he said,
"Caught you, didn't she? For once you two are right
where you belong, right between the devil and a hard
place."

Annie's enthusiasm faded as she accepted B.C.'s
verdict mutely and sat down beside him. Miss Florence
would probably fix her wagon good. She hunched her
head down into her still-damp raincoat and cupped her
chin in her hand so that she looked like a beige version of
the contemplative B.C. Cookie had come out on the
porch to watch Rose go up the hill, too, but now she
banged back through the screen door to finish her piece
of chicken.

Annie often sat like B.C., walked like B.C., talked soft
and slow like B.C. If he was nearby, or she'd just seen
him, the likeness was comical—or it would have been if
anybody had taken the time to notice. When B.C. was
angry, which was fairly often when Annie and Cookie
were around, his face seemed to grow darker and darker
like a rolling thunderhead before a deluge. He could lash
you with words until you thought he would bruise your

skin. But his hands were something else. In fact, some part of Annie knew she loved B.C's hands. When he careened down Mount Airy on his latest sliding, rolling, bouncing contraption, she worried that he would hurt his hands. His fingers were long and narrow and never still. The dark, dusty-brown backs of his hands were always scratched and scraped, the nails broken or packed with grease from his tinkering. Their specialness seemed to lie cupped like a secret in his soft pink palms—like the ocean's roar is wrapped in the curving pink inner chambers of a spikey conch shell. He had an old whittling knife he had traded for somewhere. Whenever he picked up a piece of wood and started on it, it seemed to go soft and malleable in his hands, more like putty than wood.

Two Christmases ago, without telling anyone, even Cookie, Annie gave B.C. a bottle of Corn Husker's lotion. On Christmas Eve she walked slowly down the hill and found B.C. sitting on his haunches in the half-dark, still struggling to get a rusty chain off a junked bicycle.

"Here you are," she said, bracing her knees against the expected reaction to the small red package she held out to him.

"What's that?" he asked, not reaching out for the package.

"Your Christmas present," Annie said, placing it on the ground beside him, anxious to be gone.

"I know that. What is it?"

"Hand lotion."

"You mean hand lotion for girls?"

"Miss Mackey at the drugstore said it was made especially for men with dry, chapped skin," Annie explained, wishing she had never come.

B.C.'s head snapped back as he peered up into Annie's face.

"My hands aren't any drier or chappier than anybody else's, especially yours," B.C. said. He picked up the package and slammed it down again at Annie's feet.

Annie hadn't really expected B.C. to understand. She didn't know exactly what she meant herself. Still, she was anxious to see if the bottle were broken or cracked. Squatting by the dry-docked bicycle, she opened the package and felt the bottle for leaks. Then, setting it in the shoe box where B.C. kept his few tools, she said quietly into the gathering darkness, "You should take care of your hands, B.C. They're important."

B.C. never answered, and Annie could see nothing of his face except its silhouette against the purpling sky. In a minute she left, cutting back up the hill toward the faint yellow glow of the kitchen lights. Two days after Christmas, the first time she had used her bike since vacation started, she found a small squirrel carved from a pink bar of Sweetheart soap in the basket.

She put it in a cigar box with her baby spoon and her father's swimming medal and fifteen Dixie Cup ice cream lids. She and B.C. did not exchange gifts again for birthdays or Christmas, though she and Cookie always did.

Cookie banged back out on the front porch with a chicken thigh in one hand and a wing in the other.

"Chicken, B.C.?"

B.C. shook his head without taking his eyes from some vague spot between him and the Petus house, now almost hidden behind fragile new foliage.

"Chicken, Annie?"

Annie repeated B.C.'s gesture.

"Well, I know why Annie's not talking. She's saving her strength for supper tonight. What's got your tongue, B.C.?"

"Nothing, not a damn thing, except too many girls." B.C.'s frown deepened to a scowl as Cookie came to sit on the other side of him.

"Where's silly Willy Petus, then?" Cookie asked, rubbing greasy fingers on the knees of her blue jeans.

"Did you already forget he's got company, girl company?"

Cookie threw back her head. "Hah! Not likely, when Annie pretty near drowned her not more than an hour ago. Besides, I don't believe William Petus is staying around home to play with anybody named Mary Ellen."

Annie frowned at the cabin's listing porch. "Cookie, you couldn't count to ten without exaggerating."

B.C. ignored Annie's protest and glared at his sister.

"Well, I was up there yesterday afternoon, so I know, don't I? Anyway, he goes to Froggy Bottom next week to Boy Scout camp. That'll take two weeks."

"I thought Mr. Edwards kicked William out of the Boy Scout troop, after he let the brakes off of Mr. Edwards's car and it rolled into Froggy Bottom Creek last summer."

Reluctantly B.C. smiled at the picture: thin, knobby-kneed Mr. Edwards in his Scout uniform, footsore and mosquito-bitten after a five-mile hike, watching the bubbles come out of the windows of his new Ford coupe as it sashayed gracefully to the bottom of Froggy Bottom. From Froggy Bottom, it had been another five-mile hike over rough chert roads to the state highway.

Miss Florence had protested vigorously that Mr.

Edwards had endangered William's life, leaving his car parked on a hill that way. But Mr. Edwards was adamant; William had to go.

William had bicycled all the way out to Froggy Bottom the next morning to take pictures of his achievement for his photography merit badge, not knowing yet of his excommunication. But the wrecker from Tate's Service Station passed him before he was halfway there. It retrieved the car and repassed William as he neared the last curve before Froggy Bottom. Stopping and twisting on his bike seat, he was able to get only one quick picture as the dripping coupe flashed by with its rear end in the air, already covered in a thick layer of red dust.

Cookie, Annie, William's little brother Joe-Joe, and B.C. were invited to the first showing of the picture. They ran all the way to the drugstore on Tuesday afternoon, the day the week's prints came back from Montgomery. After William's vivid descriptions (he'd talked about nothing else all week), it was a disappointment, to say the least. The first eleven pictures were William and Joe-Joe in their Easter suits in various scenic spots around the Petus house. The last picture on the roll had been *the* picture. It looked, as far as Annie could tell, like a creature from a horror comic book. Below two small eyes, a wide mouth curved into a smile, or maybe it was a leer, and saliva dripped from the gaping jaws. The rest of the picture was blank. William said the eyes and mouth were the headlights and the bumper; the blank part was the dust, any birdbrain could see that. Cookie said she couldn't even see any eyes and mouth. B.C. sighed and said that that was one sweet car to be sending into Froggy Bottom.

Now B.C. spoke in a harsh voice, as if he'd just told

Cookie and Annie the whole story. "Maybe that's how it was last summer. This summer, he's back in with both feet and going off to camp next week."

"Wow! I guess we know how come you're as sour as a green persimmon today," Cookie said, slapping B.C.'s knee with her hand. "If William goes off to Scout camp next week, how can you two be in the Mount Airy Derby?" Sympathetic in spite of herself at this catastrophe, Cookie touched B.C. lightly on the shoulder. Angrily, he jerked back from her touch.

"You've worked all year on your crate," Cookie persisted. "He ought to be ashamed."

B.C. growled softly, "He'll be back in time for the race."

"Well, then maybe you can get everything ready by yourself; and William will be here to help you drive it."

"No!"

"What's the matter now?"

"Don't reckon I can enter without another rider."

"But you said . . . " Cookie began in exasperation.

"William is riding with Hoyt Greely."

"Hoyt, the one that beat you last year?" Annie asked incredulously. "Why, William didn't talk about anything else all winter except beating him."

B.C. snorted. "Not anymore, he don't."

Cookie suddenly stooped and peered into B.C.'s face. "What did you do to William to make him so mad at you?"

"Nothing. Mind your own business," B.C. snapped.

"He wanted to be up front this time, didn't he?" Cookie accused.

"I reckon."

"And you said no. Mr. Big Shot."

B.C. rubbed a hand across the back of his neck. "I didn't. I only said we'd take the best three trials for each of us, and the one with the best time could be up front."

To Annie, B.C.'s voice seemed too high and tight, like it had been pushed through a keyhole, and she laid her hand on his arm. A little shirttail breeze raised a long row of goose bumps along her arm from where her hand touched B.C.'s hot arm to her shoulder. B.C. shivered as if he, too, had felt the heat of their skin touching.

Cookie persisted, "That's not all. Why don't you tell it all? Bet if you did you wouldn't come off sounding so four-square."

B.C.'s head dropped into his hands, as if it had been axed. "He called me a dumb nigger," he said in a voice still tinged with disbelief; but the last word was closer to a cry than a word.

Cookie's face turned in on itself until she looked like a raisin. Angrily she cried at B.C., "He's called you 'nigger' hundreds of times. Why'd you have to go make something out of that?"

B.C. raised his head and looked toward the Petuses' gabled rooftop.

"Not like this," he said. "Not like this—damn his soul."

Annie's whole body shuddered; the damp raincoat clung to her like a shroud. "Don't talk like that, B.C. Rose will skin you alive," she whispered.

"You don't like it, go on up to your house and tell her." He turned on her so fast she thought he might hit her with his clenched fists and sink his square teeth into her shoulder. Instead, he just stared at her, then sank back again.

"Don't do that," Annie said.

"Don't do what?"

"Don't. . . " Annie groped for what she meant, but it eluded her. "Don't give up, B.C.," she finished uncertainly.

B.C. shook his head. "It's not that important. Just an old soapbox derby."

"It is important. It's everything. William's wrong, I know he is," Annie cried.

"You mean he's wrong, I'm not a nigger?" B.C. asked with a sudden wicked smile.

Annie gasped and drew back. No other word was so sternly forbidden in her house. Even on B.C.'s lips it seemed sacrilegious. "No, you're not," she managed to stammer. "Besides, he only said it because he's jealous."

Cookie and B.C.'s mouths both dropped. Their eyes opened wide, and laughter rolled over the waving broomstraw.

When B.C. stopped laughing, he looked like a different person. His face was smooth, his eyes round and shiny.

Annie protested. "Really, B.C., you can do things he couldn't do in a hundred years. William knows that."

B.C. looked straight at Annie. "Maybe, but it seems like no matter what I can do, I'm gonna be the one to wind up eating a pile of shit."

"Well, I'll tell you one thing," Cookie said, "if this summer gets any more special, Annie Trammell, I'm not having any part of it."

No one spoke until the stillness was disturbed by a rough-throated bell that rang five jerked-short notes, as if the bell ringer didn't like the sound of his bell.

Annie half-rose, then slumped back beside B.C. "That

can't be Rose; it's hours till dark."

"You're forgetting Miss Florence's coke party," Cookie reminded her.

Clank, clank, clank. The abrupt summons came again.

"See you in the morning," Cookie called after her, as Annie climbed the hill toward the barn.

Annie paused and turned around. "If I'm not here by the time you finish your chores, it's because I can't leave my room. Come up through the crab-apple tree."

"Good luck, Sister Annie," Cookie called out, as Annie stepped into the cool, pungent shadows cast by the barn.

CHAPTER 5

THE BARN was built into the top of the steep slope that rose from the creek in the pasture to the edge of the big house's broad, rolling back lawn. The double front doors were on the first floor and opened onto the back lawn. The side door, at the rear of the stall for Annie's pony, opened onto a small sloping paddock, and the back door was cut into the thick whitewashed stone walls of the basement. There were ten cow stalls in the basement, but all the cows had been gone since Grampa Trammell had died. He had been a farmer at heart and had kept cows, hogs, and chickens, as well as four beautiful horses and a huge garden in the side yard.

Gramma Trammell's flowers had made the house a showcase in the spring; and she had patiently led dozens of strangers around the grounds to see the azaleas, flowering quince, grancy graybeard, and beds of jonquils, narcissus, tulips, and hyacinths. Since Gramma Trammell's death, Louise, who found open air, especially spring air, disquieting and depressing, had let the flower beds go. But enough of Gramma Trammell's spirit lingered to coax a still impressive display of unkempt, overgrown opulence each spring.

The only remnants of Grampa's animals were Black Gal, the horse Annie's father used to ride, now turned out to pasture, and Chewing Tobacco, who belonged, at least technically, to Annie. Chewing Tobacco had been nothing but a source of aggravation to Annie from the moment he scrambled out of the back of the furniture-store van. She had never wanted a horse, but got one anyway because "all the Fairbaults ride." Then when she had named him Chewing Tobacco because he was exactly the color of the chewing tobacco stains on the court-house steps, her mother insisted on calling him Toby and reminded Annie every time his name came up that there had never been a Trammell or a Fairbault who chewed tobacco.

Now Annie hit him on the rump as she went through his stall on her shortcut to the house.

Half wild and grossly fat, he shied clumsily against the far wall, then put his head into his feed box again. "Should have named you Two-by-Four," she told the oblivious little horse, as she pushed open the barn's front door and squinted into the blinding afternoon sun. Rose was still holding the clapper, waiting to ring the bell again if necessary.

"Hold everything," called Annie. "I just got two legs."

"I hope you got the same two in the same shape next time I lay eyes on you," Rose said as she smoothed Annie's hair with the palms of her hands.

"Has Miss Florence come to see Mama?"

Rose wagged her head dolefully from side to side. "That isn't the half of it. Your daddy came home from the store early, and Miss Elvira Cotton from the beauty parlor is still here, too. Seemed like I might as well ring for you before they started looking."

At that very moment, a long wavering wail came from

the house. There was a moment's silence, then the same rising wail came again.

"It's time," said Rose, turning back toward the kitchen door.

Rose went back to the stove where, as usual, every burner was covered with a bubbling pot. Annie crossed the room and pushed open the swinging door to the breakfast room. With the door half open, she looked back. From the waist up, Rose was enveloped in a thick cloud of steam; but she must have missed hearing the door swing to for she said peremptorily, *"Exodus 20:12."*

The door swished to behind Annie, and she headed down the hall toward a fresh wail.

When she got to the living room, her apprehension turned to confusion. It was Miss Elvira Cotton, a large, buxom woman in a pink nylon uniform, who was crying. Annie's father was standing at military attention behind the woman's chair, offering what consolation he felt proper—patting the Queen Anne chair lightly on the back. If Miss Elvira had known, Annie was certain that she would have been surprised and touched.

Usually, Laurence Trammell carefully avoided the house on the afternoons Miss Elvira came to set his wife's hair. He had nothing against Miss Elvira; indeed, her father had been the finest blacksmith in the county. But the woman's presence in his home made him extremely uneasy. She was not a servant who could be expected to blend inconspicuously into the warm supportive world around him. Yet, in the ordinary course of events, she certainly would never have called on Louise Trammell. There were simply no manners prescribed for a woman like this in his home. Since Laurence Trammell was first and foremost a gentleman, a situation was always to be diligently avoided if there was any risk of being unmannered, not to mention bad-mannered.

Annie walked as far as the center of the room, then stopped. Miss Elvira continued her regular wail-pause-wail without lifting her face from her hands. Her father looked at Annie with stricken eyes, a knight without his armor. Annie decided that her mother had either fainted—her head was thrown back, and one arm hung gracefully over the side of her chair—or was looking at the ceiling for cobwebs that Rose might have missed.

Only Miss Florence seemed aware that Annie stood in the center of the room waiting. She twisted impatiently in her chair and leaned toward her. "Oh, Annie, you poor child! To think what a terrifying morning you had, all because of William's old alligator."

Miss Elvira let out an especially piercing wail. "He got it through a catalogue," Miss Florence continued, after an irritated glance at Elvira Cotton. "Came right to the post office. To think I brought it home in the trunk of the Buick myself.

"William wasn't home, so naturally I took a peek to see what had been sent to him that weighed at least twenty-five pounds, the postmaster said, and smelled like . . . well, just smelled, that's all."

Miss Florence paused for breath, then plunged on. "I tell you, when I finally got that lid open and saw that brute lying there, I ran straight out to the kitchen and got a butcher knife to defend myself, hollering all the while, 'Alligator! Alligator!' "

Just then Miss Elvira let loose another wail that made everyone in the room jump.

"But do you think that a living, breathing soul came?" Miss Florence asked, glaring about the room. With a sigh, she let her thin body slump back in her chair. "Looking back, I think it was nearly dead. He didn't blink an eye 'til William had worked on him about two days."

Miss Elvira Cotton raised her tear-streaked face in consternation at the sudden silence, looked about her, then began her steady wails again, this time looking straight ahead, her eyes bulging, her soft round face quivering.

"Miss Elvira seems mighty upset," Annie observed as casually as she could to Miss Florence.

Miss Florence frowned, and Miss Elvira's scream edged upward two notes. "She says an alligator ate her father's leg," Miss Florence explained. "I don't suppose he actually ate it. Just bit it off, sounds more . . . He was coon hunting in the Okefenokee Swamp. At least, I believe she said it was her father; it could have been her brother. There are a great many Cottons, you know. Stepped right into his mouth, I believe she said, though I can't see how you could overlook an alligator in your path."

Miss Elvira pulled a bright, flowered handkerchief from the sleeve of her pink uniform and snuffled loudly. "It was my cousin Hank, and it was pitch-black night. The way it *always* is when you hunt for coons," she said stiffly.

"Yes, yes, Miss Elvira. Terrible," Laurence Trammell mumbled. In desperation he seized the woman by her dimpled elbow and started escorting her to the door, making little bows from the waist as he walked, as if she were a princess.

Miss Florence rose from her chair also, patting her too

curly hair that was now held in place by a light, golden net that looked like the web of an over-zealous spider. "I only meant to apologize for William's terrible alligator and reassure myself about Annie; she simply disappeared during all the confusion. It never occurred to me that my harrowing morning would be the cause of Miss Elvira Cotton's falling to pieces. You'd never guess that she was that emotional about alligators from all the blood-curdling stories she has for me on Friday mornings. At any rate William's alligator is now the fire chief's concern; and it's about time he did something useful, I say." Miss Florence moved toward the door, nodding absently toward Annie as she went. "Don't you get up, Louise. Oh, I forgot, you don't get up, do you? Well, that's just fine."

The front screen clicked lightly, and she was gone, though her shower of words seemed to have left a bluish haze in the air behind her.

Everyone else stayed still and silent, afraid that any sound or movement might pull Miss Florence back into the room.

After several moments, Annie's father walked slowly back toward the middle of the room. He spread his fingers and tapped the fingertips of both hands lightly together in his habitual preface to speaking. "Have we had dinner?" he asked with a small frown, looking at no one in particular.

"No sir," Annie answered.

Turning toward Annie, he frowned again. "Annie, why are you in that awful coat? Every time I've seen you lately you look as if you had slept in your clothes."

"That was just this morning," Annie suggested, "and that was my nightgown."

"Oh. Oh yes." Her father nodded, already thinking of something else.

Her mother was not so easily diverted. Stretching out a slim, blue-veined hand, she touched the hem of the offending coat.

"Heavens, Annie, you're sopping wet. Where have you been in this coat?"

"Only to the coke party. It came in real handy when the sprinklers started."

"To the party, in that coat? Oh, Laurence, things are worse than I imagined. This is the last straw. Something must be done." She sighed. "If only I had my strength."

"Now, Louise, dear," Laurence murmured, his voice suddenly as soft as a freshly plumped pillow. "This has been awful for you. Let's have a bite to eat. That's what we need." Moving past Annie, he extended both hands to help Louise from her chair.

"The trouble is, Annie has never played with other little girls," Louise said. "William is the only child Annie's age on this side of town."

Annie frowned and started to protest, but her parents had both turned to walk arm in arm from the room.

"There's Cookie," her father was saying easily.

"Oh, Laurence, you know what I mean, children with her background, with some breeding."

"Should I get us a little house in town, then?" her father teased.

"Don't try to distract me, Laurence. Something must be done. Lessons, I think."

As they walked down the hall arm in arm, Annie trailed reluctantly behind them, only the sharp pangs of hunger preventing a discreet disappearance. "My goodness,

Louise," she heard her father mutter, "how long has it been since you've been to town?"

Her mother patted her father's arm. "Too long, dear. Much too long," she said, but her voice held no sound of regret.

To Annie, dinner seemed a long, drawn-out affair, and, like the aftermath of many exciting days, tinged with a subtle melancholy. In the kitchen, Rose was humming hymns as usual; but tonight they were the kind that her father said were "full of chastisement." Her mother busied herself with the supervision of Ruth-baby's "simply unmentionable table manners," which was some help; but her father, whom Annie loved to hear talk about what he had seen and heard downtown all day, seemed preoccupied with thoughts of his own.

Then, just as Annie was scraping the last morsel of sweet potato out of the shell, her father cleared his throat and spoke, not addressing his remarks to anyone in particular. "The city manager fired Ben Reilly today."

"What?" her mother asked, pausing with her napkin outstretched toward Ruth-baby's mouth.

"Ben Reilly, the street sweeper who got in that argument with Mel Decker. Or more precisely, the new pastor—Reverend Henton, I think his name is—got in an argument with Mel, defending Ben."

Her mother nodded. "And the upshot of it is that Ben Reilly doesn't have a job anymore, while that preacher has gone on his merry way. Laurence, can't you see that you're worrying about the wrong man?"

Her father seemed not to have followed her mother's line of reasoning. "Otis said Ben has six mouths to feed and another on the way."

"There, you see. That's what happens when some outsider tries to change the natural order of things. Whites and coloreds always get along just fine until someone else butts in."

"But, Louise," her father protested, "the man who butted in, as you say, was a colored man, too."

Her mother drew erect, her usual lethargy seemingly dispensed by the strength of her feelings on the subject. "He's not Winton colored. He's not one of our own, is he?" she demanded.

Slowly Laurence shook his head. "Still, it isn't fair for Ben Reilly to have to suffer. There should be something I could do."

Louise Trammell concentrated on a spot between Laurence and Annie. "Of course, it is pointless for me to discuss this with you, Laurence. I don't know why I never seem to learn."

Annie gave a tiny sigh. Her mother always did seem to be trying to explain things to her father and to her, even to Ruth-baby. Maybe one day she would finally just give up.

"For four generations the Trammells have been prominent in Winton," her mother went on. "You are expected to carry on, to be a leader in this town. You might say you were born to see that certain things never change. That's not the same thing at all as worrying over every little trouble the down-and-out get themselves into. Everybody in this town heads for the store if they have so much as a hangnail bothering them. I'm afraid of going to town for fear of whom I'll see you with."

Laurence Trammell watched his wife apprehensively with something like pain crinkling the corners of his eyes. Instinctively Annie wanted to protest her mother's words, but she had been taught since birth that whatever her mother said or did was outside all judgment. To question this brought not only her mother's disapproval but her father's as well, so she bit her lip and willed herself to watch as if from afar, listening for a break in the conversation that would allow her to escape into the kitchen with Rose.

"Sometimes," her mother said, "I think that you refuse the privileges and responsibilities you were born to just to upset me."

"I would never deliberately upset you, Louise," her father replied, "you know that."

"Well, then, if you really want to do something, something constructive, you could see to it that so-called preacher is horsewhipped."

As Annie put her hand to her mouth to stifle a gasp, she sensed rather than actually heard her father's own start of surprise.

"Louise, you don't mean that."

Her mother's brows narrowed. "I do mean that, Laurence. I have watched my father whip men. Ordinarily he could handle a dozen men without raising his voice, but he knew when stern measures were called for."

She glanced surreptitiously toward the kitchen. "You mark my words, Laurence, that preacher is trying on this town for size. If there is a man of courage here, he had better stop the troublemaker while he is stoppable."

Annie watched, caught up in the conversation in spite of herself. Her father slowly folded his napkin and pulled it through his silver napkin ring. His face seemed paler than ever.

"Times have changed, Louise. Men don't go around

thrashing each other anymore. I was thinking more of
something I could do to help Ben Reilly get his job back."
In the tight silence that followed, Louise Trammell
paled, then turned her attention back to Ruth-baby.
Annie couldn't remember when she had seen her mother
so angry about anything. Her fingers trembled as she
lifted her napkin to Ruth-baby's face. Seeing so much
emotion on her mother's face was like hitting a cold spot
in the creek in the summer. You couldn't believe it was
there. You gasped, and it was already gone again.

Her father spoke into the silence. "Louise, I'm sorry I
brought up such an unpleasant subject at the table."

"So am I," her mother replied stiffly. "Twice now we've
spent nearly our whole meal talking about two colored
men I've never laid eyes on." Her glance touched the top
of Annie's head. "You might also give some thought as to
what Annie and Ruth-baby ought to be hearing their
father say.

"But as long as you've brought the subject up, I have
one last thing to say. If you can't take care of that man
properly, Laurence, stay away from him. Do you hear?
I've seen farm workers like that. Behind those smiling
eyes lies nothing but hate. He'll bring disaster to whoever
gets near him."

She frowned. "It's like the Lord occasionally makes a
mistake and gives a white man black skin. No matter how
the world grinds him down, he just can't settle down to
being black, and the world can't see him as anything else,"
she said, then shook her head at such a ridiculous idea.

In the long silence that followed, Annie escaped. She
could not stand for her mother to bring such an unhappy
look to her father's face.

The next morning, while Annie and Cookie sat on the back steps, skipping rocks down the sidewalk that led to the garage and waiting for Rose to inspect Annie's room, Annie tried to tell Cookie about her parents' strange conversation about the new black preacher Reverend Henton; but Cookie was more interested in talking about the fiasco at the coke party. Cookie and Rose and Otis went to the Reverend Williams's church, and the Emanuel Methodist was on the far west side of town, part of another world.

"Maybe," Annie persisted, "it would be a good place to investigate when it isn't so hot." Today, although it was only eight o'clock, the heat already lay like a hot iron across her shoulders.

Cookie was strangely disapproving of the fiery young preacher. "Mama wouldn't want us to have nothing to do with him," she said flatly.

When Annie told her how he had stuck up for Ben Reilly, Cookie did not answer at all. When she spoke again it was to dismiss him completely.

"Let's go crawdad hunting," she suggested.

"No," Annie answered, after a moment's hesitation, "water's still too cold."

"Well, then, let's go see what B.C. is up to."

"The first thing you ladies are going to do is take this mess of greens over to Dr. Matt's house," Rose called through the door.

Both girls smiled at once. Miss Lessie Carter made the best scones, pound cake, and oatmeal cookies of anybody in the world. And besides, it was sort of like going to visit the city jail or the mausoleums in the old part of the cemetery; no matter how many times you went, it never seemed an ordinary place to go.

Now Rose came out the back door with a heavy iron stewpot full of savory new turnip greens that had been on the stove's back burner since six that morning. Whenever there were extra garden vegetables, Rose cooked a huge batch and what she didn't use at the big house or the cabin, she sent across the street to Dr. Matt's house—that is, to Miss Emma and Miss Lessie, for Dr. Matt had been gone about eight years now.

To Annie and Cookie, he was only a yellowed picture, a ramrod-straight man with white hair and gold-rimmed glasses in an old-fashioned striped suit and a high-collared shirt. Yet the whole town, especially Miss Emma and Miss Lessie, his unmarried daughters, still thought of the house as Dr. Matt's.

Annie stood up and reached for the handle of the caldron. More fun going to Dr. Matt's than going to a Coca-Cola and alligator party, she thought and half-smiled.

But her mother's strange burst of anger and her unsettling suggestion that perhaps the Lord sometimes gave white men black skins would not let her be. After all, hadn't she often felt she was closer to being a child of Otis and Rose? And did it have to be such a terrible mistake— why did it have to matter at all?

CHAPTER 6

DR. MATTHEW CARTER had been the school principal for thirty-five years and had prided himself on being a progressive educator as well as a firm disciplinarian—an exemplary blend of the old and new. Annie's father said he was called doctor because he had taught so long. His oldest daughter, Miss Emma, short and more than stout and still full of driving energy at sixty-five, had taught under Dr. Matt—and later under that *other* man—for thirty-four years. It was the general consensus that she was the best teacher the school had ever had and could have certainly gotten another extension to teach two more years. Those closest to her on the faculty said she had retired because she wouldn't have it said that she taught longer than Dr. Matt.

Miss Lessie, her younger sister, had never worked outside her childhood home, but she was a veritable dervish in her own tiny domain. A dense grove of pin oaks kept most of the Carter yard bare of grass; and every afternoon Miss Lessie swept the whole yard and the street all the way out to the middle, stooping to pick up stray twigs and pebbles and stuff them into the sagging pockets of the apron she always wore. Annie had often watched her from her bedroom window across the street, picking up fallen oak leaves and twigs late into the summer twilight.

She wondered if Miss Lessie didn't prefer the stark neatness of her yard to the more unkempt lushness of the green ones all around her.

When she worked in the yard, Miss Lessie wore a heavy hair net pulled down to the middle of her forehead, an old cotton housedress, her long white apron, and tennis shoes. Every time she stooped, her neck flushed a deep, pretty pink except for a tiny white ring around the mole just below her left ear.

If they were sure none of her relations were within earshot, folks said Miss Lessie was strange—not strange like Hank Ketchum, who couldn't even talk plain and never took a bath, but something else—and Annie was never sure just what that something else was.

Cookie said maybe she was just dumb and trying to hide it because she hardly ever said anything that wasn't a proverb, like "Lie down with dogs, get up with fleas," or "Blood is thicker than water." If she was ever questioned about anything she said, her nostrils quivered, and she would elaborate only by saying, "That's what Papa always said."

But just try getting an extra cookie, Annie had answered. It was more than dumbness, all right. Take her feelings about men: No matter what anybody said or did to try and dissuade Miss Lessie, Dr. Matt's house was locked tight as a tick, day and night, summer and winter—windows down, shades pulled, doors locked, and screen doors latched, as if the whole family had gone on a trip around the world. In the summer, she would leave the kitchen door open, but she double-latched the screen door top and bottom and got the kind of door that had a solid lower half.

When you knocked, Miss Lessie peeked out at you

from at least two windows to make sure no men were around before she opened the door. If she was working in the yard, as she did for many hours every nice day, she retreated to the porch any time a man on foot went by. If he as much as turned his head her way or crossed to her side of the street, she was in the house and had the door locked fast behind her before he was close enough to speak. There were no exceptions, not even Laurence Trammell, whom she had known since he was born.

Miss Lessie's precautions did not include young boys, so up until two summers ago, B.C. as well as Annie and Cookie was a frequent visitor. B.C. liked Miss Lessie perhaps better than he liked anybody else. He admired her neatness and the way she kept at every job until it was done just right. He would often work behind her for hours, as silent as she, her shadow.

There was a very simple test of manhood. Annie had overheard Miss Lessie explain it to her father through the screen door in her simple, hesitant way when he had tried to convince her to let a grocery boy in. Once a boy's head came far enough above the top half of the screen door to throw a shadow on the faded kitchen linoleum, he was a man.

The spring B.C. turned nine, he and Cookie and Annie went running across the street one morning with a sack full of lady peas. The ground was still cold under their tender, newly bare feet. Banging on the door with his fist, B.C. called out, "Fresh peas," like the vegetable vendor did when he came down the street in his old truck on summer mornings.

Miss Lessie, as thin and stringy as Miss Emma was short and padded, got halfway across the kitchen before she saw B.C.'s shadow and recoiled toward the broom she kept standing in the corner by the stove for just such emergencies. "Get," she hissed, brandishing the broom above her head and making small scurrying charges at the door like a mongoose warding off a snake.

Stunned, B.C. called out, "What's wrong, Miss Lessie? What's wrong?"

"Get. Get out of my kitchen," she kept saying.

"Miss Lessie," B.C. said, almost pleading, "I *am* out of the kitchen. I'm B.C., and I'm out here on your porch, and look what I've brought you—fresh peas, just now picked."

"No men allowed! No men allowed!" she fairly screamed, and at last B.C., Annie, and Cookie understood.

Annie was always a little in awe of B.C. after that. For in that strange rite, some part of him really did metamorphose from boy to man. Granted, Annie thought she saw a suspicious wetness in his eyes as he backed off the porch, still clutching the sack full of peas. But his shoulders drew back, his jaw hardened, and his head lifted a little higher as he absorbed the full impact of his new standing with Miss Lessie.

When he reached the pin oaks in the front yard, Miss Lessie set the broom quietly in the corner and softly called through the screen, to ask the girls if they'd care to come in for just a taste of chess pie.

Shut up as it was the year around, Dr. Matt's house always smelled cool and musty, like trunks of old clothes kept under houses. This morning was no exception, though the early summer air outside had vibrated with freshness as Annie and Cookie sprinted toward Dr.

Matt's, the hot turnip-green liquor sloshing over their fingers.

As Annie and Cookie lifted the heavy wrought-iron pot to the kitchen counter, Miss Emma called out from the front of the house, "Who's there, Lessie? Have you let someone in the kitchen?"

The sound of Miss Lessie screaming "Get out of my kitchen" never raised any comment from the practical Miss Emma. She heard that every time some innocent delivery boy or encyclopedia salesman came to their door. But the sound of the screen slamming and kitchen chairs scraping back—that was a much rarer sound, and her curiosity was immediately aroused.

"It's Annie Trammell from across the street with a mess of cooked greens."

"And Cookie," Annie called out.

"They are going to try my chess pie." Miss Lessie gave the girls a smile just over the tops of their heads that was more like a little grimace. "It isn't good as I can do."

While Annie and Cookie ate their huge pieces of pie and drank the cold milk Miss Lessie set before them, she stood silently by the stove watching each bite as it went from plate to mouth. You never really saw Miss Lessie's face because she kept her eyes so resolutely away from yours. You can't remember a face with no eyes, Annie thought as she bent over her plate.

"It's going to be a scorcher, Miss Lessie," said Cookie. "You better take it easy today."

"From rising sun to setting sun, a woman's work is never done," answered Miss Lessie, wiping her bony fingers absently on her apron front.

"Yes'm," Cookie agreed solemnly, her mouth full of chess pie.

Annie envied Cookie her "Yes'm." It had a special moist earnestness that served in almost any situation. When Annie was at a loss for words or sensed that her next words were crucial ones, to say "Yes'm" was very chancy. Sometimes it eased her past a sticky place in a conversation with a grown-up, but more often the grown-up stopped as if disturbed by a sudden draft, and Annie would be scrutinized through narrowed eyes, as if she had been the one who had raised the offending window.

Now, Annie heard Miss Emma pushing the heavy swivel chair on its rollers back from Dr. Matt's huge old rolltop desk—the only thing of Dr. Matt's she allowed herself to use. Annie gave Cookie a swift kick under the table; payment for their chess pie and milk would fall due any second now.

Miss Emma cleared her throat noisily and called down the hall, "Lessie, tell them I have exactly fifteen minutes this morning to show them the latest work on Papa's papers—not one minute more."

Cookie sighed, and Miss Lessie grimaced almost directly at her in keen appreciation of her disappointment. "Another day, another dollar," she said solemnly.

"Yes'm," Cookie answered immediately, and this time Miss Lessie's long eyeteeth showed.

"Their fifteen minutes starts *now*," Miss Emma called out in warning.

Annie bolted a piece of crust that brought tears to her eyes and pushed back from the table. "Coming, Miss

Emma."

The bare hall floor under her feet was cool and satiny smooth. The boards ran longways, and the edges of each plank had warped just enough over the years to make contoured tracks for her feet, holding her straight and steady on the path to the large front room that had been Dr. Matthew Carter's bedroom, sitting room, study, and library. The shades were down here, as in all the other rooms, but the organdy curtains were freshly starched and snowy white against the wallpaper's faded fleur-de-lis. One whole wall was covered with every picture Miss Emma and Miss Lessie had been able to find in which Dr. Matt was either featured or a member of a group.

Miss Emma swiveled to face them, her short legs barely reaching the heavy chair's pedestal. Her gold-rimmed glasses were perched on top of her head, the earpieces disappearing under two rows of stiff white curls that looked just like the curls of the marble angel Annie had seen on Dr. Matt's tombstone.

She lifted her plump ringless hands palms up in a delicate, helpless gesture. "Papa's spirit still calls out to the young," she said. "That's the real wonder of the man I'd like to capture on paper. Can it be done?" she asked, suddenly catching both girls in her piercing gaze.

"Yes'm," Cookie answered immediately, as she had her answer always ready.

Annie's hesitation brought Miss Emma's dark-brown eyes full upon her, cutting away the cluttered room, the stacks of magazines and books on the floor, the narrow bed, and the rocker against the wall. Annie felt that her eyes might leave their sockets before they pulled loose from Miss Emma's grip on them.

"I believe it can be done," Annie said, emphatically slapping her thigh to compensate for her tardiness.

"What?" asked Miss Emma with a puzzled frown.

"Put Dr. Matt down on paper?" Annie asked, again uncertain of what was expected.

Miss Emma snatched at her glasses. "Of course it can't be done. You don't think you can just put visions down on paper, the way you can your multiplication tables, do you?" she demanded.

Annie closed her eyes, trying to review the conversation from the beginning. Cookie gave a small tentative yank on her blue jeans. Quickly Annie opened her eyes and gave Miss Emma a solemn, "No'm."

"Well, that's what I've got to do—something you think can't be done at all; or else Papa might as well be . . ." She stopped abruptly and turned toward Cookie, leaving Annie to slump gratefully against the door frame.

"Yes'm," Cookie agreed woefully, her eyes wide and knowing.

Miss Emma's eyes suddenly softened. "It's wonderful to find someone who understands. It's what keeps me going. Though Heaven knows, hens' teeth couldn't be any rarer."

She pushed herself back around toward the desk and, with her back to them, began sorting through a tall stack of index cards, jotting notes on the edges every few seconds.

Annie backed slowly out of the door after Cookie. Her eyes were free again, and she paused briefly to savor the room's strangely exciting atmosphere.

Over Dr. Matt's bed hung a huge ram's head with glass eyeballs and long shaggy hair that seemed to have dandruff. Under the head was the gun Dr. Matt had used to kill the beast. Miss Emma said he had decided never to kill another animal after that long-ago hunting trip to the Colorado mountains. He kept the ram's head as a memento of his decision and the gun as the burden of a man raising two young, innocent girls in a hostile world.

Dr. Matt's highly polished, high-top shoes (which Miss Emma had the very devil of a time finding, even back in 1935) stood primly together, ankles touching, at the foot of his narrow bed. He had liked them because they supported his slender ankles, weak from so many years of pounding up and down hard school corridors and across baked clay playgrounds.

Beside Dr. Matt's large desk stood a towering dumb cane plant that Annie knew would be fifteen years old this summer. The plant's care, plus the daily dusting and cleaning of the room, was Miss Lessie's contribution to Papa's immortality.

To Annie, the room looked just like Jefferson Davis's room down at the Little White House of the Confederacy in Montgomery, except that Dr. Matt's room was even better, because you could go in the bathroom and see his toothbrush and razor and shaving mug, just where he'd left them in a precisely tilted row. Maybe that's why he was always so neat, thought Annie. He knew he might be called any time and how he left things would be exactly how the whole world saw him forever after.

In the cool gloom of the hall again, Cookie and Annie felt along the wall, not waiting for their eyes to adjust to the darkness. About halfway down the hall, they bumped into Miss Lessie, who stood waiting silently for a report.

"Dr. Matt's dumb cane looks awfully good, Miss

Lessie," Annie offered.

"Yes'm," Cookie agreed.

Miss Lessie gave a satisfied grimace and stood aside. Reaching for each other's hands, Cookie and Annie ran through the kitchen on tiptoe and, both pushing with their free hands, slammed the screen door against the porch wall and burst out onto the porch. In the sudden sunshine, they stumbled down the steps and, holding each other around the waist, danced crazily, joyfully, round and round toward home, lightly leaping bare oak roots as they went, never missing a step.

* * *

The twelve o'clock whistle hurled its hungry cry across the town. Like those of Pavlov's dogs, countless mouths began to water, and impatient stomachs growled. Clerks waited restively for laggardly customers to clear the store, and businessmen began rattling their car keys in their pockets.

Annie and Cookie, just barely halfway up the magnolia tree, immediately reversed themselves and began swinging out and dropping earthward with the assured ease of a blind man walking in his own garden.

"Dibs on the pot liquor," Cookie called, remembering that Rose had been cooking turnip greens that morning, and headed for the kitchen door.

"Over my dead body," Annie cried, cutting toward the front door, hoping the shortcut would get her to the kitchen and the steaming, dark-green, pungent broth that both she and Cookie loved to pour into a cup full of hot, crumbled cornbread.

With practiced swats at the swinging doors, Annie burst into the kitchen without breaking stride. Cookie stood by the stove, triumphantly holding out her cup.

"Save me some, Rose," Annie cried, opening a cabinet to get a cup.

Rose grunted and peered over her shoulder at Annie. "You don't look like you missed many meals so far. Get in yonder to the table. I'll bring your cup. I'm going to see you beat your daddy to the table yet."

Cookie's eyes widened. "Mama, I was here first," she protested.

"So was Eve. That don't mean she got the whole apple."

"Just keep my cup in here," Annie said, turning toward the breakfast room. "I'll be eating in the kitchen in a few minutes anyway."

"That's premeditation," snapped Rose. "That's worse than coveting the whole apple."

Cookie nodded vigorously, and Rose raised rheumy brown eyes toward the ceiling. "Lord, have I scattered my seed among thorns?"

"Elizabeth Anne! Lunch is served," her father announced in stentorian tones from the breakfast room.

"Child, you going to be late to your own funeral," Rose mumbled with a worried frown. "Now, scat."

* * *

Laurence Trammell tapped his fingers impatiently on the breakfast-room table, his stern face holding Louise and Ruth-baby silent in their seats. Tardiness was so foreign to him that each time he confronted it, it was not only an aggravation, but a shock, a rediscovery.

Unfortunately, for some reason that he had never allowed himself to dwell on, his firstborn's most characteristic trait seemed to be tardiness. Maybe it was because she came so late in his life. He was almost forty, thirty-eight to be exact, when he married; and Annie came five years after that. Perhaps it was because of all those long, scream-filled hours Louise had to suffer just to prod her out into the world. Whatever the cause, it sometimes seemed to him that their only relationship through the next twelve years had been countless summonses: Get up, come in, wash up for supper, get in the car so that we can start for church—and so it went.

Now, she was finally in her chair at the table, but his soup was lukewarm and his appetite had diminished considerably. Annie sat on the very edge of her chair, kicking at the rungs with her feet, looking for all the world as if she had been held there for days against her will, a bird cruelly tied to a branch. Noticing the first pink tinges of sunburn on her small, heart-shaped face, Laurence looked ruefully at his own pale, freckled hands extending from the blue seersucker jacket that he wore even on the hottest August day.

"Stop that noise, Annie, and eat your soup," he said, his voice sounding angrier than he had meant it to. I wonder what she does all day, he thought.

"Elizabeth Anne, what has happened to your hair?" her mother wanted to know.

"What's wrong with it?"

"It's, it's . . . " Louise paused, at a loss for words.

"She's probably just not combed it yet today," Laurence suggested.

"Probably," Annie agreed.

"Elizabeth," Louise sighed, "a lady's morning toilet might possibly be the whole key to her success in life." She looked wanly at Laurence as if to say, "You see. Something must be done."

Laurence nodded, submissive to female mysteries, and turned his head toward the kitchen.

"Rose, I have a furniture store to run. Where's the rest of my lunch?" he called loudly, to reaffirm his place as head of this house full of women.

"I didn't hear any grace," Rose said, poking her head through the door.

"ThanktheeLordforthisandallthymanyblessings-
                                                        Amen."

"Jesus wept," Rose added solemnly.

Laurence Trammell hesitated before he unfolded his napkin and laid it across his lap. She always did that, even the night the mayor and Henry Warren, the new district congressman from Dothan, came for supper. He never meant to mind, because he knew she had learned the habit from her mother before her, but he always did. It made no sense and always left something hanging in the air, a gentle reproach—guilty as charged.

He'd even gone so far as to suggest she learn a new verse, although he knew it was pointless. If a white woman could turn her husband this way or that—mold, shape, press him by endless years of soft, intransient Being—a black woman could turn you inside out and leave you dangling helplessly by the scruff of your neck time and again without you ever knowing, until after the fact.

Ruth-baby, crumbs of cornbread sticking to her chin

and squeezed between the fingers of one fat fist, gave an ear-piercing scream as she disappeared backward from the table. Lunging wildly, dragging his best silk tie across his plate, Laurence caught her by the hem of her dress. Rose reappeared at the door. "What's the matter with her?" she asked, glancing toward Laurence.

Laurence turned toward Annie.

"She stuck out her tongue at me," Annie said.

Laurence felt the blood surge to his face. "You mean you tipped Ruth-baby's chair back deliberately?" he asked.

Her mother's hand fluttered to a pin at her throat. "You might have damaged her brain."

"I will not tolerate this kind of disruption at the table," Laurence shouted, banging down a fist that raised every dish on the table half an inch and plainly including Rose as well as Annie in his angry glare. "Annie, finish your lunch in the kitchen."

"Yes, sir," Annie answered quickly, her soup bowl, glass, and silver already stacked precariously on her plate.

* * *

As Annie disappeared through the swinging door, Laurence felt a strange sense of defeat. Staring at his half-empty plate, he wondered if the three women had discussed him that morning. Were they working together against him, or were they working at cross-purposes against each other? They were like three rivers: each one vastly different from the other; each one different every day from herself the day, the hour, before; yet each one unceasingly moving past him toward something. At least with Annie the movement was always on the surface. Every thought she had seemed to ripple across her face. Her cloudy lilac eyes caught light like tiny whirlpools spinning off submerged rocks. They were the eyes of Louise Fairbault as she had raced to meet him at the Selma depot. The first time he saw Louise, Laurence thought he had never seen such loveliness, such exquisite softness, so much so that it hurt him just to look at her. As she had stood beside him on the platform, tapping her feet impatiently while he gathered his bags, her dark-red hair had just brushed the top of his shoulder. He never tired of watching her long slender fingers fluttering, jabbing, curling, as if to help each word she spoke find its proper place in his thoughts.

Laurence knew he had never been handsome; he was small-boned with pale parchment-paper skin. He had kept growing until he was too tall for his slight, almost delicate frame. Self-conscious about his tallness, his awkwardness, his thinness, he moved stiffly, lest he bump into something or trip on the stairs. Once, while watching him try to learn to ride his bike, his father had told him that when he was born someone had ordered, "Heavy on the starch," and kept on ironing, when they should have ordered "Hang it up!"

Only under the teasing eyes of Louise Fairbault had he ever been able to dance, almost frolic, that sweet, short time. He had never known anyone who seemed so light and gay and pleased with everything he said and did. He had raked his brain for the culprit who had cut in on his first, his only, dance. Maybe it was bringing her here, away from the flat Delta and her father's big farm to the eastern Alabama foothills crowded with pines. Maybe it was her father's dying so soon after the wedding. After all, the old man had ordered and protected every moment of her life until then; while Laurence, on the other hand, had never relished authority over anyone, especially women. To him, women seemed dark, mysterious forces one never understood and only rarely subverted from their private purposes. He had even tried, tried so hard he ached from it, to blame Annie and Ruth-baby—after all, she had almost died in childbirth twice—but it was no good. He knew who had stopped the music—for him and, more terrible, for the only woman he had ever really loved.

When he was a small boy, he was terrified of the dark, and once he had trapped a lightning bug in a mason jar to carry to bed with him. It had worked. For hours the tiny light had chased the shadows, and he fell asleep with the jar pressed against his cheek. But his sleep had cost the small insect dearly. It had beaten itself to death, trying to escape the invisible walls of its glass prison. When Laurence saw the creature dead at the bottom of the jar, he had cried into his pillow.

For a moment he watched Louise as she fed Ruth-baby; her lips, even slightly parted in unconscious mimicry, seemed to droop a little at the corners. A part of his mind still found it inconceivable that, after his experience with the lightning bug, as a grown man, he would do the same thing to another human being. He shuddered, remembering his elaborate attempts to seem witty and gay during his courtship of Louise. His parents were dead, his brothers and sisters all married and gone, Otis married. Night after night he had sat alone in the big, empty house, planning each word he would say to Louise the following weekend in Selma. If he did not win her, he had thought, he would surely die.

After they married, he had been unable to uphold the deception a single day. Before his very eyes, Louise seemed to pale. Her lighthearted chiding took on a new, sharp edge. One morning he had awakened to find her, still asleep, curled into a little ball sobbing. It was then that Laurence had first remembered the lightning bug. When she woke up, Louise remembered nothing, but it was shortly after that she was ill for the first time. For Laurence, the days and months afterward were a blur, as the horror of his sin gripped him.

One rain-chilled January night, the last meeting of the winter revival, he had submitted to his guilt. He had vowed to set Louise free. When he got home she was waiting up for him, sitting up in bed, pillows piled behind her back. Her long redwood hair, tangled in a peach-colored ribbon on the shoulder of her nightgown, lay curled against her neck like a kitten playing with a string.

His anguished sense of loss was suddenly softened, like the feeling of honey on a wound. Was it relief? Not to be guilty anymore. Kneeling beside the bed, he confessed. Not what she already must know, being the victim, but his unforgivable sin: he too had known that he was a stone to her butterfly, and still he had taken her, kept her for his own sake.

Louise stroked his head absently, as she might have Ruth-baby's. "There, there now. Don't make a scene, Laurence."

"Louise, I offer you your freedom," he whispered.

"Freedom. Freedom to do what?" she had said, her

voice petulant. "Get into bed, Laurence. It makes me shiver just to think of the draft there must be down on that floor."

He had been too late. There was no more fire, no remembrance, even, of fire. From that night, they had both thought and moved with a single accord, to make her glass cage as comfortable and invisible as possible.

* * *

"Laurence, you're not listening, and you've hardly touched your lunch."

The breakfast room swam before his eyes. Even Ruth-baby was watching him silently from her round, blue eyes.

"I better get back to town," he said abruptly. "The boys are laying carpet all over Elsie Turner's downstairs this afternoon. They'll be short-handed at the store."

"What color?"

"Persimmon, I think it's called."

"Wouldn't Elsie just."

Laurence gave a guilty start. He had filed the little irony of sharp-tongued Elsie and her persimmon carpet away yesterday morning when she bought it (all 500 square yards, right off the floor), knowing Louise would appreciate the humor of it. He collected these little female ironies and brought them home, presents for Louise. It was the closest he ever came to striking a spark in her inward-looking lilac eyes.

Other women seemed to sense intuitively the fine difference between his gathering gossip for another female and being a male gossip (whom they all would have shunned), for they often commented, with a sigh or shake of the head, "That poor man. He just lives for Louise Trammell." He had overheard such comments in drugstore booths several times himself. Other times he just read the sympathy in their glances. He would have been terrified had he known how much more several of those warm glances suggested to more objective observers.

"I'm sorry, dear, I meant to tell you sooner," he apologized. "Yesterday morning I think she was in, but while she was there, there was something—the fire at Florence's, that's it. Elsie rushed off, and I let it slip my mind in all the excitement afterward."

"Never mind that now. I've been thinking about something much more important. I have the solution to our problem."

"What problem?"

Louise exhaled impatiently. "Annie, of course. I want you to go straight from this house to Miss Emma's and arrange for Annie to begin deportment lessons tomorrow."

"Does Annie know?"

"We'll discuss it at dinner tonight. It's summer, the ideal time, and the only other alternative is finishing school. There are some lovely ones around Mobile," she said.

"Louise, she's only twelve."

"That's just it. If we wait until she's any older, I'm afraid it will be too late. If only I could be a real mother . . ."

"Hush, dear. You're the most beautiful mother a girl could ask for. Tonight I'll bring you some of those good hush-puppies from the cafe if you'll promise me to rest this afternoon and not fret about Annie. After all, Emma

Carter had no trouble whipping two generations of
Winton citizens into shape."

Rose stuck her head through the door. "Y'all about
through in there?" she asked.

"Yes, Rose, you may clear the table now and bring us
some dessert." Louise answered without turning her head.

As the door rebounded behind Rose, Laurence could
see Annie at the kitchen table, laughing at Cookie over a
dripping spoonful of pot liquor, smooth, shiny, brown
hair swinging back and forth across her cheek as she took
a diving bite, then licked the spoon front and back. The
door closed silently, and Laurence turned back toward
Louise.

" 'Deportment,' you said? I'm not sure I know exactly
what that cures."

Louise tapped a slippered foot impatiently. "Well, you
learn how to behave properly—in Annie's case that would
mean like a lady. I think to make it perfectly plain to Miss
Emma what our needs are you should broaden that a
little. Just tell her you'd like her to take up where breeding
leaves off."

Laurence wanted to throw back his head and laugh at
what he thought of as her droll Delta wit. But he just
nodded like a boy taking down a list for the grocery, for
she did not recognize her own humor—and it hurt them
both when he laughed alone.

"What's for dessert?" he asked.

CHAPTER 7

FROM THE KITCHEN Annie watched Rose back through the door, balancing two plates of apple cobbler in front of her. Rose stood peering down expectantly while Laurence and Louise took their first bites. One foot in a felt slipper slit at the sides to allow room for her corns still held the door open behind her.

"It's fine, Rose," her mother said.

Her father nodded his head and lightly kissed the tips of his fingers.

"Y'all all set then?"

"Yes, thank you. Everything's fine," Annie heard her mother say again.

"Good," Rose said emphatically, " 'cause I'm fixing to rest these bones." She gave the door a shove with a dimpled elbow and was back in the kitchen.

"Move over, you two," Rose said, waving her arm at Cookie and Annie. "I done mopped and washed windows and hung out a lineful, and it's not one o'clock. This afternoon Miss Louise is going to be after me to clean closets. She's the best woman I know for getting up work for other folks."

"Where's your plate, Mama?" Cookie asked, used to her mother's laments.

"Think I'll just set a bit—give my appetite a chance to

catch up with my stomach," Rose answered, exhaling heavily as she sat down at the small table. Her heavy bosom heaved, and the buttonholes of her dark-green dress strained against the buttons until the satiny pink of her slip showed like a row of rosebuds down to her waist.

"What you two been up to this morning?" she asked, resting a broad hand on each knee.

"Just taking greens to Miss Emma and Miss Lessie like you said. That took the whole morning," Cookie complained.

Annie nodded. "We're going to spend the rest of the day helping B.C. fix a bike."

"Where has William been this whole week?" Rose wanted to know.

"Oh, Mama, who cares about that nasty old William Petus?" Cookie blurted, wrinkling her nose.

Rose raised an eyebrow in surprise.

"He called B.C. a dumb nigger, and they had a big fight. B.C. says he won't ever have anything to do with William again so long as he can draw breath."

Rose put her hand gently, probingly, under her left breast. Her eyes on their faces seemed to lose their focus. After a minute, she said in a faraway voice, "So that's what's been eating the boy. It had to happen."

"What had to happen?" asked Annie.

Rose came back to them with a wry grin. "The Holloways and the Petuses were never meant to ride the same track long. Still, I'm sorry for B.C. The first time is always the worst." With sudden intuition, Rose looked sharply at Annie. "Is that all that's bothering B.C.?"

Annie shifted uneasily, thinking of Wadine Pratt. But now it seemed so faraway, she nodded her head. "I guess so."

"Well, I reckon he'll live, though they was awful close," Rose said, her voice low and faraway again. "*Deportment*," she said slowly, rolling the word off her tongue. "No, that can't be it."

"Can't be what?" asked Cookie.

"That's like sending somebody back to their own country. Like that skinny little Mexican fellow that worked at the hardware store a few years back."

"What Mexican fellow?" said Annie, leaning forward as she tried to follow Rose's strange conversation.

"What Mexican fellow is neither here nor there. You were born and bred right here in Beacon County, so it don't apply. But whatever it is, that's what you fixing to get, Annie," Rose said glumly, shaking her head and tugging at the waist of her dress.

Annie paled. "Just for messing up one little old coke party?"

"Honey, I don't rightly know. But just now, while I was clearing the table, I heard your mama telling your daddy to ask Miss Emma would she give you depo . . . anyway, them lessons. Maybe, if you do real good on your lessons . . ."

"Won't she ever give up on lessons?" Annie cried. "Mrs. Hargrove already told Mama last fall that if she insisted on one more violin lesson for me, Mrs. Hargrove was afraid she'd find herself tone deaf."

Cookie turned her eyes upward. "From what I heard from the front porch, she started worrying some too late."

"It's just a good thing I quit taking lessons before she keeled over this winter. She'd probably have left a note saying my playing did it."

"Honey, I don't think these gonna be music lessons. These got something to do with stretching out your breeding. Let's see, I believe she said she wants Miss Emma to take up where your breeding left off. Something like that."

"I won't do it. I just can't," Annie cried, shoving her plate back. "I promised B.C. I'd help him fix that bike. He needs us now that William isn't his friend anymore and Cookie and I, we promised, we swore . . . " Her voice faded away. She could not tell Rose about their secret pact.

Rose brushed a lock of straight brown hair back from Annie's cheek. "Baby," she said sadly, "B.C.'s time has come. From now on, nobody can help him much. Getting used to hard knocks is part of getting to be a man, and a black man's got to get positively partial to them. The sooner the better."

Cornbread crumbs clogged Annie's throat. Her eyes stung. Flinging herself into Rose's lap, she clutched her around the neck, hiding her face in Rose's neck as hot tears trickled down both cheeks.

"I don't want to be stretched any way at all. It's hopeless. They ought to just let me be. I'll never come out right."

"Hush now," Rose murmured, rocking back and forth on the creaking chair. "I 'spect any problem you got is half my fault. I don't know 'bout raising white babies past a certain point," her voice fell, "once just loving them ain't enough.

"Your mama's just trying to give you some advantages,

especially since she can't do much for you herself—her health and all being what it is."

"Oh, Rose, I did it," Annie whispered into the soft dark neck. "I made her sick. She was never meant to have such an ugly daughter. It makes her sick."

"Don't say one more word like that! You not too big for me to turn across my knee, even if your feet do drag the floor. Maybe your mama's just naturally sickly, and it's such a burden it's all she's got time to mind." She paused. "But sometimes I think she's just plain scared of living. Heaven only knows she hasn't had much chance to practice."

She shifted her legs under Annie's weight. "Besides, baby, everybody's beautiful to the folks that love them. Don't I think that scrawny, little squint-eyed Otis is a vision? You'll see. You'll see how it is one of these days," she crooned softly, pulling Annie's cheek down against her soft shoulder.

"What on earth is going on out here?" Laurence Trammell asked leaning through the door, his voice hurried and anxious. "We thought we heard crying. Is someone hurt?"

"No, sir, Mr. Laurence, just a little growing pain, I reckon," Rose answered over Annie's head. "You needing some more cobbler?"

"No, no. If everything is all right, I better get back to town. I'll help Miss Louise back to her room before I go, though." There was a little silence. "See you this evening at dinner, Annie. I may have some special news for you."

Annie kept her face hidden in Rose's damp shoulder until she heard the soft swish, swish of the door.

After a moment Rose spoke. "Up you get, young'un.

My neck's got a crick in it won't wait—not to mention a kitchen full of dirty dishes. Take you some cobbler and some more ice tea out on the back steps. Then you can take some down to B.C."

Annie sat on the bottom step, her eyes half shut so that the sun made a golden fringe of her brown lashes, and spooned the cobbler into her mouth—hot sweet cobbler, cold lemony tea; hot cobbler, cold tea.

"Well, I for one don't know any cause for you to be sitting around purring unless you're some kind of cat that favors being skinned," Cookie snapped.

"Cookie, I'm not going to take any lessons from Miss Emma. Haven't I talked Mama out of Miss Rebecca's School of the Dance three years running? I wouldn't let B.C. down for anything."

"Forget B.C.," Cookie screeched. "You are in dangerous, horrible trouble, Annie Trammell, if I've got those deport . . . whatever-they-are lessons figured right."

"Who cares what kind they are if I don't ever take any?"

"Don't make no difference, I'm thinking," said Cookie. She dropped a thin, brown arm around Annie's shoulder. "Annie, they fixing to marry you off."

"Marry me off!" Annie cried, jerking her eyes open. "I'm only twelve years old."

"That's just what I heard your papa say when Rose went into the kitchen, but it didn't discourage Miss Louise any."

"You have finally flipped your wig, Cookie Holloway."

Cookie leaned toward Annie. "Do you remember sitting all afternoon in Mr. Abe Welch's hayloft, watching them men and boys wearing themselves out trying to get

Big Mac interested in that heifer? Well, that's breeding, and folks just fancy that up a little with cake and preachers for weddings."

Annie's eyes felt so dry, she thought she might never be able to shut them again, might be doomed to see everything the rest of her life. She pulled her face away from Cookie's. "Well, those grown men finally gave up on Big Mac, didn't they? They'll just have to give up on me too."

"You'll be fighting powerful odds: your mama, your daddy, Miss Emma, Miss Florence. . ."

"Miss Florence! How does she come into this?"

"Don't bust my eardrums," Cookie said, rubbing her ear. "I didn't think this up; I'm only letting you in on it."

"What does Miss Florence have to do with it, then?" Annie whispered.

Cookie's eyes widened, and her narrow chest expanded beneath her white T-shirt as she delivered her knockout punch. "Who do you suppose your intended is?"

Annie watched two young gray squirrels chase across the garage roof and leap unsteadily into the nearest pecan tree.

Slowly she shook her head. "They wouldn't marry me to William Petus without even telling me." Her voice was still a whisper she couldn't seem to break.

"Your daddy said he would have some special news for you tonight, didn't he?" Cookie squeezed her eyelids shut until her lashes almost disappeared. "What you gonna do, Annie?"

Seeing tough, reliable Cookie at the point of tears brought the full weight of her problem crashing down around Annie, as if the big pecan tree in front of them had been uprooted and toppled across her.

Rose stepped out on the back porch balancing an old, chipped enamel bowl covered with a piece of newspaper. "Get this on down to B.C., will you, Cookie? And don't get too filthy working on that old car of B.C.'s, you two."

"Yes, ma'am," Cookie sighed, lifting her arms for the dish.

* * *

The pasture was full of midday quiet as Annie and Cookie knelt in the dust, waiting impatiently for B.C. to speak.

"I still don't know," B.C. said, shoving another cinder block under the back end of the wheelless chariot in front of him. "It just don't sound right. Even if Miss Louise is that desperate over Annie William Petus would rather be dipped in honey and drug through a hill of ants than get mixed up with any girl, especially Annie Trammell."

"Listen to the pot calling the kettle black," Cookie said, tossing her head.

Without warning, the vivid black-and-white memory of Wadine Pratt's and B.C.'s twisting bodies shook Annie, and the newspaper-wrapped bowl almost slipped from her hands. With trembling fingers she wiped some sweet apple juice onto the shoulder of her shirt.

B.C. seemed not to have heard Cookie, but he stared at Annie until she turned away to watch a fretful mockingbird tugging at last year's dried berries in a low tangle of wild blackberry bushes.

"And besides, B.C., you know mamas don't count feelings like that," Cookie added.

"That's a fact," B.C. said, shaking his round shaved head. "What you figuring on doing, Annie?"

Annie, still numb from Cookie's revelation, had not figured on doing anything at all. Now with B.C. watching her intently, she felt a quiet sense of pride and unhappy sureness.

Slowly, she rose to her feet. "I guess I'll be leaving," she said, her words dropping like pebbles in a pool. As if someone had flung a blanket across the pasture, the world was suddenly still and empty. B.C. and Cookie stared up at Annie like dwarfs in a magnetized circle.

With a wild, balancing flutter of his wings the long-tailed mockingbird settled fearlessly on Annie's shoulder and pecked jerkily at the sweet apple syrup drying there. As a last peck caught her skin, Annie shuddered and swung angrily at the bird with her hand. "Get away," she shouted, as strong wings caught in her hair and were gone.

Released from her silence, Cookie whispered, "You mean leave Winton?"

With an effort, Annie pulled her eyes down to rest on Cookie's awestruck face. Groping for details, she reviewed her possible avenues of escape. There was Uncle Titus in Fayetteville. He'd just send her right back home on the afternoon bus. In one week last summer, she had given him a bad case of the hives. Last winter she'd had an Eskimo pen pal, but she hadn't answered her last two letters. Besides, the thought of all that snow and darkness depressed her almost as much as William Petus.

"Detroit," she suddenly blurted out.

"You don't have bus fare to Montgomery, Annie Trammell. How you figure to get to Detroit?" B.C. asked, wiping greasy hands on his faded plaid shirt.

"Well, I . . . I was planning to hop a freight."

B.C. squinted skeptically. "Why you going to Detroit?"

"'Cause, that's where all the colored people go to find freedom and easy times. I heard Daddy say so to Mama when Tom left the store so suddenly and ran off up there, and after Daddy'd been so patient with him about his drinking all these years. So if that's the best place for all the colored people to run to, it'll probably be the best place for me."

"I still reckon it's not true," B.C. said, absently rubbing a scraped place on the back of his hand.

"It is too," Annie protested. "Why, I'm leaving this very afternoon on the three-oh-five."

"I mean, maybe it's not true they mean to marry you off to William Petus. After all, he's due to leave for Boy Scout camp in a week. Don't seem like there's hardly any room in a week to get a wedding in. Besides, Two-Time said that girl's gonna be there most all summer."

Annie whirled on Cookie, whose cheeks darkened suspiciously.

"Cookie Holloway . . . "

"I'm right. I know I'm right," Cookie cried, backing toward the front porch. "In fact, B.C. just proved it! It even explains why William Petus picked a fight with you."

B.C.'s eyes hardened, then flicked away. "Never mind that," he said.

Cookie began pacing back and forth, her hands behind her back. "B.C., if you thought marrying a girl was staring you in the face, would you rush off to admit it to William Petus, who'd laugh you clear to Fayetteville, after all the talking you done against girls?"

"Maybe so, maybe not," B.C. answered noncommittally.

"Well, you know what Mama says, 'Pride goes before a fall,'" Cookie said, rearing back with her hands on hips that were no bigger around than her mother's knee, "and William Petus is ninety-nine and forty-four one-hundredths percent pure pride. He'd rather never be your friend again than have you be able to lord it over him, especially about a girl."

"I reckon he might," B.C. agreed skeptically. "Cookie, you really think that might be it?"

"You sound like you hope it is right. Don't you have any human feelings, B.C.?" Annie cried.

"I didn't sound any way at all. I'm just trying to get the facts."

"Well, here's some more then," Cookie said, beginning to pace again. "The wedding has to be after Boy Scout camp, don't you see? It's plain as day. No matter what a burden Annie is to her mother, Miss Emma has to have time for the lessons to do some good, so as to have Annie ready to be a married lady. Mary Ellen has come down to be in the wedding. She's probably up there practicing her part right now." Cookie's eyes widened. "Why, she's probably gonna be your maid of honor."

"No!" Annie cried, jumping to her feet.

Cookie stopped pacing, and the two girls looked at each other, remembering the long day down by the creek last summer when they'd planned their weddings. Their bridesmaids' dresses would be pink with green sashes—like the wild primroses that covered the creek banks.

They would be each other's maid of honor. B.C. and William were not to be invited—just Rose, Otis, Ruthbaby, and Annie's mama and daddy. Now Annie realized that they had never discussed husbands. It had been a lovely all-girl ceremony. Now that reality in the form of William Petus had been dashed in her face, the ceremony seemed cold and scary as a funeral.

Cookie finished the defense of her case in a quavering voice, her shoulders hunched, her hands jammed into her jean pockets. " . . . and William is being sent to Scout camp to keep him quiet and pay him off for marrying Annie." She paused, silenced by the overwhelming evidence she had just marshaled. "I guess I better pack and come along too. You'll probably need saving before we're halfway to Fayetteville."

The breeze quickened, sending chicken feathers swirling across the bare yard.

Annie licked her dry lips, and the salty taste of dried tears seemed a promise of faraway oceans and singing seashells. "B.C., why don't you come, too? It'll be fun. We'll go everywhere, not just Detroit."

A small smile touched the corners of B.C.'s full mouth, as if he, too, tasted a salty sea breeze.

"Please come," Annie urged, sinking to her knees beside B.C. "It won't be anything without you."

B.C.'s face seemed about to succumb to one of his dangerous scowls, but instead it quivered and became still again.

"You know what they make in Detroit, don't you?"

B.C. nodded.

"You can probably buy one up there for a song. Maybe even get a job working on real cars if you tell them you're eighteen. I bet you could show them a thing or two about cars."

"I don't know if it would be right. Someone ought to stay here to help Mama. She seems awful tired lately, and I don't reckon she could manage without one of us. Leastwise not while she's still so tired out. She's probably got the high blood again. Maybe she could get some medicine from Dr. Mason, and I could catch up to you girls later."

"We liable to be anywhere—even China," Cookie pointed out. "Besides, without us around, Mama won't have half as much to do. And Mama is always after us to make something outta ourselves. She'll be proud if we go to Detroit and get rich."

B.C. kicked the dirt in frustration. "Hey, wait a minute," he cried. "Why you girls in such an almighty rush? You're safe 'til William gets back from Scout camp, and maybe by that time Mama will get some medicine. We could make a real careful plan and save up some money, too. We could pick up scuppernongs and sell them in town."

Cookie clapped her hands. "We could collect drink bottles and old coat hangers and get the refund."

As mythical piles of money mounted around them in the dust, the three children joined hands, and their shadows slowly lengthened behind them until they were leaning forward to read each other's faces in the summer dusk. When the bell from the big house rang across the meadow, they started as though caught by eavesdroppers.

Cookie dropped Annie's hand, but for a moment B.C. did not. "I reckon you hate William Petus as bad as I hate him, and some other people too, I might say."

Annie held carefully still. She knew William was awful

and Wadine Pratt was worse, but somehow she had not thought of hating them.

"Just wait, Annie. We'll show them all," B.C. whispered into the darkness.

Reluctantly Annie rose. "I guess I better go get some supper and find out about my lessons from Miss Emma Carter."

"Don't worry, Annie," Cookie called after her. "It's just 'til we're ready to leave."

CHAPTER 8

TEN O'CLOCK the next morning found Annie reluctantly entering Dr. Matt's room in a starched sun dress and white sandals still wet with polish. After a brief flurry, when Annie scandalized Miss Emma by casually sitting down on Dr. Matt's bed when Miss Emma invited her to be seated, the first lesson proceeded more or less according to plan—Annie's plan, though Miss Emma seemed happy enough for all that.

Miss Emma wrote *de-port-ment* on a small slate that had been Dr. Matt's when he was a boy. After making certain Annie was aware of the historical interest of the little board and its ultimate destination in the Dr. Matthew Carter Museum, which she envisioned as a room behind the school gymnasium, she handed the board to Annie.

With hope born of desperation, Annie asked, "Does deportment *always* have something to do with breeding?"

"I certainly like to think so," Miss Emma said, "that is, in its broadest sense."

After walking down the hall and back three times with a book on her head, Annie asked how the work on Dr. Matt's papers was progressing. For the next hour Miss Emma read while Annie listened to ten of Dr. Matt's most moving letters to the state legislature suggesting modern improvements—and the brief, impersonal answers promising continued study of Dr. Matt's suggestions and thanking him for his concern. The replies were often identical and signed by a flattened-out, unreadable scrawl at the bottom. Miss Emma said that people with handwriting like that were always bureaucrats who spent their lives seeing how little they could get done for how many people. "You see, Annie, in Alabama, education is at the bottom of the heap," she said, her voice rising in indignation.

Pinning Annie's face between her two moist, plump palms, she searched her face as if looking for some sign of intelligence. "Ach," she cried, turning away, "do you want to know why you're so mistreated, neglected, ignored?"

Annie nodded her head vigorously.

"It's because you don't have a vote. So, who decides where the money for your education goes? I'll tell you, the legislators and the tycoons in this state split it fifty-fifty."

Staring at a picture of Dr. Matt in a black robe and a four-cornered hat, she sighed. "Perhaps that was his greatest idea—though you ought not to set up priorities on great ideas."

"Exactly what did Dr. Matt have in mind for us children, Miss Emma?" Annie asked hesitantly, not wanting to break Miss Emma's mellow mood.

"Why, the vote, child, like I have been telling you. How old are you, Annie Trammell?" she demanded, straightening in her swivel chair.

"Twelve, going on thirteen."

"You're overdue then. By Papa's reckoning, you'd have been a responsible, law-abiding, *voting* citizen since the eve of your tenth birthday."

"Is that anything like as good as grown?" Annie asked, rising to stand at solemn attention.

Rising on the little footstool in front of her chair, Miss Emma nodded and tapped Annie lightly on the head and each shoulder. "There, Elizabeth Anne Trammell, you're good as grown. But remember, with privilege and the right to choose comes the responsibility not to choose foolishly. You must choose what's really best for you and for the majority. Thanks to Papa and you dear children, we may get Alabama off her knees yet."

There was an awkward silence, and Annie realized the ceremony needed ending, like revival meetings that had lasted too long into the night.

Tentatively she murmured softly, "Amen." Then, seeing Miss Emma's favorable reaction, she gave her loudest, most fervent, "Amen to that, sister. Amen to that."

Miss Emma came down off the stool with a flat-footed little thud. "I think that's all for today, Annie. I need to get back to my cataloging now. Your father said an hour every day, so I'll see you tomorrow morning at ten o'clock. You practice walking up and down stairs at your house three times with a book on your head. And remember," she said, "one of the attributes of a lady is that she is punctual—no matter what you may have heard to the contrary." She swiveled back to the desk, and Annie retreated quietly down the hall toward the kitchen.

Annie was almost to the back door when a soft voice behind her made her jump. Miss Lessie was sitting still as stone on a cane-bottomed chair squeezed between the refrigerator and the stove.

"Wouldn't you like just a small piece of prune cake?" Annie glanced toward the sun-filled back door.

"It was Papa's favorite cake," Miss Lessie added in her hesitant, breathy voice.

That settled it; Annie pulled out a chair at the kitchen table. Her whole outlook on Dr. Matt had changed. He had indeed been an unsung champion of the young and defenseless. If he were alive today, he would take her hand, and together they would eat prune cake and challenge anyone to marry her off to the meanest, ugliest creature this side of the Okefenokee Swamp. Lord, she'd rather spend the rest of her life with William Petus's alligator than William and Miss Florence. Worst of all, she suddenly realized, she'd be kissing kin to Mary Ellen Parker.

Miss Lessie carefully cut a gigantic piece of cake and placed it on a chipped Blue Onion saucer. Then with both of her long-boned, brown-spotted hands, she held out the plate toward Annie as if it were some sort of offering.

"Would you care for a little cold milk to wash it down?"

Annie looked down doubtfully at the huge piece of cake.

"Perhaps just a little coffee-milk, then?"

Annie nodded. "Aren't you going to sit and have something, too, Miss Lessie?"

"Well, maybe just a swallow of coffee," Miss Lessie said, smiling shyly over Annie's head. Taking a cup with no handle from the windowsill behind the curtain, she poured half a cup from a huge pot she always kept hot on the stove and poured another for Annie, half coffee, half milk.

"Nice day today," she said after she had pulled her chair

up to the table.

"Yes'm," Annie mumbled, her mouth full of cake.

"Think it might rain tonight?"

"No'm, I don't think so."

Miss Lessie's conversation, regular and limited as it was, was years familiar to Annie and easy to take. It seemed to be spliced together across the long pieces of silence with kitchen noises—a pot simmering, a faucet dripping, a clock ticking, the refrigerator's hum (Miss Lessie still called hers an icebox). It was when Miss Lessie suddenly cleared her throat and kept going that Annie felt ill at ease.

"Lesson over?"

"Yes'm."

"Going to be a lady, are you?"

"My mama sure is counting on it," Annie answered evasively, keeping her eyes fastened on the spotless white front of Miss Lessie's apron.

" . . . I'd like that."

"Well'm, I'll do my best," Annie said, shuffling her feet against the rungs of her chair.

"I mean, I'd like to be a lady," said Miss Lessie in a soft rush of words, her head bowed, her hands clasped tightly around her cup.

Annie looked up from her cake in surprise. "I suppose you are a lady, Miss Lessie. I'd sure count you for one," she added more emphatically.

Miss Lessie shook her bowed head. "Never even been to school. Not one day. Papa said some people are meant for learning, some for doing."

"You sure do a lot. I'll vouch for that, Miss Lessie," said Annie anxiously to the small gray head across the table from her. Then with horror she watched Miss Lessie's pale blue eyes, moist now with effort, rise slowly to hers. Her narrow nostrils quivered like a hound's, sniffing hopefully upwind.

"I'd like lessons on being a lady," she whispered, leaning toward Annie until the bib of her apron was almost in her coffee.

"Miss Lessie, I'm the last one . . . "

"It's not like you got to read or do numbers, is it?"

"No'm, it's not that. It's more like the blind leading the blind."

"I saw you hit a squirrel with a slingshot clear to the top of your mama's biggest magnolia," Miss Lessie said flatly.

"You did?" Annie asked, pleased to have found a witness for the disbelieving Cookie.

Miss Lessie nodded, folding her hands with an air of finality. Then she turned her head away from Annie and looked steadfastly at the wall. Annie felt she had never seen this proud, hawk-nosed woman with the iron-gray hair before. She knew Miss Lessie was letting her go and would never ask again, and she ached to be leaping down the steps toward home.

"Being a lady can get you in all sorts of trouble with men," Annie warned.

"I can keep secrets," Miss Lessie said, never turning her head.

Annie sighed. "For today, I had to learn proper walking. Do you have a book handy?"

Miss Lessie's eyes widened in apprehension. "A book?"

"It's just to set on top of your head."

Miss Lessie rose stiffly, as if unaccustomed to sitting for so long, and opened a deep cabinet drawer. First wiping off the dust with her apron, she laid a large black cookbook in front of Annie.

Annie stood up in her chair and carefully balanced the book on Miss Lessie's head.

"Now try to walk to the sink, then back to me without dropping it."

A look of ferocious concentration on her face, Miss Lessie stepped one small step at a time toward the sink. If the book wobbled the least bit, she froze until the crisis was past. At the counter, she grasped the edge of the sink and pivoted ever so slowly back toward Annie. Just before she finished the turn, the book slid sideways, glanced off her narrow shoulder, and fell to the floor. With a cry of despair, Miss Lessie ran to her chair between the stove and the refrigerator. With her hands to her face she began banging her head against the hot-water pipe.

"Stop, Miss Lessie! Please stop," Annie cried, running to grasp her arm.

"What is all that noise in the kitchen, Lessie?" Miss Emma called from Dr. Matt's room. "Don't you know I'm trying to study?"

"It's just me, Miss Emma, having a piece of prune cake," Annie shouted back. Grabbing Miss Lessie's thin, jerking body, she whispered, "Miss Lessie, don't worry about dropping that book. Mine falls off every time. That's why we got to practice. Why, it's not even natural to get it right the first time."

Miss Lessie stopped banging her head, and Annie ran and picked up the book. "Keep this, Miss Lessie, and practice whenever you get a chance. Going up and down steps is best, I reckon."

Miss Lessie pinned the book to her chest with her long, blue-veined arms. Nervously, she glanced toward the back door.

"That's okay," Annie amended quickly, "just step high, same thing. You know, like the majorettes. They must be ladies for sure."

A thin, reluctant smile lit Miss Lessie's pale face. Maybe it was just gratitude, or maybe she saw herself in a little pleated skirt, high-stepping down Main Street past Caulder's Drug Store between long lines of people waving purple felt flags with Matthew Carter High School emblazoned across them.

Annie downed the last bite of cake and wondered when she had eaten the rest of it. "See you tomorrow, Miss Lessie. Study hard," she said, and the teacher of deportment walked—head high, shoulders back—slowly toward the door.

CHAPTER 9

IN THE MIDDAY HEAT, downtown streets and sidewalks threw up shimmering curtains around each building. Store clerks gossiped idly and drank Coca-Colas to fight off drowsiness, staring inhospitably at the occasional customer. The few customers felt unwanted as well as hot and sticky. They longed to be home, stretched out for a nap on cool sheets or nodding in a favorite chair.

Laurence Trammell and Otis Holloway stood side by side at the double back doors of the furniture store, feet apart, hands clasped loosely behind their backs. Through the big glass panes, they watched the empty alley in comfortable silence. The first time they had stood together looking into the dusty alley, waiting impatiently for their turn to go to lunch, Laurence could barely see out the windows. Otis, five years older and then a good two heads taller, was Laurence's hero, tutor, friend, and chaperone, answerable directly to Laurence's father for the behavior of them both.

Over the years, Otis's boyish slouch had become a hunch, and Laurence had grown to be a tall, wiry, stiffly straight man who stood head and shoulders taller than his old friend. Now, as then, they were nearly always together, except when Laurence was at home in the evenings or working on the books in his small second-floor office.

As a boy, Laurence Trammell had asked Otis all his

questions and told him all his dreams. On the rare occasions he had made Otis angry with him, his world stopped until they were friends again. They had discovered early the safety precaution of falling into silence when they were around other boys, white or black, or grown-ups. As they grew older, the encroachments of different schools, parents, and finally girls flowed together and encircled them, and their silences flowed together, too. But they still worked and played together Saturdays and after school; and while loading and unloading furniture and making deliveries, they caught up on what each other's day had been like and gossiped about their respective worlds.

After Laurence finished school, he and Otis worked side by side day in and day out at the furniture store. Then Laurence's father died and Laurence took over the furniture store. That was the winter, hard and bitter as a mock orange, that Otis began calling Laurence "Mr. Laurence." Otherwise the years passed and little changed.

After Laurence had been running the store about five years, Otis married Rose. Although they had often talked of girls, Otis never mentioned her name until the Friday night he told Laurence he was marrying in the morning.

Laurence felt so hurt and stunned that he only nodded curtly and gave Otis Saturday off. That evening, after he had locked up alone, he sat at his desk in the darkness until he fell asleep. When the clock over the bank struck two, he awoke, stiff and cold. As he rose, his knee collided painfully with a half-open drawer. Gripping the edge of his desk, he fought the tears that stung his eyes. How much better a good clean cut, he thought angrily, than a bone-shattering bruise.

A cold wind sucked at his neck and pushed him from behind as he walked home through the successive yellow circles of the streetlights. To either side, the streets he had known his whole life were cut-off, menacing cul-de-sacs that kept him resolutely moving toward his own big, empty house.

Otis came to work Saturday afternoon as usual and stayed to help Laurence lock up. It was then Laurence offered to build him a cabin by the stream in the pasture, not far from the crumbling ruins of the cabin where Otis's father had lived before him. The gift was made and received without question, almost without comment by either man.

The next winter, Laurence met Louise Fairbault on a rare weekend away from town, and they were married six months later to the day. Neither Laurence's nor Otis's marriage really changed things. There was now perhaps a little less time when they were alone together. Though Otis still went in the delivery van, neither he nor Laurence helped with the loading and unloading any more. They left that to the younger men. But they were never far apart—usually no more than a few feet. (If you were a careful observer, as Miss Pat the bookkeeper was, you'd see this was just as much Laurence Trammell's doing as it was Otis's.) And they still gossiped about the town's latest comedies and tragedies, as did everyone else in the store.

Now the two watched silently as three bent, dusty figures made small scurrying dashes up the dirt alley toward them. A passing truck sent them pressing up against a wall and covered them with yet another layer of dirt. They made slow progress because they scrambled under every loading dock they passed and dropped to their knees to look under every dust-covered, bush-sized weed that grew along the alley's edges. Each figure dragged a partially-full croaker sack and occasionally dropped something into it. Laurence Trammell felt as if he were watching three war orphans like you saw in *Life* magazine on a bizarre Easter egg hunt.

He glanced down and saw a small smile of recognition and remembrance light Otis's round face.

"Looking for pop bottles," he said, nodding his head that was round and shaved like his son's.

"Must have a big project under way to need that many. B.C.'s car?" Laurence asked, smiling as Annie dived under a low dock.

"No, I reckon it's almost done."

The childrens' earnest absorption in their search for the dusty treasures that littered the alley prodded Laurence Trammell past his habitual silence.

"Remember *The Mystifying Marvel's Magic Book of Tricks?*"

"One dollar and forty-five cents, plus postage," Otis answered immediately.

"Did it ever come?"

"Nope, never did."

Laurence looked out at the children again, now only two stores away. "They're almost too big for such shenanigans. Makes me feel old just watching them, Otis."

Otis's round gold-rimmed spectacles glinted in the light. "Wait until you're watching your grandkids crawling up that alley."

The children were huddled together in a patch of shade cast by the store's delivery van. Heads nodded, and Annie climbed the ramp to the store.

"Hi, Daddy. Hi, Otis. Hi, Miss Pat. It's hot as the hinges of hell out there," she said, giving the drink machine in the corner a meaningful glance.

"Annie, watch your language," Miss Pat protested. "This is a place of business." But she started rummaging through a small box of change she kept for such emergencies.

Miss Pat sat and moved as if she were always at attention before some invisible general, and spoke as if each remark were being taken down verbatim. Long ago, she became convinced that she and she alone would have to be a stern taskmaster if some semblance of order was to be maintained among the store's indolent, irascible crew. No one else shared that opinion with Miss Pat. In fact, every man at the store spent most of his day trying to outdo the others in teasing, courting, cajoling, nagging Miss Pat until her dark eyes glittered.

To reinforce her all-business image, Miss Pat restricted herself to wearing only three colors or combinations of these three: black, red, and white. In return, at least a dozen times a week for the last fifteen years one of the men had asked another one, "What is black and white and read all over?"

The other would gape, scratch his head, then finally the light would dawn. "A newspaper!" he would cry, delighted with his astuteness.

"No!" his companion would reply, throwing up his hands, "Miss Pat!" Both would hang in the office door, laughing at their cleverness until Miss Pat routed her tormentors with a barrage of erasers and was chided, from a safe distance, for such unladylike conduct in a place of business.

"B.C. and Cookie are outside, too," Annie informed Miss Pat now.

Miss Pat looked sternly over her glasses and put her hand to the huge iron-gray chignon she wore at the nape of her neck. "What is this, a raid?"

Annie grinned and waited.

"Thank you for that grin," Miss Pat said, her face still stern, but her eyes betraying her. "Now I know where your eyes *and* your mouth are. If you'd kindly wiggle a few fingers, I could see where to put these nickels."

After one long swig on a big orange drink, Annie gathered all three drinks and started toward the back door.

With a mock-serious face and a small bow, Laurence opened the door for her. "Don't forget to bring the bottles back."

"Oh, Daddy," Annie said, pausing only long enough to give him her I'm-going-to-be-patient smile.

The men resumed their posts and watched Annie, Cookie, and B.C. work their way on down the alley.

"B.C. really shot up this winter, didn't he?" Laurence said, watching B.C. standing with his too-long arms up over his head to pull the kinks out of his back.

"Yep, already passed me by," Otis answered, squinting out into the sun-filled alley.

"I understand how boys just gradually become men, hard a job as that is," Laurence said, pulling a handkerchief from his pocket and slowly cleaning his heavy, dark-framed glasses. "What for the life of me I

can't make out is how girls—girls like Cookie and
Annie—become women, soft, round . . . " he chuckled,
"clean."

"It don't bear thinking about," Otis answered, shaking
his round head.

"I guess you're right, Otis. Did Mr. Harper like that
desk you and Sam delivered this morning?"

"Yep, said it fit him like a glove. But it'll be back by
Wednesday at the latest."

"Why do you say that?"

" 'Cause the new Mrs. Harper was there, and she said it
was positively stifling."

Laurence laughed. "Guess I better get upstairs and see
if there's something less stifling we could order him out of
Atlanta then."

Upstairs the heat was already gathering in the dark
cubbyhole he called his office. Papers, catalogs, and
account books were stacked on the desk, the extra chair,
and the floor. It had been almost a week now since he had
done any of the paperwork, and he shuddered at the
thought of Miss Pat discovering his laxness.

Every morning, he resolutely climbed the stairs and sat
behind his father's heavy desk, but a terrible lassitude
seemed to come over him as soon as he sat down. Maybe it
was the hot stale air up here. Maybe it was the poor light.

The last two mornings he had spent sketching plans for
a real office, partitioned off from the rest of the floorful
of stored furniture waiting silently in the half-light to
become part of some family's rowdy, love-filled life. A big
window with a window fan, fluorescent lights, and shelves
would complete the transformation.

The plans were hidden now under one of the stacks of

paper, but he didn't look for them.

Last night he had dreamed again that he and Louise were going to Tennessee to spend a few weeks in the mountains. The dream was vivid and full of details: Louise bent over the open suitcase asking how many shirts to bring; the long, tortuous road up the mountain; the rambling summer hotel that he actually had visited with his parents every summer when he was a boy.

It seemed he could smell the pines and hear the creaking boards as he walked across the wide veranda. Monstrous rocking chairs cocked against the balustrade saluted his arrival as they always had.

As if he were at the movies, he watched himself turn and drop a bag to ring the door bell. He looked just as he looked every morning while he shaved: a long, thin nose with fine lines running from just below the inner corners of his eyes down to his nostrils; pale, undistinguished blue eyes, washed out by light brown brows and nearly invisible eyelashes; a chin a shade too short; and the glistening stubble of an unexpectedly golden beard.

Long, long ago Louise had rubbed his rough, shining cheek and said it made him look wicked. "My satyr," she had called him.

As he watched himself retrieve the bag and step into the cool, dark lobby, he realized that only his bearing, almost militarily straight, commanded attention; a slight stoop, a drooping, and he would immediately disappear.

Louise waited primly in the car, like a new bride. With comic haste, he recrossed the veranda to claim her. Leaping down the steps two at a time, he reached out for the door handle.

Here the camera of his dream began shooting in slow

motion, and the light flickered unevenly, like the light in the first movies he'd seen as a boy. Slowly, he pulled open the door and offered his free hand to Louise. She tucked her skirts around her knees and gathered her small straw hat and bag.

Outside the dream, the sleeping Laurence Trammell found the suspense unbearable. He strained toward Louise's shaded face, his arm eagerly outstretched. He felt that if she didn't hurry, he would never again see her lovely face.

She would not be hurried. He could hardly breathe now. She put down her purse and pinned her hat at a rakish angle on the top of her small head.

A hot yellow fog curled over the edges of the slowly flickering film. Their hands touched now, and he could see her face, laughing, eager to begin this new adventure. But the hateful, yellow fumes had dimmed the sun and swallowed the hotel in front of them and the car behind them. Still she laughed and tugged impatiently at Laurence's sleeve. Now his sleeping self, frantic at the thought of losing her in the mist, gave a piteous cry, and he was part of the slowly disappearing world around him. The air was thick and acrid, but now that he actually held Louise's hand, it didn't matter. Finally he was close enough to lean toward her and smell her familiar perfume. Nothing mattered. He was not even terribly surprised to see that she was very young, just a girl, dancing around an old man who gasped for air, shoulders hunched against the swirling yellow fog. His eyes burned and tears flowed down the fine lines of his face, until helplessly he shut them against the pain, and she was gone.

Each time, the dream ended there, and Laurence would awaken with both arms still clamping the damp pillow across his face. The faint, sharp smell of Louise's medicines and her deep, even breathing helped him find his way home.

Now he raised his head slowly from his desk and rotated his shoulders to ease the stiffness. What a young fool he had been to think he could maintain the deception he had perpetrated during their whirlwind courtship, or that if he couldn't, it wouldn't matter once he had her love. How could he have not realized that Louise with her Fairbault pride would be sickened to find herself duped by such an awkward, unsocial storekeeper.

Staring ahead of him, Laurence sighed. If only Louise really would let him take her some place cool and green— some place they could both see new vistas, breathe fresh air.

In front of him, there was a sudden, soft scrabble of sound, and he realized it had become so dark on the always-dusky second story that he couldn't see anything at all beyond the soft circle of light falling on the account book open in front of him. Mice, he thought in exasperation and reached to switch on one of the four new floor lamps standing behind his desk.

Annie flinched in the light.

"Annie!"

"It's raining out," she explained. "Me and Cookie and B.C. want to know if we can wait here and ride home for lunch with you."

Laurence's head swam in confusion. Had she seen how old and pitiful he was? Of course not. That part was dream. A dream of a dream. Had he been crying? Was that real or part of the dream? He wiped the corner of his eye as if he had something in it—dry. What had she said just now, this stranger who had always had the discomforting habit of flashing across his path when he least expected her, then disappearing just as suddenly?

"No, of course not. You're a walking dust mop. By the time you run through the rain to the car, you'll be red mud from head to toe."

The drone of the rain on the roof hung a curtain of noise between them. Laurence was surprised to see that, even in the yellow light, the eyes staring so steadily into his were not muted or subdued to some ordinary shade of blue or brown, but were a luminous lilac. It almost seemed that the straight, ordinary brown hair and freckled nose made them even more arresting than a perfect setting like her mother's lovely, oval face and dark-red hair.

"I suppose I could take the truck and let you three ride in the back."

"Yeah! That's neat. I'll go tell them. Hurry up. I'm starved!" And the spotlight was empty.

Just then the twelve-o'clock whistle blew, and he rose and turned off the lamp in relief.

Otis sat at the foot of the stairs paring the thick calluses on the palms of his hands with a razor-sharp, wickedly-curved linoleum knife. Laurence glanced around the rain-gloomed floor crowded with furniture arranged in sterile wall-less little rooms that women seemed to love and strove to imitate in their own homes.

"Where is everybody?"

Otis nodded his head toward the back of the store. "Miss Pat got them."

"Well, let's go see if she left us anything to carry home to their mamas."

From the alley came a muffled mixture of thuds and yelps. Miss Pat was belaboring the three treasure hunters, back and front, with the long-handled push broom Otis used to sweep up the packing that furniture came in. When Miss Pat paused at the sound of the doors opening behind her, Annie, B.C., and Cookie seized the moment and sprang into the safety of the van, which was backed up to the edge of the ramp, its doors hanging open like outstretched arms.

"Dusting a few britches, Miss Pat?" Laurence asked, doffing an imaginary hat.

"Yours aren't past dusting either, Laurence Trammell," Miss Pat answered, giving the broom a menacing flip in her boss's direction.

Otis sidled quickly down the steps to climb into the cab as Laurence made a hasty jump from the ramp. He saw the children watching in amazement as Annie's dignified father leapt off the ramp, and unexpected laughter rose all the way from the bottom of his pedaling feet as he felt the brush of Miss Pat's long-handled broom across the seat of his pants.

He landed lightly on the drive, crouching to absorb the shock, and jumped into the cab. As he accelerated down the alley, tires whining and spitting gravel, he felt elated, like a boy who knows he's just impressed his girl for the very first time.

At the kitchen door, he snapped off a big geranium for Louise and sailed his hat at Rose as he strode through the kitchen. Laughter still simmered just beneath the surface of his thoughts. When he stepped into his wife's dim room, she lifted her head and sniffed anxiously, like a deer catching a scent of smoke on a hot summer breeze. Presenting the geranium with a flourish, he bowed from the waist and asked if she would care to have lunch with him.

Reluctantly, scolding him as she went, she allowed herself to be half-walked, half-waltzed to the table where a still-beige Annie waited.

Ordinarily, Annie's general appearance was the first order of business before lunch was served, and it usually required several trips to the bathroom and several inspections. Today she watched silently as Laurence snapped his napkin into his lap and hummed a tune under his breath, despite the fact that he strictly forbade whistling or singing at the table. Laurence's exhilaration mounted as Annie, Louise, and even Ruth-baby watched in wonder. He forked a huge mouthful of mashed potatoes and gravy into his mouth, pretending he was completely unaware of their scrutiny.

"I didn't hear no grace," Rose called suspiciously from the kitchen.

Laurence solemnly bowed his head. "Twinkletwin-klelittlestar," he mumbled, running all the words together.

"Jesus wept," Rose answered, apparently mollified.

"Laurence," Louise gasped, "you certainly are in a peculiar mood today."

Laurence threw back his head and gave a short laugh. "Well, Otis's done it again. He just made my day."

Louise's lilac eyes darkened, and Laurence quickly

added, "Properly speaking, I should give the credit to Hank Ketchum."

The front legs of Annie's chair came crashing to the floor.

"Elizabeth Trammell, how many times must I tell you not to lean back like that in your chair? That's just the way your second cousin Alf ended up a vegetable. Would you like to finish your lunch in the kitchen?"

Annie shook her head meekly.

Why, she's anxious to hear my story, Laurence thought in pleased surprise.

"On the way home today, Otis told me old Everett Williams tried to draft Hank Ketchum this morning."

"Hank Ketchum! What on earth for? He knows as well as I do . . . "

"Thoroughness, my dear, military thoroughness." Laurence saluted his audience sharply.

"Well, what happened?"

"Never got past the first question, as Otis tells it. Everett said, 'Where do you live, Hank?' Hank was standing at attention in front of that rickety old desk Everett sets up in the post office lobby.

"'Same old place, Everett,' Hank told him."

Annie giggled.

"Everett gets huffy and snaps, 'What is your present address, Mr. Ketchum?' "

Laurence chuckled, then continued, "I can just see Hank standing there grinning, turning that old railroad cap in his hands, completely unperturbed by 'General' Williams.

"'Down behind the bottling plant,' Hank drawls out

slowly, still grinning. All the other men in the room start guffawing, and old Everett turns purple as a ripe plum.

"'I mean, you simpleton,' he shouts, rising from his seat, his knuckles white on his desk, 'how do you get your mail?'

"Hank's grin gets broader than ever. He nods his head eagerly up and down. 'Why, Everett, the postman brings it,' he says proudly."

Laurence and Annie laughed happily at the thought of Hank Ketchum besting the pompous, overbearing Everett Williams, who always strutted around town in his uniform thumping kids on the head.

Ruth-baby looked at the faces around her and decided to take her cue from her mother. Puckering her small mouth, she watched Annie and her father silently, a little frown creasing her smooth forehead.

"And what was Otis doing spending the morning at the induction office? I thought he was supposed to be helping you down at the store."

"He wasn't there. He saw Scat Mackey when he went to the post office for the mail, and he told him." Laurence grinned. "Scat will be around this afternoon to tell us again himself."

"I don't doubt it for a minute! Laurence, when will you stop consorting with all the low-life in town, especially. . ." Louise raised a significant eyebrow toward the kitchen. "I'm not at all surprised that they would take pleasure in poking fun at a poor, unfortunate white man like Hank Ketchum."

"What!" Annie blurted out, unable to believe that her mother had misunderstood so.

Laurence gave Annie a sharp look and pushed back from the table abruptly.

"I'm tired. I think I'll lie down a little bit before I go back to town."

"I declare, I don't know what comes over your father sometimes," Louise said to no one in particular. Then with a bright smile, she turned toward Annie. "How was your lesson this morning? I want to hear all about it."

Annie started in her chair.

"Laurence . . . ?" Louise began, her voice rising, "I thought you told me the lessons were to be every morning."

Laurence paused, one hand already on the door into the hall, and turned back toward his chair.

"As a matter of fact . . . " he turned and looked at Annie. "Cookie and B.C. and I were so busy this morning. . ."

"Laurence!"

"I'm sure she can make it up this afternoon, dear," he responded. Then, catching a glimpse of the despairing eyes at his elbow, he added, "Of course, she's likely to bring home a terrible cold sitting an hour in damp clothes over at Miss Emma's."

Louise glanced anxiously at the silver, rain-sheeted window. "I suppose you're right," she said, turning to give Annie a searching glance, "though she does seem to have a cast-iron constitution. Heaven only knows where she gets it. Could you help me back to my room before you begin your little siesta, Laurence?"

Laurence had stretched out on the living room sofa when Annie tiptoed hesitantly into the room.

"I was wondering," she said, "about Ben Reilly."

Drowsily Laurence shook his head. "I wasn't able to get his city job back for him . . . "

The small face before him fell, and Laurence pushed himself up, strangely anxious to wipe the disappointment from Annie's lilac eyes.

"But I spoke to Mr. Meecham at the hardware store, and he's going to start work for him Monday morning."

His daughter lifted a thin, brown arm in partial salute and with a touch of a smile left as quickly as she had come.

Laurence lay back again and slept more deeply than he'd slept in a week. The sound of rain merged with the color and smell of pines and danced him far, far away.

CHAPTER 10

ANNIE MOVED AROUND her room restlessly, opening drawers and shutting them, forgetting to look inside. Ruth-baby slept with her favorite blanket, her "pinkie," pulled up over her head. The whole house was still except for an occasional metallic rattle from the kitchen.

Outside the rain ceased as suddenly as it had begun, but there was no sense of relief. The sky was still a dark, motley gray; and a yellowish-green light, the color of an overripe pear, cast an eerie glow over the front yard. The light seemed inverted, steaming up from the ground, as if all the earth's ills were rising upward only to be fiercely repudiated by a lowering sky. Annie found herself thinking of the carbuncle boil she'd had on the back of her leg last summer and the sweet shooting pain as her father lanced it with his sharp pocketknife, releasing the putrid, gray-green poison over his clean handkerchief.

With Ruth-baby sleeping upstairs and her mother and father sleeping downstairs, Annie felt as trapped and oppressed as the air outside. What was it her father always said? No place to go but up. She grinned. She'd ring the bell for Cookie, and they'd play in the attic. As she slid down the banister, then tiptoed down the hall, the silence now seemed exciting and the air full of summer lightning.

Instinctively Annie restricted her visits to the attic, sensing that her mother's favorite saying, "Familiarity breeds contempt," would apply to the attic as well as to people her father always seemed to be fooling around with downtown. But now the atmosphere was just right—equal to an attic full of old dreams and dresses fit for princesses from other worlds. And there was another problem with the attic: Cookie wasn't normally allowed the run of the house, other than the porches and the kitchen, of course. "Underfoot," Rose called it. Annie paused at the kitchen door, then decided to tackle Rose head on.

"Rose, everybody's asleep except me and you."

"Well, if you're waiting for me you're backing up."

"Can Cookie come up, please, Rose?"

"How I'm supposed to get this kitchen clean with two of you underfoot? No, ma'am."

Annie scratched her head. It looked like Rose was going to have to be a silent partner in the plan. "Rose, I got a place to play figured out where we won't be under anybody's feet." She paused. "You'll be under our feet, but we won't mind."

Rose's felt-slippered feet slapped at the linoleum as she moved between the kitchen table and the sink.

"Look out that window, child, and quit studying any playing this afternoon. Even if we don't all get blowed into Jefferson County, we fixing to have us a trash-moving gully-washer. If I had my say, we'd all be downstairs in the cellar."

Annie gave Rose her most winning smile. "Aw, Rose, the noon whistle will blow if there's going to be a tornado. Please, can I ring for Cookie before the rain starts again?

Please? I want us to play in the attic."

"The attic? You so anxious to meet your maker, then?"

"We'll be out of everybody's way, and we'll come down first toot on the whistle."

Rose shuffled closer to the window for another look into the midday gloom. "I would feel a sight happier if Cookie wasn't down there by herself in this weather," she conceded reluctantly.

"Okay, then? B.C., too?"

"Not B.C. He's in town helping at the store. Go ahead and ring the bell just twice; don't want to wake up everybody and his brother."

Annie hurried toward the back door. "Thanks, Rose," she sang out, giving Rose's broad waist a squeeze as she went past the sink.

Cookie came running on tiptoe across the backyard, as if Chewing Tobacco were nipping her heels. Her eyes were round and shiny with excitement.

"Ooooh, Jesus! Something's fixin' to give!" she called. Her orange shirt bulged with a pint jar that held their accumulation of pennies, nickels, and dimes.

"Thought I'd better bring this in case a tornado hits our house."

"What if it hits this house?"

"Don't talk that way," Cookie said, glancing at the sky.

"Want to play in the attic?"

"The attic? You got termites in your brain?"

"We'll come down first toot on the noon whistle. Anyway, suppose a twister hits us; had you rather be on the bottom or on the top of the heap when she sets us down?"

Cookie looked nervously over her shoulder at the dark

clouds gathering behind her. "You sure know how to make a body feel welcome."

They tiptoed up the stairs, and Annie used her father's long-handled bone shoehorn to pry open the waist-high attic door which opened off the top of the stairs. It had warped so out of shape her mother no longer thought about locking it. After several moments of struggle, she and Cookie were able to slide their fingers around the edges and give a jerk. A flesh-crawling screech tore the still, heavy air. Just beyond the dwarfish door, raw beams soared steeply to a point, and pale, cloud-deflected light lit the edges of strange unrecognizable shapes.

Cookie rocked back on her haunches and looked at Annie nervously. "If this is okay, how come you sweating?"

Annie swatted at Cookie's head and duck-walked through the small opening into the attic's dusty gloom. "Cause it's hotter than a ginger mill up here, that's why. Once we're in we'll shut the door and open some windows and watch the storm coming."

"How come, shut the door?"

"Do *you* want Ruth-baby in here bawling, messing into everything?"

"I reckon not."

"Well, then?"

Cookie turned and pulled the door shut with one hand, still clutching the jar half full of coins in the other.

"Let's count the money first, so we'll know how far we've come," Annie suggested. "Then we can put on a show. There are trunks of old clothes up here. Some of them are a hundred years old, I bet."

Cookie crept on her hands and knees over to a small

west window. Sitting cross-legged in front of it, she poured the coins out in a small mound in front of her. "They look like more in the jar," she said. Behind Cookie, puffy, rigidly-correct Annabelle, Annie's mother's old padded dressmaker's dummy, watched in disapproval as Cookie sorted the mound of coins into small heaps of nickels, dimes, pennies, and quarters.

"All right, how much?" Annie asked.

"One dollar, fifteen cents."

Annie bit her lip. "Even if we do hop a freight, we need more than that. We've got to make some money fast, or I'm going to have to feed myself to William Petus's alligator."

Cookie raised the window and cool, rain-scented air set tiny motes of dust dancing in the hazy light.

The fresh air that raised the dust from the floor seemed to clear the dust inside Annie's head too. "We've got to sell something. Have a sale!"

"What have we got to sell?"

"My toys?"

Cookie shook her head. "That don't seem fair with Ruth-baby coming along after you. Especially since she's fixing to be an only child."

"Chewing Tobacco!"

"Somebody dumb enough to buy that fat, mean, ugly critter's not just going to fall in our laps in the next two weeks. Besides, how'd you explain that to your daddy?"

"Well, what have you got?"

Cookie scratched at a tight braid. "I heard of second-hand and third-hand junk, but counting on fourth-hand junk to get us all the way to Detroit is pretty farfetched."

A sudden crack of thunder rattled loose window panes,

and a cold gust of wind toppled Annabelle. The rain began again, harder now and laced with summer hail. It pelted the roof just over their heads, furious at its long confinement.

Cookie's mouth shaped words soundlessly as they both jumped to tug at the open window. Lightning seemed to be dancing on the sun-parlor roof below them, and the thunder clapped louder and louder at their frenetic antics.

Both girls sat back on the floor, breathless and shivering from the sudden chill in the air and the excitement of their struggle against the rain.

"Let's get out of these wet clothes before we catch our death," Annie said. She undid the wide leather straps from an old traveling trunk, while Cookie peered over her shoulder. On the faded paper lining of the curved lid and the top tray, faint peacocks strutted among tiny hearts entwined in fancy pink curlicues. The trays were a mad jumble: heavy pieces of jewelry, watches on long gold chains, fans, lace handkerchiefs, and a faded picture of a man in an old uniform with knickers instead of grown-up trousers.

"He must have run away from home to join the army," Cookie suggested. "B.C.'s gonna do that."

"He won't have to," Annie reminded her. She lifted out the heavy tray and set it on the floor. Leaning over the trunk again, she pulled a heavy, sequined, sea-green dress out of the trunk. "We'll already be in Detroit."

Cookie chose a black dress with a plunging neckline punctuated by a large pink silk rose that hit her just above her navel.

"Not if that pile don't grow faster," she said, glaring at the pile of coins.

Annie pulled her dress on and squatted to see if she could find a reflection in the small window. "Being gorgeous isn't very warming," she muttered, rubbing her arm. Cookie swirled a pale blue cape of tiny pleats above her head. "Ma'am," she said with an elegant bow, draping the cape around Annie's shoulders, "your taxi to Detroit is waiting at the curb."

By the time the heavens had exhausted their fury at being held back so long and had settled into their regular work of wetting the world, Cookie and Annie had moved into a Detroit mansion, and both had been to glittering, fancy-dress balls and fallen in love with tall, dignified men who looked strangely like Annabelle, the dressmaker's dummy.

Waltzing around the ballroom floor, Annie grinned and hugged her mysterious admirer fiercely. "I bet you could show William Petus," she challenged. Suddenly Annabelle lay stiff and heavy in her arms, the music stopped, and Cookie sighed sadly from her place on the trunk.

"Annie, we've got to sell something," she whispered, "even if it's the clothes off our . . ."

"Cookie! That's it. I know how we can get to Detroit."

"Yippee!" Cookie yelled. Jumping to a crouch on top of the trunk, she sprang toward Annie.

"Cookie, don't!" Annie cried, as she and Cookie fell on Annabelle. "You are going to tear the merchandise."

Cookie stared down in amazement at her glittering dress. "You mean you going to sell THIS? Your mama will skin you alive."

"That old dress?" Annie scoffed. "Why, I bet it's a

hundred years old. Besides, Mama doesn't go to dances—
or any place. That was probably my Grandmother
Trammell's, maybe even Great-grandmother
Trammell's."

Cookie untangled her legs and skirt and sat erect, her
face long, her mouth held straight only with difficulty. "In
that case, Sister Annie," she canted in a preacher's
sonorous voice, "you are saved. Saved and sanctified!"

"Did you land on your head?"

" . . . and for the fifth time, I might add," Cookie
finished with a grin, dusting her long black satin sleeves.

"Oh, no, you don't! I was the one . . . " Annie jerked
upright, and both of them saw poor Annabelle lying
crushed beneath them and laughed.

"Your fellow is looking a bit peaked," Cookie
commiserated with a cluck of her tongue.

"Not at all," protested Annie, "he's just getting his suit
pressed."

"Well, he might oughta try taking it off first," Cookie
suggested.

Outside the rain came to a final, ragged halt, and the
sound of the front door closing told them Laurence had
gone back to town. In the sudden stillness, Cookie yawn-
ed and, carefully smoothing her skirt, leaned back, resting her head on Annabelle's soft, dented stomach. Annie
brushed her own skirt halfheartedly, then leaned back
beside Cookie. Her bare arms and legs inside her silken
dress felt cool and boneless. The whole house seemed to
exhale a languorous breath, and the two girls drifted
silently between waking and sleeping, relieved and
content to have an idea, the beginning of a plan. The
grandfather clock in the living room struck the hour and

then the half hour before they moved again.

First there was the foray to Annie's room to find dry clothes for them both, then the trip to the barn for rough brown croaker sacks. To avoid disturbing anyone's nap or Rose, whose slippered feet still slapped back and forth across the kitchen in time to fragmented, mournful tunes she sang under her breath, they climbed down, then back up again with the sacks, through the dripping crab-apple tree. Carefully they stuffed each sack with the contents of three trunks, tied it with a sash or a belt, dragged it across Annie's room, past the sleeping Ruth-baby, through the window onto the sun-parlor roof, and watched solemnly as it dropped over the edge of the roof, to fall with a loud smack into the sodden flower beds below.

On the last trip, dragging the tenth heavy sack between them across the rough attic floor, Cookie drew her eyebrows into pained peaks. "I been tiptoeing so long, I don't know if I'll ever be able to come down again."

"Never mind, you are on the runty side anyway," Annie comforted her. "Now you'll have that much less growing to do. Pull."

When they were halfway across Annie's room, the covers of the big bed heaved and a small voice, still struggling with the weight of sleep, asked, "What you and Cookie doing, Annie?"

Annie loosened her grip on the heavy sack, stuck out her lower lip, and blew straight up at her hot sticky bangs. "Hi, Ruth-baby," she answered. "Cookie and I found this bear in the attic. Must of come in out of the rain. If you're real good and just lie right back down, I'll carry him out of here for you and drop him off the roof. Bet he'll think twice before he decides to bother us again."

Ruth-baby clutched the edge of her pinkie and dived back under the covers.

As Annie and Cookie eased the bag from the window-sill to the roof, a faint, muffled voice asked, "Is it gone, Annie?"

"Almost, Ruth-baby," Annie answered, sticking her head back into the room. "You stay put a little while longer, just to make double sure."

The small mound under the bed covers quivered and gave a big yawn. The clock on the mantel ticked to slow, steady breathing again.

Cookie gave Annie a big wink that collapsed one whole side of her face. "Good thing your mother's not as fussy about her flower beds as Miss Florence," Cookie said, looking balefully at the shattered camellia bushes, grotesquely splayed under the weight of the bulging croaker sacks.

Annie finished loading a wheelbarrow and began dragging another of the rough brown burlap bags toward the rusty red wagon that had once been hers and now belonged to Ruth-baby.

"If you don't get a move on," Annie said between her teeth, "everybody's naps are going to be over. By the time we explain one thing and another, we'll be too old to catch any trains."

"Besides," said Cookie, laughing, "you'll be an old married lady with six kids."

Annie shivered. "I don't think the women in our family are good at having babies. You going to push or not?"

The sidewalks on Magnolia Drive were as old as the houses they fronted and had long since bucked and buckled at each joint, undermined by root, rain, and drought. Learning to skate here was a test of courage and agility that had resulted in an impressive array of bruises and cuts for Annie and Cookie; but at the same time, it had made them the best skaters in town.

Pushing the heavy wheelbarrow in front of her, Annie could close her eyes and predict each lunge and roll of the wheelbarrow and steer accordingly. After three blocks, houses, pavement, and sidewalk stopped abruptly and the rough chert road to Northside began. The road sloped sharply downward on each edge into deep gullies that carried off the rain. Now they were full to the brim—twin rust-colored torrents. The tall, saw-edged Johnson grass and goldenrod on the far side of the gullies were covered thickly with red dust that even the rain had not budged.

Walt Hazy's pasture, with its tottering barbed-wire fence, formed a bumper zone—a no-man's-land between Magnolia Drive and Northside, where about half of Winton's black people lived.

At the first house, the privet hedges began. They were anywhere from knee-high to taller than Annie could reach on tiptoe, living screens thrown up against the ankle-deep dust, the knee-deep mud, and the last line of defense against ugliness, deprivation, and exposure.

Cookie glanced obliquely, furtively into each opening in the hedges, her need to know only a little stronger than her appreciation of the message of the beleaguered living shields. For Annie, Cookie's obvious unfamiliarity with Northside was disturbing and embarrassing. Cookie's covert eagerness to see everything seemed a warning that she would resent Annie's knowledge, her easy familiarity with M Street.

Annie kept her head down, watching the soft red stain

of Northside's mud creep slowly over her sandals, between her toes, and over the edges of her feet.

Every Thursday afternoon for as long as she could remember, she had traveled this road with her father so that each hedge, each naked baby and scraggy, yapping dog was as familiar to her as their immaculate counterparts on Magnolia Drive, while Cookie had been here no more than half a dozen times.

* * *

Thursdays were the days Annie and her father drove over to Northside to the third house on the right-hand side of the road, to pick up the week's laundry. The hedge here was only waist high, and, from the road, you could see the small, unpainted, weatherbeaten house with the wide front porch full of asparagus ferns, begonias, and geraniums planted in cans, pots, jars, and boxes. There were several straight-backed chairs for the frequent visitors and one large brown armchair for the house's oversized owner.

One of Annie's first brushes with the refreshing pleasures of logic had come when she had discovered that the laughing black giantess who ironed her sheets was named Ina. Why, she had wondered ever since, weren't all people like that—so sure of who they were and what they were they called themselves that for all to know. Like Ina—the "ironer." Monday to Friday, year in, year out. She never seemed to need anything else. Soon as she saw your car in front of her house, she began laughing from way down inside her thick man's chest, one laugh pushing the one in front of it.

There were no in and out curves to Ina. Her neck was as thick as her close-clipped head; her shoulders were cleanly right-angled above a flamboyant shift, which she visibly filled from shoulder to hem. Huge, taut-skinned, and (you knew instinctively) painful stovepipe legs completed the plumbline from shoulder to ground.

Every Thursday Annie's father got out and walked around the back end of the car as Ina came ponderously down her steps, her full weight falling with a heavy thud on first one foot and then the other.

"Don't come down those steps, Ina," her father would protest as he hurried through her waist-high hedge. Ina would laugh, roar out at the two of them, as she kept rocking down the steps, her laughter flicking away Laurence's manners as if they were pesky but inconsequential flies.

"And how is Miss Annie today?" she would call out from the bottom step between gasps for air. If there were two packages, she would hand Annie the smaller one and laugh again as Annie pressed her face against the smooth, still-warm sheets, neatly stacked and tied with string.

Up close, Ina always gave off warmth—like her sheets. She smelled of strong soap and starch.

Once Annie had seen her father watching Ina's descent with something like pain pulling his mouth down at the corners. "If cleanliness is next to godliness," he had said to Ina, "I know who's going to be on the right-hand side of the throne."

Though the words had seemed brave and hard to say to Annie, Ina's laugh came back quickly, no different. "Sure enough," she said slapping at her thigh. "I bet you dead right, Mr. Laurence." She stopped then and looked speculatively upward. "I wonder, do I get a footstool—do thrones have footstools?" Laughter like echoes from a deep, dark well smoothed the lines of her father's face and pushed Annie and her father, laughing, laughing, back to the car, the warm bundles of laundry pressed tightly against their chests like mustard plasters.

As soon as her father started the car and pulled away from the curb, their laughter subsided into an easy silence, as if Ina had only let them use her laughter. They couldn't bring it away, but it would be there next Thursday when they returned to borrow it again.

But what, thought Annie, with a small sigh she was careful not to let her father hear, are we laughing about?

* * *

Today, as Annie and Cookie appeared in the break in Ina's hedge, pulling the loaded wheelbarrow and wagon behind them, Ina sat in her overstuffed chair. Each foot (in a size-ten, unlaced, man's shoe) rested on the edge of a huge iron pot filled with pink begonias. She waved at Annie and Cookie, as they deposited their burdens at the bottom of the steps, as if they were just the two she had been expecting. Her legs, swollen to the bursting point, glistened in the silvery, rain-scrubbed light.

"Well, Miss Annie," Ina ventured, as Annie and Cookie took the straight-backed chairs she waved them to, "and this must be Rose Holloway's Cookie. See you coming out of the Baptist Tabernacle, Sundays, don't I?"

Cookie nodded. "Yes'm."

"Well, it's trying to clear off and turn cool, but mostly

this rain has just left me stewing in my own juice. How about you girls joining me in some lemonade?"

Annie had finished her second glass and was stretching her tongue for the last dribble of undissolved sugar at the bottom of her glass when Ina mentioned the wagon and the wheelbarrow loaded with croaker sacks.

"Heavy load," she said, glancing down appreciatively. "Looks a little like clothes bags, and then again a little like croaker sacks."

"You're right both ways," Annie said, eager to get down to business.

"All those for me, then?"

"No, no. They're all nice and clean. Good condition, too."

Ina knit her eyebrows and looked cautiously down the road as if expecting trouble—or help—to arrive any second now.

"Taking a little trip, then, are you?" she asked very casually, still looking off somewhere else.

Cookie suddenly gave a loud giggle and slapped her thigh. "We're not running away from home, if that's what you mean."

Annie shifted uneasily at this half-truth, but Ina's face cleared, and she gave Cookie one of her rumbling laughs, throwing back her head until it rested on the back of her chair.

"Well, then, what can I do for you girls? What's in all them sacks anyhow?"

"Clothes, like we said. We want to have a rummage sale and use your front hedge," Annie explained.

Ina tugged at one knee, then the other, to help lower her

legs gently to the floor. "Now you talking. I can sell a fur coat to a weasel," she said, pushing her chair back against the wall.

While Annie and Cookie spread coats, suits, hats, dresses, shirts, skirts, and shoes out on the still-dripping hedges, Ina whistled up the mud-splattered, half-naked children wading in the drainage ditches and told them to spread the word. Then she brought out a piece of cardboard and made a crude sign, which she stuck into the front side of the hedge. Next, she had Annie and Cookie set a board across two chair bottoms to make a counter and brought out an empty shoe box—to put all the takings in, she said.

Three teenage boys walked by on their way back from town, dressed in their best clothes, their hair glistening with Vaseline. Ina waved them into the yard. Neighbor ladies on either side came with fat babies on their hips. A shriveled old man with a cane was carried over the ditch's racing waters by his son, and he set himself up in one corner of the yard on a rickety bench, telling fortunes for a penny a head.

Just then an old dusty car drove by, slowed, then went on. "Reverend Henton," Ina said with a loud sniff. "You can bet he's on his way to comfort poor Esther Pierce. That man got a nose for trouble."

A hush settled over the yard.

"Who's Esther Pierce?" Cookie wanted to know.

"Well, her name wasn't rightly Pierce, I don't suppose," muttered Ina, "unless you count living with a man twenty years. You know Amos Pierce, don't you?"

Cookie gasped. "But Ina, Amos Pierce was white."

Ina nodded. "But he liked his women dark. He was the

meanest, stingiest white man I ever knew, excepting maybe his two brothers Burt and Jeb."

The old man telling fortunes looked up and gave Ina a crooked smile. "Mean, maybe, but not stingy. He left Esther five kids to raise, I hear. A bunch of wild woods colts."

"Poor babies," Ina sighed, "there won't be no place for them in this world, and maybe not the next."

For a moment longer, she stared after the dilapidated car, then she began calling out prices as she reached into the gaping sacks and spread clothes on the hedges around them. Only the people clustered around the edges of the yard continued to whisper and stare after Reverend Henton's car, and Annie and Cookie were once again swept up in the excitement of the sale.

Suits went for fifty cents, winter coats for seventy-five, children's clothes for whatever was offered. To avoid a fistfight, Ina auctioned off the black and green evening dresses that Annie and Cookie had worn while they danced away a rainy afternoon with Annabelle.

Since they had to wait until there was hedge room to open successive sacks, everyone stayed to see what would come next, even if all their money was gone. There were matching Chesterfield coats, with dark-blue velvet collars, that seemed very like the ones Annie and Ruth-baby had once worn in spite of Annie's protests to her mother that anything that suited a three-year-old could not be suitable for an eleven-year-old. There was a man's raincoat that had a zip-out lining—Tom Landy, the outside man on the garbage truck, said it was perfect for work, and it was only a little long in the sleeves. All over the yard people laughed and held clothes up while others measured, stepped into, or pirouetted in fall, winter, and spring clothes. Who bought what quickly became a blur, as Annie and Cookie counted change, and Ina kept opening new sacks.

Once Annie heard Cookie ask Ina why she didn't buy herself a pretty dress. Ina's roar turned every head to watch her reach for a navy blue dress with red buttons down the front. The crowd laughed back in appreciation, and Cookie stared at her toes in embarrassment. The hem of the dress barely reached the middle of Ina's thigh, and it was obvious that not even one of her thick legs could have passed through the narrow opening at the back.

"Now, if you have ladies' shoes," said Ina to Cookie, grinning ear to ear, "like these . . . " She lifted one foot off the ground to show off her unlaced men's shoes split on both sides to make room for her bunions. "Size ten E, I believe."

Tom Landy stepped up, daintily holding one of Annie's father's narrow black shoes.

"Get out of here," Ina roared, giving his shoulder a thump that sent him flying back into the crowd.

"I'm surrounded by midgets," she protested and laughed until tears stood in her eyes. "One of you midgets fetch my chair down from the porch before I fall down and do in this whole crazy circus."

No sooner had several young men gotten Ina settled in her chair under a scrawny mimosa at the edge of the yard, than Reverend Henton, the new preacher from the Emanuel Methodist Church, pulled up in front of the gap in the dusty hedge and stopped his car. There was a woman with him now, and Annie knew intuitively that it must be the Widow Pierce, as she had heard several women call Esther. She was pressed back against the car seat as if she thought she could escape the stares of everyone in the yard.

Reverend Henton walked around the car's front end and opened the door and reached in for Esther Pierce as if she were a complete invalid. Expertly, he steered her across the gully and through the crowd. While people awkwardly expressed their sympathy or pointedly ignored her, Reverend Henton smiled at everyone and began handing out peppermints to the children around his legs.

So this was the man who had stood up for Ben Reilly, thought Annie, oddly disappointed both in the man and in the silent crowd around her. Why weren't they all cheering, and why did he have to be so little and scrawny looking? Why, he wasn't much taller than the tiny Widow Pierce, and he wore thick gold-rimmed glasses that slid down almost to the end of his nose. He kept pushing at them ineffectively with his index finger. But one thing she had to give him. Even on this muggy afternoon, he looked cool as a cucumber. His seersucker suit didn't have a wrinkle, and his face seemed determined but quite cheerful.

"I can't believe he had the nerve to bring that woman," Annie heard a woman behind her saying. Everyone in the crowded yard seemed to be moving, drifting with some unseen current.

"Who is running this magnificent operation?" Reverend Henton asked.

"We are," Annie and Cookie called, unable to resist grins of pleasure.

"Well, then, allow me to wish you success and perhaps

offer you a peppermint."

Cookie stepped forward quickly and popped the red and white pinwheel into her mouth. Annie stepped forward, too, but something made her glance back toward Ina's chair under the mimosa and the look on Ina's face froze her hand to her side. Mumbling something about cavities, she turned back to the table, pretending to sort change.

In a few moments Annie looked again toward Ina, certain she had misunderstood her stare. She was talking idly to several women and seemed to have forgotten Reverend Henton's presence altogether. But still, something had changed. People seemed to have regrouped all over the yard. Now on one side of the center walk, Reverend Henton stood with a shy Esther Pierce by his side, talking intently to several young people, including the three teenage boys with the Vaselined hair.

On the other side of the walk were more people, but they seemed much quieter with no real center of concentration. They drifted, talking to first one friend, then another, but dispiritedly, as though all the time they were talking they were trying to listen to what the people on the other side of the yard were saying.

Then, just as surely as he had divided the waters, Reverend Henton stirred them up again. After leaning down to pull on little Nathan Lee's ear, he turned abruptly and crossed to the other side of the yard, grinning like he thought he was stepping over the Jordan into the Promised Land. He came to a standstill directly in front of Ina.

Slowly she pushed herself out of her chair until she towered, scowling, above him.

"We've come to buy a dress," he said, "a black dress."
The crowd gave a collective gasp.

Ina squinted down at the pair before her. Esther was
visibly quaking, and something like pity seemed to touch
Ina's broad face. "That's a nice thing, Reverend. Maybe it
would make her feel better." She spoke as if Esther
weren't there at all.

Reverend Henton's expression didn't change. "We
need a black dress because we have a funeral to attend."

Now the crowd really gasped. "Have your brains been
scrambled?" Ina roared. "Isn't this poor woman bound to
have enough trouble settling with the Lord without you
getting her and her five woods colts killed?"

For a moment Reverend Henton's face seemed to
register surprise, then it closed again, revealing nothing.
"Talking about your woods colts . . ." he said, staring
pointedly at Annie.

Annie saw Ina's big hands flare open, and for a
moment it looked as if she meant to grab the Reverend
Henton and shake him good. But instead she said in a
strained voice, "This here's Annie Trammell, Laurence
Trammell's chile." She paused, then added flatly, "Mr.
Trammell is a good man."

"A good white man," Reverend Henton answered just
as flatly. He reached out and pushed the reluctant Esther
forward. "I've heard about your daddy. He'd be the
perfect one to tell. You tell your daddy that if Esther here
doesn't get some kindly remembrance from Mr. Pierce's
estate, then we are going to attend his funeral." The tiniest
smile lightened his severe face. "Just to show our respects,
you understand."

Esther gave a muffled cry as the Reverend Henton

turned her toward the hedges, and the crowd fell back as if they did not wish the small man to touch them. He picked up a dark-blue dress and held it up to Esther, shook his head and replaced it on the hedge.

Ina still stood angrily in the center of the yard. "What you trying to do, tear this town apart?" she demanded now.

The Reverend Henton whirled to face Ina so suddenly that Esther was spun aside. "What is she supposed to do? Starve respectfully to death? Esther will be at that funeral, on the front row, unless she gets a remembrance— something for the five little remembrances Mr. Pierce left for her, you hear? Now can we buy a dress or not?" he added more calmly, and he turned his searching gaze directly on Annie.

Trembling, Annie nodded, and once again the current in the yard seemed to reverse itself and people eddied uneasily back and forth in confusion.

With one hand, the small preacher pulled a trim black dress with bone buttons from a stack of other clothes. On the other arm, Esther slumped against him, barely able to stand. Fishing in his pocket, Reverend Henton found a dollar. "Keep the change," he said brusquely to Cookie.

As he drove off, noise erupted as if a flock of starlings had been frightened from their perches and were angrily trying to resettle, unable to find a suitable place again.

Ina glared down at Cookie and Annie. "Ain't no good gonna come of this." Her scowl deepened. "Of course, he's dead right. That Pierce was as worthless a man as ever drew breath in this town. Kept Esther and all those kids since she wasn't no more than a kid herself, then didn't have the gumption to leave her or them kids one penny.

Her family is all gone, so she got no folks, no money, no friends, not even a name for her and them kids." Ina sighed. "Looks like Esther Pierce is one of those women bound to be taken over by some man—each one with his own ax to grind, each one more dangerous than the last."

* * *

"Good thing Ina agreed to give away what we couldn't sell," Cookie said as she pushed the empty wheelbarrow tiredly ahead of her. "I never would have made it home if I'd had to lug stuff back again."

On quivering legs, both girls retraced their steps with the empty wagon and the wheelbarrow rattling eerily along the silent street.

A wild sunset, a layer cake of orange, red, and violet, urged them to hurry, to ride the thin edge of darkness that had covered all the houses behind them and lapped now at their heels.

"You gonna be late for supper again," Cookie predicted.

"That'll just get me to the kitchen that much faster."

"How much we make?"

"The last money I could see to count for sure was twenty-one dollars and seventy-five cents."

Cookie sighed. "Too bad we can't just stay home and open up a store. Inside of a year, we could own this town and pack up William Petus and let him see how he likes Detroit."

"Yes," Annie agreed.

"Annie, do you reckon he didn't love her at all?"

"I don't know," Annie answered, knowing she meant Amos Pierce and Esther. "Ina did say he was the meanest man she'd ever met."

Cookie shook her head. "I'm thinking he didn't leave her nothing because she was colored; and colored just don't count at all, not to the likes of Amos Pierce."

Someplace close by, a magnolia had perfumed the air with its heavy fragrance, and Annie's exhilaration seemed to be draining away with the sun. "Oh, Cookie, don't pay any attention to people like that," she protested.

Cookie turned and grimaced in the gathering dusk. "That's kinda hard to do, I bet, when they leave you five young'uns to watch starve to death." She paused. "And look at B.C. He and William Petus been friends since they was born—just like you and me. Now William tells him he's just a nigger. B.C. ain't ever gonna get over that, Annie. Not as long as he lives." Her voice fell. "I wonder if they were ever blood brothers like you and me are blood sisters?"

Annie made a face. "They're brothers all right—Cain and Abel."

Cookie sighed. "Yeh, I reckon, only this time Abel's got to do the running as well as losing everything. I sure do hope Detroit is like everybody says, or I declare I don't know what on earth is going to become of B.C."

Walking silently, Annie thought about the afternoon: the crowds, the smells, and the laughter. As the wagon bounced onto Magnolia Drive's tilting sidewalk, Cookie asked, "You gonna tell your daddy about Esther Pierce like the Reverend told you to?"

Annie nodded and saw Cookie's chin lift.

"I hope she goes to that funeral."

Annie shook her head doubtfully. "I don't know. Ina didn't think it was the right thing to do." Suddenly she had a thought. "I bet my daddy can fix everything. He got Ben Reilly another job."

"It's better to fix things yourself and not always be asking somebody to fix it for you."

"All right, then," Annie shot back, irritated, "I won't tell him."

Cookie shrugged. "Maybe you should. Reverend Henton did say to, after all. That makes it different."

"You like him?"

Cookie frowned thoughtfully. "I reckon," she said finally.

As Annie and Cookie turned into the driveway, Annie let out a low whistle. "Wow, I didn't know we were that late . . ."

CHAPTER 11

EVERY LIGHT in the Trammell house was on from the basement to the attic. The whole lawn was striped with long fingers of light that probed the darkness accusingly. Cautiously the two girls began circling the house toward the back door.

"What you reckon we better do with this?" Cookie asked, giving the mayonnaise jar that Ina had put their money in a shake.

Annie glanced around quickly, and her eyes fell on the large rectangular flower box at the back door, still ablaze with late spring geraniums.

Quickly she gave tentative, then determined, yanks on the two largest plants at one end of the planter. "There," said Annie, "stick it down in that hole, and we'll stick the geraniums back on top." Just as they finished tamping the soil around the plants, Rose opened the back door wide and stepped out onto the back porch, backlighted by the flood of yellow light streaming from the kitchen. She lifted her arms above her head—like an avenging angel, thought Annie.

"Well, mercy, mercy, the prodigals have returned." Rose's clipped words were uneven around the edges, like she had been trying to file them sharper but didn't get the chance to quite finish the job before they came up.

"Hope you two not expecting a fatted calf—maybe a piece of rawhide strap."

Grabbing both of them in her arms, Rose pressed them against her apron. But before Annie could catch even one breath of Rose's baking powder and flour smell, she had pushed them away again and was shaking them back and forth like she did the dust mop. Annie fully expected to be dashed against the side of the house and hung in the little dogwood tree beside the steps.

"Mr. Laurence, Miss Louise, I got 'em. Big as life and twice as natural," Rose hollered right into their faces.

"Mama, you want to bust my ears?" Cookie protested.

"For a start, maybe. What do you two girls mean, disappearing in the middle of a storm and staying gone the whole livelong afternoon and half the night?"

Annie and Cookie looked at each other for an answer, a plan.

At that moment, Laurence Trammel stepped into the kitchen door. Silhouetted by the light, he was long, sharp, and thin—a knife blade to Rose's ladle.

"Annie, Cookie, are you all right?"

Both girls nodded solemnly, still trying to sort through the emotions thick around them and their own knowledge about where they had spent the afternoon. For the first time, uneasy feelings began to stir in their stomachs and chests.

"Your mother has been frantic. She thought there might have been some sort of—well, foul play."

Cookie looked at Annie, then back at Mr. Laurence. "It's all right, Mr. Laurence, we weren't playing. We were out working."

"Don't you see, when you two disappeared while we

were all sleeping, and the attic—torn apart, all the trunks emptied. Your mother's dummy battered and thrown in the corner. It seemed impossible, but—well, what were we to think. Your mother was hysterical. I finally had to call Dr. Mason to come give her a shot, and . . ." Breaking off suddenly, he looked down at Cookie and Annie. "If you two weren't dragged out of here, you certainly have some explaining to do."

He rubbed a finger over his drawn brows. "Your mother better hear this, too, I suppose." He turned on his heel, and Cookie, Annie, then Rose, followed him silently across the kitchen and down the hall.

As they walked, Cookie kept looking back over her shoulder at Annie until Rose reached over and gave her a hard thump on the top of her head.

"Well?" Laurence Trammell stood on the far side of the bed, holding one of his wife's hands in both of his.

"We were playing in the attic . . ." Annie began.

Cookie nodded. "So as not to disturb you folks' nap."

"Then there was this really bad storm up there and . . ."

Cookie balled up both fists and shook them at the ceiling. "I wish you could have heard them hailstones, big as Mr. Laurence's fist. Lightning was practically curling our hair."

Louise Trammell pushed herself up on one elbow and waved away Cookie's stream of words. "But the attic . . . the place is demolished. And all this talk of bears. Why, you had poor Ruth-baby believing you had been eaten alive. Then we discovered you two were missing . . ." Louise sank back onto her pillows. "At least we don't have to worry about all our winter clothes. You two had them all the time—though I hate to see what shape they are in." The thought made her pause and twist her head anxiously back toward Annie and Cookie.

For once words failed Cookie. Caught in Louise's demanding gaze, she groped for Annie with one hand without turning her head.

Annie felt a strange pressure building up behind her ears and eyes, as if she were a submarine diving further and further away from a noisy, jostling world above her. There was a sharp nudge in her side, another one, and Rose's echoey voice said, "Answer your mother."

Annie saw her mother's fingers twist a small piece of pillowcase between her fingers.

"There were three trunks full of clothes. Don't tell me you and Cookie could have mislaid them. Even your father's good cashmere coat is gone and all my evening dresses—everything. Rose has checked twice."

Her mother gave a nervous little laugh. "Why, if I thought for one minute . . . Annie! Are you listening?"

Her father, keeping his eyes on Annie's and Cookie's faces, patted his wife's hand. "There now, dear. I'm sure . . . poor dear," he said softly, like a mother trying to pacify a child and go on with the book she's reading at the same time.

"Annie, I'm waiting," her mother said.

"We don't have the clothes," Annie said, her voice a whisper.

"We thought they were at least a hundred years old," Cookie added. "They sure smelled old."

"Well, who does have them, for goodness sake?" Louise asked, ignoring Cookie's remarks.

"I . . . we don't know."

"Don't know!"

"Well, not exactly."

Louise struggled forward again, tugging impatiently at the hand Laurence still held.

"There now, dear," he said turning toward her, a small frown creasing his forehead. "Don't upset yourself."

"That's it," Annie heard someone mutter. It sounded like her own voice. It was so hard to tell, when she felt like she was under water. "We gave them to the poor."

Louise stiffened. "Well, you'll just have to go and ask for them back again."

"That's out of the question, Louise," Laurence Trammell snapped with such unaccustomed firmness that a hush fell. "What a Trammell gives is given."

Louise gave a small scream and fell backward. With a collective gasp, everyone stepped toward the bed.

"Sweet Jesus," Rose groaned and placed a protective arm around Annie's and Cookie's shoulders.

Louise's small heart-shaped face was bloodless, and her mouth hung open in quiet surprise. She lay limply still, oblivious of her curls crushed against her pillow, her eyes closed.

That, thought Annie, in some cool, efficient part of her mind, is the difference between fainting and swooning.

"And just where did you two manage to find that many poor people?" her father asked sternly. "If I'm any judge, there were enough clothes in that attic to clothe half of Winton."

"We went over to Ina's," Cookie offered, watching the pale Louise out of frightened eyes.

"Ina's! Ina couldn't get any of those clothes over her hand, much less her head."

"She didn't *keep* them," Annie explained hastily. "She

just let us use her hedge. We spread everything out, and people just sort of appeared from everywhere." Annie shook her head remembering. "You never saw anything like it. When we first got there, there wasn't a soul around except Ina sitting on her porch and a couple of kids playing in the drainage ditches. We spread out a few sacks of clothes on those hedges, and before you could say scat, you couldn't get from one side of the yard to the other for people."

"And it wasn't even Saturday," said Cookie. Catching a grin just in time, she pursed her lips and looked anxiously down again at Louise Trammell's still form. "Is she all right?"

Laurence Trammell seemed to consider the question a hard one, and he looked down at his wife as if searching her still face for an answer. There seemed to be none, and he laid her hand gently on the coverlet and turned back to Annie.

"Let's you and I go into the living room for a while, Annie. Rose will watch your mother."

They sat side by side on the long brocade sofa, the grandfather clock across the room ticking like a bomb inside Annie's head.

"What am I going to do with you, Aunty?"

The almost-forgotten nickname brought tears to Annie's eyes.

"You still are my serious, little, old Aunty, aren't you?"

He gave a tug on a strand of hair just behind her ear. "I admit that your extravagance is going to put quite a crimp in our budget this fall, and you really should have asked before you gave away all our clothes as well as your own ... but damn it all, Aunty, I'm proud of you. All these

Thursdays going over to Ina's. I never realized that you saw past Ina's clean sheets and big laugh." Her father took her hand. "Now tell me about it. Everything."

Annie stared without blinking at the fireplace where two ornate Chinese urns with dark-blue tops seemed mocking reminders of the mayonnaise jar lying quietly beneath the geraniums on the back steps.

Her father's forgiveness seemed to hinge on the fact that she had given the clothes away, not sold them. Then, too, if he knew about the money, he might want to know what they planned to do with it.

"Well, Annie," her father urged.

Slowly Annie told her father about dragging the heavy wheelbarrow and wagon to Ina's house and spreading the clothes on her hedge. She told him about the crowd gathering and what a good time everyone had had. And the more she told him, the stronger the urge became to tell everything, about the money and most of all about leaving. Somehow it didn't even seem very real or urgent any more. She wished Cookie would come out of her mother's room and help her decide what to do. She had never imagined how it would make her feel to deceive her father.

In an attempt to delay making a decision, she began to tell him about the Reverend Henton and the Widow Pierce. Instead of smiling or slapping his knee awkwardly the way he did when he was recounting a funny story he had heard downtown, he leaned back and became strangely quiet.

"Whew," he finally said softly, "looks like your mother's premonition about the Reverend Henton was correct."

"Will you have him horsewhipped?" Annie whispered.
Her father frowned. "Of course not—don't you know
better than that?"

Annie nodded and, despite her own burden of
deception, felt better. Her father looked so calm and sure
sitting there. He would know how to help poor Esther
Pierce—even better than the Reverend Henton. He might
even know how to solve her problem, if only she knew
whether she dared tell him. Rose had as much as told her
not to bother her father about anything that concerned
her mother. Annie searched his pale eyes for some sign.

Just then there was a moan from the bedroom.

"Miss Louise is coming round, Mr. Laurence," Rose
called, and her father rose quickly.

At the door, he turned back a moment. "Don't worry.
I'll speak to Reverend Henton. You were right to tell me."

Annie nodded again, and her father was gone.

CHAPTER 12

AFTER THE RUMMAGE SALE, summer day after summer day unfurled and lay limp and motionless at Annie's feet. It seemed as if time itself had snagged on some cosmic thistle.

Secretly Annie watched Ruth-baby hurrying about in her funny, headlong trot, clutching her bedraggled doll protectively to her chest. If Ruth-baby saw her watching, she would dance around Annie's legs begging her to play, but her energy only made Annie feel heavy and stiff and anxious to be alone.

As punishment for the unauthorized attic raid, her parents and Rose had decided that she and Cookie were not to see each other for one week, the barn being no-man's-land for each of them.

With Rose busy with Ruth-baby and the housework, her mother recuperating from her latest "setback," and her father and Otis at the store, the punishment would have been easy to circumvent. In fact, Annie did slip into the barn twice and stand in Chewing Tobacco's stall, leaning on the half-door, watching the cabin below. Both times she saw B.C. squatting in the bare yard beside his derby car, but she did not wave or call out.

Though she didn't quite admit it even to herself, the only part of her day she looked forward to was the time she spent each morning at Dr. Matt's. The moment she placed a bare foot on the cool, faded linoleum, she seemed beyond time. Here the rules were so simple—"Yes, ma'am. No, ma'am. Thank you, ma'am. Please. Open the pot and give me some peas."—and Annie was teacher as well as pupil. She wouldn't have admitted to anyone, even Cookie, how wonderful being a teacher made her feel.

She lay on the couch now, oblivious to Ruth-baby's tugs on her shorts. In her daydreams, she and Miss Lessie walked regally through the crowd up to the President and his wife. The books balanced on their heads were motionless despite their long easy strides.

Both wore long gowns and spotless white gloves.

In front of the President, they paused, their hands folded demurely across their stomachs. After a flawless, genteel conversation with the President and his wife, a murmur of admiration ran through the glittering crowd, and the President's wife nodded pointedly to her secretary. At the door an impertinent newsman stepped directly in front of Miss Lessie.

"How do you explain your great success today?"

Miss Lessie's polite smile did not waver. "Yes, ma'am. No, ma'am. Thank you, ma'am. Please," she said, her head held high.

As they stepped forward, the rude reporter fell back, his pencil still poised to write.

Rose gave one of Annie's toes a tentative tug. "Time for your lesson, Annie."

"Me, too. Me, too," crowed Ruth-baby.

"No," Annie said, more sharply than she'd meant to. "You'd only interrupt and get in the way."

"Well, well. I think we got us a dedicated lady here,

Ruth-baby. Let's you and me go get us a gingersnap and some milk," Rose said, grinning down at Ruth-baby.

Annie slammed the front door behind her, but she didn't stay mad long. Who could stay mad thinking of Miss Lessie's big gray eyes solemnly watching every move you made, one hand nervously twisting at the top button of her housedress as she slowly, awkwardly repeated each move of her lesson. If Annie nodded her approval, she lowered her eyes at once, but her smile would spread, slow and golden as melting butter, until she turned away in embarrassment toward the sink or the stove.

The first part of every lesson she still spent in Dr. Matt's study with Miss Emma. Between them, they had worked out a very satisfactory routine. First, Miss Emma would bring Annie up to date on how Dr. Matt's biography was coming. Then she would read a couple of Dr. Matt's letters to the state legislature or other educators around the state. Sometimes she even asked Annie's opinion about where a certain document should come in the book. Then in the remaining time she would demonstrate some facet of "ladyhood": how to set a formal table; how to sit with your legs crossed without your foot going to sleep; who had to offer you his seat; and who you had to offer your seat to—or was that to whom?

Today Annie had to practice rising and offering her seat to her elders, and she hurried across the street; Miss Lessie would love today's lesson.

"Morning, Miss Lessie," Annie called through the screen door. Miss Lessie turned from the sink and wiped her sudsy hands on the bottom of her apron, a shy, one-sided smile lighting her face as she crossed the floor to unlatch the screen, top and bottom. Though obviously glad to see Annie, she never spoke until after Annie's lesson with Miss Emma. Now, a small smile still on her face, she turned to the breakfast dishes in the sink.

Miss Emma, already busy at her desk, merely grunted as she heard the scrape of Annie's chair beside the bed. "Vision," she said, lifting her head and peering at Annie over her glasses. "Vision is the key word. The ability to anticipate the inevitable future and prepare the world for it. That's the gift Papa had—the gift of vision."

Miss Emma cleared her throat. Her eyes peered over the tops of her glasses as she scrutinized Annie for some sign of comprehension.

Annie squirmed. Miss Emma's opening remarks were always the most difficult part of a lesson because you had no idea where she was starting from. Now she wondered what the most ladylike answer would be.

"It's the children of the children warned who can hear, can finally see the visions of the great and thank them," Miss Emma added.

"Ah," said Annie, catching the drift now. "Thank you, ma'am."

"Not me," Miss Emma said in exasperation, "Papa." She sighed and poked two fingers over her glasses and rubbed her eyes hard, erasing some depressing vision of her own.

"Me and Cookie think Dr. Matt was the greatest man there was. Any kid who heard his ideas would," Annie said earnestly, thinking of his petition to give the ten-year-olds the vote. "When you get your book written . . ."

Miss Emma snapped her notebook shut. "There," she said, "you're just what I need. The optimism of youth. Don't know what comes over me sometimes. Now let's get to work. It takes time to make a silk purse out of a sow's ear."

Annie nodded. Miss Emma always said the same strange thing before they started the day's lesson.

*   *   *

Pausing in the dark hall, Annie took a deep breath; the whole house was full of the warm smell of gingerbread. The spicy smell was familiar, yet sharp and exciting, like the first time you smelled burning leaves in the fall. When she got to the kitchen, there was a huge square of the dark, crumbly cake at her usual place at the table. Miss Lessie was already seated opposite Annie's chair, the ever-present mugful of steaming black coffee in front of her.

Annie pulled back her chair. "It sure smells good in here."

"Gingerbread always has a sad smell to me," said Miss Lessie, flushing slightly at her sudden burst of words.

"How can something smell sad?"

Miss Lessie's eyes flickered past Annie's. "It's the only thing I can remember about our mama dying. She had baked gingerbread that morning early, to beat the heat. Afterward, Papa wouldn't allow any flowers at the house here. He shut all the windows and doors to try to hold the living smell of Mama baking gingerbread in the kitchen."

Both Annie and Miss Lessie jumped at the sound of something like a loose shutter banging against the house.

The bang came again, and this time the screen door was flung wide. A tall, redheaded boy, balancing a cardboard box of groceries on one knee, blocked the rebounding screen door with an elbow.

"Wow, you ladies must be talking a blue streak," he said with a wide grin. "Where you want me to set this here box of groceries?"

Miss Lessie seemed to explode so that everything around her disintegrated. Her coffee washed across the cloth, her chair cracked like a whip as it hit the hard linoleum floor.

"Don't come in," Annie shouted, her glance shifting from Miss Lessie's crouching form to the grocery boy standing in the middle of the floor, still holding the box of groceries in his arms.

Annie didn't hear Miss Lessie move and didn't see her pick up her broom. She saw a look of incredulous fear spread across the boy's freckled face, then a narrow blur as the broom handle fell across his shoulders.

The heavy box split on the floor at his feet, and tin cans rolled in every direction. A large glass jar of pickles shattered, and the air was full of the smell of vinegar and alum. Annie's chair tipped backward.

"For goodness sake, what is going on in there?" came Miss Emma's angry voice from the study.

Annie grabbed Miss Lessie from behind, her arms tight around her bony hips, but she was only dragged back and forth as Miss Lessie advanced and retreated from the grocery boy, who had crouched in a corner, his arms over his head, his face to the wall. As the broom fell again and again, he gave one low cry and sank to his knees. He never struck back, only folded both his long arms across his head.

Miss Lessie seemed completely unaware that Annie was behind her, her face pressed into her back as she struggled to pull her away from the fallen boy.

Suddenly, a force stronger than either of them catapulted them backward. Annie's elbow scraped painfully against the screen door.

"How many times do I have to tell Jake Carruthers to get his boys to leave the groceries on the steps? Now see what he's done," Miss Emma shouted, looking around the kitchen.

Miss Lessie stared straight ahead, frowning as if she were trying to remember something for her grocery list. When Miss Emma said sharply, "Lessie, go to your room," she moved noiselessly, gracefully avoiding cans and jars without ever looking down.

"Miss Emma," Annie began in a high quavery voice, "he isn't moving."

"Who's that?"

"The boy from the grocery."

Miss Emma shook her head impatiently. "I suppose I better call Dr. Mason."

* * *

Rusty Henshaw sat in a kitchen chair holding a dish-cloth to a deep gash over his left eye. Miss Emma paced up and down, each heavy step shaking china hidden behind cabinet doors.

"Well, now this really isn't so bad," Dr. Mason said. He

grinned down at Rusty. "Just enough of a scar to impress the ladies."

Rusty grinned uncertainly and looked at the wreckage all about him. "This was my first day on the job."

Dr. Mason gave a hearty laugh. "Well, they say the first day is always the hardest one. Now, I want you to ride back down to my office with me. Want to take a picture of that red head of yours just to be sure. Wait for me in the car, will you?" he asked, steering Rusty toward the door.

Annie stood awkwardly by the stove not knowing whether to go or stay. Then Dr. Mason turned toward Miss Emma, his face grave, his eyes dark with worry, and it seemed too late to move.

"Has this ever happened before, Emma?"

Miss Emma stirred uneasily. "Of course not. I told that Jake Carruthers!"

"The truth, Emma," Dr. Mason said, his shoulders sagging forward.

"There was only the time she threw that flowerpot at Arthur Gates when he came creeping around the back porch and scared her half to death."

Dr. Mason shook his head. "Even little ordinary fears like you and I have sometimes get worse as we get older, Emma."

"Do you think Mrs. Henshaw will make trouble then?"

"Mary Henshaw has five other boys. He looks to be the smallest of the lot. Chances are she won't even notice a little gash like that."

"What, then?"

"It's Miss Lessie I'm worried about, Emma. What's to become of her?"

Suddenly big tears gathered behind Miss Emma's

rimless glasses, and her large chest rose like a pouter pigeon's. "Lessie, Lessie, Lessie. That's all I've ever heard. What's to become of Lessie? Who's to look after Lessie? Well, I'm not as strong as Papa. It's too much for me." She gave a sob that sounded as rusty and protesting as an unused door. "But who ever asks what's to become of Emma? Poor Emma Carter."

Miss Emma's curls quivered, and Dr. Mason patted her broad shoulders awkwardly. "Now, Emma, don't you give way on me. You've always been a pillar. You always will be. It's your nature. You can't quarrel with your nature, any more than Lessie can quarrel with hers."

Miss Emma pulled a handkerchief out from under her belt and gave a strong blow.

Dr. Mason opened his black bag. "That's better," he said. "Keep Lessie quiet today and give her two of these to take to sleep tonight. She'll be right as rain tomorrow. Take two yourself. Do you good."

Dr. Mason went out the back door to his car, and Miss Emma walked heavily down the hall without seeing Annie pressed back in Miss Lessie's chair between the stove and the refrigerator.

For a few moments there was the void people leave in their wake, then slowly, sound by sound, Annie heard the life of the house going on: the drip of a faucet, the soft sputtering of the water heater, the distant scrape of a chair. Annie let her head rest on the wall behind her. It was still warm from the heat of the stove. Her pounding heart slowed and synchronized its beat with the rhythm of the house itself.

It was a long, dreamlike time later that Annie knew no house could mete out such sad, deliberate blows.

Opening her eyes, she looked around the kitchen to focus on a sound so low that just turning her head seemed to obliterate it. She closed her eyes again, and, without her ears or eyes, she knew the sound came from behind Miss Lessie's closed door.

With every step down the dark narrow hall, the sounds became more intense, like the beats of a heart that must burst.

Annie leaned against the heavy door at the end of the hall. "Miss Lessie, don't," she whispered. "Don't, Miss Lessie. It won't help."

Still the thudding continued.

"It's not right," Annie said, wondering as she said it what she meant.

The only response was the steady thudding. Even without seeing, Annie knew exactly where Miss Lessie had fled, how she crouched against the wall in the darkness of her small room; she knew without being told that now she banged her head violently against the wall to alleviate a far more bitter hurt and a fear that threatened to consume her.

Annie pressed her hands against the door. It almost seemed that she could feel the pounding stinging the palms of her hands.

"Miss Lessie, our lesson. You forgot our lesson," she said, groping for something to touch Miss Lessie in her dark world.

The pounding grew louder, echoing in the hall, making her ears ring. Surely Miss Emma had heard, too.

Annie caught her breath. Miss Emma would be very angry with Miss Lessie. She had caused enough trouble already.

Annie rapped sharply on the door. "Miss Lessie, stop that this minute. Don't you know a lady never makes that kind of racket?"

There was a sudden silence.

"Miss Lessie?"

No answer.

Annie turned and ran back toward the kitchen. Opening her notebook, she grabbed a pencil and drew a series of clumsy stick figures.

The first drawing showed two stiffly erect figures, one much taller than the other. They stood back to back. The taller figure had an angry scowl on its face. The smaller one had a large tear on its cheek.

The second drawing halfway down the page showed the same two figures, still stiffly erect, but now facing each other shaking hands. At the bottom of the page, the small figure stood behind a chair. The tall figure, her arms outstretched, wrists elegantly dropped, poised before taking the proffered seat.

Ripping the page from her notebook, she hurried back down the hall and pushed the page under Miss Lessie's door.

"Look at the door, Miss Lessie. It's your lesson." Silence. "Please look, Miss Lessie. I'll wait for you in the kitchen."

In the kitchen, the spicy smell of gingerbread was mingled now with the strong smells of pickle juice and antiseptic. It was not unpleasant: a cool hand placed on a feverish brow. From down the hall came the faint uneven pecking of Miss Emma on Dr. Matt's old black typewriter.

Then there was a soft scurry, like little mice playing in

the darkened hall. Miss Lessie stepped hesitantly into the doorway; her eyes were on her open-toed shoes; her arms were folded tightly across her stomach, each hand gripping an elbow as if she were cradling some tiny unseen infant. Her hair was mussed, and one side of her face was badly discolored and swollen.

Slowly she lifted her eyes and swayed visibly as if the sight of her familiar kitchen staggered her. Annie stepped toward Miss Lessie. With a hesitant smile that just touched her soft, gray eyes, Miss Lessie tilted her chin higher and stretched out her hand toward Annie.

Tentatively the bony fingers, rough and dry from too many dish-washings, touched Annie's and squeezed.

"Won't you take my chair, ma'am?" Annie asked, stepping behind her chair to hold the back as Miss Emma had shown her.

Miss Lessie pivoted on one heel and, flaring out the skirt of her dress, lowered herself slowly, precisely, into the chair.

"Thank you, Annie. Don't mind if I do," she said softly.

* * *

Though Miss Lessie and Annie started every time a car passed the house or the phone rang in Dr. Matt's study, it seemed, after several days, that there would be no repetition of Miss Lessie's nightmare. With slowly growing hope, Annie wondered if Dr. Mason could possibly have been right when he predicted Rusty's mother wouldn't notice a new gash on the head of one of her six boys.

Friday, Rusty even delivered groceries to Miss Emma's

again, though he was careful to leave them on the bottom step, and he sprinted out of the yard as soon as he had set them down.

Watching from her front steps, Annie sighed, wishing sadly that he'd gotten amnesia while he was getting his nasty gash. She could just hear Rusty and William Petus and Hoyt Greely chanting Miss Lessie's name.

Rusty crossed the street and came to stand in front of Annie, staring at his tennis shoes, both of which had been cut to allow more room for his big toes.

"How's your head?" she asked.

Rusty squirmed, twisting his feet back and forth as if someone had nailed him to the spot on which he stood.

"Ah, that wasn't anything. I mean . . . a little old woman like Miss Lessie . . ." Rusty scowled at the magnolia tree. "I never woulda cried or anything like that, you know, if she hadn't come at me so sudden, and it being my first day on the job and all."

Annie watched Rusty's scowl deepen. She wanted to explain for Miss Lessie and plead for her, but the words rolling through her mind seemed so garbled.

Rusty's voice dropped. "I mean. . . Emmett and Willy, and then there's all my brothers. . . Annie, look at it my way. They would never give me any peace again."

His words sifted brokenly through Annie's own thoughts. "You mean, maybe we should just forget the whole thing?" she asked in disbelief.

Rusty blushed furiously. "I might of known." He spun away.

"Rusty, don't go! I really meant it," Annie called after him.

He turned back toward her slowly, suspicious of some further torment.

"That's the best idea I ever heard. Let's shake on it," urged Annie.

A wide smile lit his freckled face. "You're supposed to spit first."

Annie spit vehemently at the pavement and reached to grab Rusty's hand, still at his side, and pump it up and down. Then she paused.

"This does work both ways, doesn't it?"

"How's that?"

"You won't ever mention Miss Lessie if we don't mention you, right?"

"That's sure a deal with me," Rusty said, pumping Annie's hand now.

"Bye," called Annie over her shoulder, as she ran to tell Miss Lessie about the promise she'd made for both of them.

At the bottom step of the back porch, Annie stopped. Miss Emma was nailing a small sign onto the end of the banister.

"What is a *tres-pas-ser*?" asked Annie, sounding out the long word.

"In this case, anything at all with pants on," Miss Emma answered dryly.

Miss Lessie peered cautiously out the screen door, then waved shyly when she saw Annie.

"Was Rusty a trespasser?" Annie asked.

Miss Emma started as if Annie had said a dirty word. "He certainly was. Ought to be taken into court. Scaring people to death."

Miss Lessie edged onto the porch, her hands fluttering in gentle protest. "Forgive us our trespasses as...."

"As we forgive those who trespass against us," Annie finished quickly.

Miss Lessie smiled and nodded. "That's right, isn't it, Emma?"

Miss Emma seemed to have difficulty breathing. "Would you stop looking as though it was I ... if you two had remembered that scripture a little sooner, we wouldn't be teetering on the brink of ruin."

"Miss Emma," Annie burst in, "I forgot. You're not teetering anymore. Rusty and I made a deal. That's what I came over to tell you."

Miss Emma's eyes narrowed. "And what did Rusty want?"

Annie clapped her hands in anticipation, "Only that we not tell a soul that the first day on the job little Miss Lessie Carter scared a big boy like him half to death and had him bawling like a baby."

"Well, Lessie," said Miss Emma, "you've squeezed through again. But I hope this will be a lesson to you. This time you almost went too far. . . Lessie?"

Miss Lessie was pressing back against the screen, her eyes a wide, glazed stare. Miss Emma and Annie turned to follow her eyes.

"Oh, Lessie, that's only the garbage truck. It's Thursday, you know."

Miss Lessie didn't move, and Miss Emma shook her head hopelessly. "Go on inside, Lessie. Go on, get."

CHAPTER 13

ON FRIDAY Annie heard Rose and Otis talking in the kitchen as she stepped onto the back porch. When she heard them mention Reverend Henton, something made her stop just outside the screen door to listen; she had forgotten all about him.

"If it wasn't for gossip," Otis was saying in a dry voice, "I reckon the Ladies' Aid Society would have to disband for lack of business."

"There's no more gossiping in this town than goes on down at that furniture store," Rose retorted. "That Reverend Henton is lucky he didn't get no more than the bruises he did."

"I know for a fact Laurence tried to talk them out of going to the funeral, and he tried to talk the Pierce brothers into giving Esther and her kids some money, too," Otis said. "He knew before he went that it wouldn't do no good, but he tried."

Outside on the porch, Annie gave a little gasp of surprise at this news, but Rose had turned on the tap water and did not hear her.

Over the sound of the water, Rose spoke in a voice charged with bitterness. "Lilly told me that that Jeb Pierce pushed Esther so hard she stumbled off the curb, skinned her knees and tore her dress. Reverend Henton got considerable worse. Maybe it's no more than he deserved.

"What makes it so bad is her cousin told me she loved that no-good Pierce and never could see one thing wrong with him. Poor little thing. That Henton gonna have to answer to the Lord if he brings her more grief than she can stand. Where did he come from anyway?"

Mentally Annie supplied Otis's resigned shrug.

"I guess that child's fixing to spend the rest of her life paying for her foolishness," Rose said. "She won't have no place among black folks or white; and nobody can help, Laurence Trammell no more than Reverend Henton."

Annie's mind wandered, uncomfortable at Rose's belief that here was something her father could do nothing about. Suddenly she heard Otis talking.

". . . going to have a service of his own Sunday afternoon, they say. Gonna have everything 'cept the body. Esther got to be crazy with grief or something, cause I reckon she agreed to it. That preacher's sure that'll fetch her some money."

Rose sighed. "Lord save us and keep us."

Annie heard chair legs scraping and hastily retreated toward the pasture.

* * *

B.C. was sitting on the porch with Cookie, and between them they had a small pile of money. "What's here plus what we got from the sale makes fifty-two dollars and seventy-five cents," B.C. said as Annie walked up. He grinned at the two openmouthed girls.

"Does that mean we can buy tickets?" Cookie wanted to know.

B.C. shook his head. "We better not. Too risky. Old Ridgely down at the station might call up Mr. Laurence. Besides, we'll need food and stuff until I get my job working on cars in one of those plants. What it does mean is we better leave pretty soon—before Mr. Laurence makes another trip to Ina's and hears about the money."

"Oh, B.C., I'm so glad you're coming," Annie cried, stooping to give him a quick hug. For a moment he seemed about to return her hug, then he snapped, "Cut that out. You want to get me hung?"

Annie fell back. "How could I do that?"

"Black boys are not supposed to have nothing to do with white girls."

Now Cookie protested. "What you mean?"

B.C. did not answer, but to Annie's horror, warm knowledge rushed through her body, heating her face and making her hands and feet tingle.

Impatiently Cookie stamped her foot. "Now look at you, Annie. What in thunder you turning red about? You two both been out in the sun too long."

B.C. spoke in the awkward silence.

"I still haven't promised I'd go for sure; but if I do go, we should tell Mama."

Cookie threw up her hands. "Tell Mama? You are crazy. She's going to just let us go off to Detroit without raising a hand?"

"I mean tell her just enough so that she'll know

afterward we had to do it. So she'll know that we didn't leave without saying good-bye."

"Well, it'll take a genius like you to do telling like that," scoffed Cookie.

"No. Not me. Annie."

"Why me?" cried Annie.

"Because," said B.C. flatly, "you got a way with words, from reading all those books, I reckon, and because Mama can read our minds across the room. That's why."

"She reads my mind, too. All the time."

B.C. shrugged. "Well, tell her while she's real busy, supper time or something."

Annie shook her head adamantly. "This is your idea. You tell her."

"If you want me to come . . . " B.C. began.

"Okay, okay. Just don't blame me if I ruin everything."

B.C. smiled as slow and easy as a sunning cat. "It's your wedding."

Annie glared helplessly at B.C.; then she remembered the news she'd come to tell them.

"They wouldn't let Esther and Reverend Henton come to Mr. Pierce's funeral, so Reverend Henton is going to have one of his own! They are going to have everything except for the body. I guess that's already buried."

"Oh, Jesus!" cried B.C., his face full of wide-eyed amazement.

"He's gonna win. You know that. He's gonna get that lady what she and them kids deserve. I know he is."

Cookie shrugged. "Maybe."

"I'm gonna go," B.C. announced. "I wouldn't miss it for the world."

"Me too," Annie said.

Cookie shook her head. "You know Mama knows when that funeral is gonna be as well as we do, and she's gonna have us at her side the livelong afternoon."

Reluctantly Annie agreed. "Still, it seems like we should go. I've never been to a real funeral." She paused, thinking of the timid Esther Pierce. "Wouldn't it be awful if nobody was to go?"

B.C. rose abruptly. "What do we care—we're leaving this town. Don't forget," he said, turning to Annie, "tell Mama. Be sure she knows it's got nothing to do with her. Later, when we've gone, she'll understand we had to. That's what's important."

* * *

Rose was at the kitchen table stringing beans into a big enamel bowl when Annie got back. Ruth-baby sat between her feet, playing with the beans that dropped.

"Want some help?" Annie asked.

"If the offer don't drop me dead in my tracks," Rose answered. Without looking up, she took a handful of beans and put them on a piece of newspaper for Annie.

"Where's your shadow?"

"Home. B.C. too."

"He's some better, don't you think?" Rose asked, lifting her head to wait for Annie's reply.

Annie shifted uneasily. "What do you mean?"

"He's not so hurt anymore about William, I don't think."

"Oh, yeah," Annie replied noncommittally.

Rose went back to snapping beans in an easy clickety-clack rhythm, but she kept her eyes on Annie.

"People do get over things," she said. "Look at your mama. She's already over her little setback over the clothes. She seems right cheerful this morning."

Annie chose her next words carefully. "Rose, my daddy can fix a lot of things, can't he?"

Rose nodded. "More than most I reckon. He's a good man, Annie. Got a natural good eye for the way things were meant to be and not afraid to try for it."

"Do you s'pose he could stop something if my mama were really set on it?"

Rose's smile just touched the corners of her mouth. "Everybody's got their blind spots, baby, and I reckon I wouldn't put Mr. Laurence to any tests over some whim of your mama's."

Annie sighed, "Rose," she said, dropping her hands in her lap, "Cookie says you can read our minds. Is that true?"

Rose's hands were still for a moment over her bowl and then began moving quickly again. "Not unless what you're thinking is written all over your face—which it usually is."

"But Rose, if you couldn't see our faces, you'd always know some things, wouldn't you?"

Rose snapped a long bean slowly down its succulent spine. "That would depend, honey." She laid a hand gently across her heart. "Now take me, for instance. If I was to ever . . . not be around, I'd want you to know I still felt exactly the same way about you children. You and Cookie and B.C. and Ruth-baby will always be my babies to me."

Annie was so relieved she felt limp. "Me, too, Rose," she said softly. "I feel just the same way, exactly, and so do

Cookie and B.C." Happiness seemed to flood the kitchen like morning sunshine. Rose understood. She would know exactly how they felt when she found out. Jumping up from the table, she gave Rose a fierce hug.

"Raining beans," Ruth-baby said, laughing. "Rose, it's raining beans!"

"Now," said Rose briskly, catching what beans she could with her skirt, "enough of this tomfoolery. I got to get dinner on the table or Mr. Laurence gonna skin me alive." She cupped Annie's chin gently in her warm palm. "And I want you and Cookie not to do any beforehand worrying about me leaving. The Lord sets his own time for everything."

* * *

By seven o'clock the next morning, Cookie and Annie had already congratulated themselves on their good fortune. Everything was going to be all right. Rose understood. Nothing else seemed to matter. In a burst of enthusiasm, Cookie clapped her hands. "Let's us go over to the Emanuel Methodist Church."

"The funeral isn't until tomorrow afternoon."

"That don't make no difference," Cookie persisted. "We can watch them getting ready. Besides, we haven't ever seen the church, even, and before long we'll be gone forever."

Annie blinked. She couldn't conceive of something existing in Winton that she had never seen. The bright sunlight seemed to dim. Was this what leaving would be like—only worse, much worse?

Cookie jumped to her feet. "Come on. Don't always be

turning everything over in your head. Life's for doing, not thinking," she urged.

The Emanuel Methodist Church was a dark-red brick building. The grass had been trampled flat and brown by the coming and going of worshippers' feet.

"It's just like Bethel Baptist," said Annie, as they climbed the steps to the double front doors. "All this way for nothing." The Bethel Baptist was Rose's church, and she and Cookie had been in and out of it all their lives.

"Not inside," Cookie said. "It's bound to be different on the inside."

"You going to bust right in in your jeans?"

Cookie appraised the situation. "No-o-o. I guess I'll go around to that side door. It'll lead up in the loft. Let's just have one good look and then skedaddle." She gave Annie a little shove, and they started around to the side door of the church.

Crickets buzzed and the air was heavy and still. In a steep gully that cut around back of the church, someone had left an old pickup that was covered in red dust. Annie could just barely make out that it was dark blue or maybe black and the fender on one side was all crumpled.

Inside, steep stairs led directly upward into darkness that was only a little cooler than the air outside. She could feel the heat increase as they went upward. The backs of the pews were filled with hymnals and paper fans just the way they were in her own church. Just as she got ready to lean over the balustrade and look down, she heard a scraping sound that made her heart leap in her throat. Cookie had obviously heard it, too, for she dropped to her knees.

Cautiously both girls raised their heads until they could

peer down on the sanctuary. Stained glass windows cast crazy-quilt patterns across the empty pews. Cookie suddenly squeezed Annie's arm so hard she had to cover her mouth to keep from crying out. Two white men in dirty overalls were crouched against one wall of the church, just about halfway down the aisle. One of the men was much bigger than the other, but somehow, it was the smaller of the two with his dark, greasy hair and quiet scuttling movements who made Annie feel as if someone had just put a cold, clammy hand on the back of her neck.

Slowly they moved along in low crouches, whispering back and forth to each other, unwinding something as they went. Once they paused and laughed low and moved on again. Up the steps and into the choir loft they went. Something about the size of a lunch box was pushed under the big flower box that stood on the edge of the baptismal pool. Then the men stood up, brushed their hands and knees, and gave each other silent, playful punches on the shoulder—like boys who had just pulled off a clever trick.

Annie and Cookie dropped out of sight again, just as the men turned and retraced their steps up the side aisle and out the same door through which Annie and Cookie had entered the church. Somehow, the look of secret pleasure on their faces made Annie wish she had never seen them at all.

Suddenly she was aware of the unbearable heat in the balcony. Cookie's face glistened with sweat, just as the men's had. Hers must, too. She shook her arms then her legs to loosen cramped muscles. Her heart was pounding strangely, as if she and Cookie had witnessed something important and dangerous.

"We should get out of here," Cookie whispered.

Annie tried to shake off her strange feelings. "What you scared of? We didn't do anything!"

"What are two white men doing in this church?" Cookie asked.

"You said yourself. They've got to get the church ready for the funeral."

"They didn't have no flowers."

"Maybe they were fixing the lights. They had all that wire."

Cookie seemed unconvinced. "Let's get out of here anyway."

Holding hands, Annie and Cookie scrambled down the narrow steps. At the door Cookie paused, peeked cautiously outside, then flung the door back and they raced across the churchyard. Just as they ducked behind a large clump of rhododendrons, Annie noticed that the old pickup was still there, but she saw no sign of the two rough-looking men.

They were almost home before Cookie spoke again. "I never have seen such ugly-looking men in all my life. Who do you guess they were?"

"I don't know, but I hope I never see them again, especially the short one," Annie answered.

Cookie quickened her pace. "Let's get back home, before we get skinned at the other end of this deal. I swear I don't know where you get such crazy ideas."

"Me?" Annie spluttered, her fear forgotten. She swung at Cookie a second too late. She was already running again. Annie grinned with her teeth closed, to keep the dust out of her throat.

At lunchtime, when Annie came to the table, only her

father was waiting for her. Her mother was indisposed and Ruth-baby had eaten and been put down for a nap. Annie slipped into her chair sideways, glad she had remembered to wash her hands before she came in. Her father looked sternly at her over his rimless glasses. Then without warning his narrow face broke into a smile, and he made a strange choking sound. "Annie," he said, "you look like a barn owl. Your eyes are the only thing on you that isn't covered in dust. Where in the name of all that's holy have you— and Cookie, too, I suppose—spent the morning?"

Automatically Annie shrugged her shoulders, but something, the memory of the two crouching men, their laughter, something, made her want to tell her father, just as she had wanted to tell him about Esther Pierce. It would be his problem then, not hers. For another moment Annie remained silent. It seemed as if she had talked to her father more in the past few weeks than in her whole life put together. The thought made her feel funny and a little bit scared.

Hesitantly, watching for his smile to fade and his napkin to be snapped into his lap, Annie began telling him about her visit to the church with Cookie.

Her father did not interrupt, and though his smile did fade, he looked more concerned than angry. "And you're sure that they did not hurt anything?" he asked.

Annie nodded.

"They didn't take anything that belonged to the church?"

Again Annie shook her head and her father frowned. Finally he, too, shook his head. "It's probably nothing. Don't worry about it. I'll tell Reverend Henton about it the first chance I get. He's got that funeral tomorrow."

Annie's eyes widened. "Are you going to the funeral?"

"No. I really didn't know any of them. And what I knew about Amos Pierce I didn't like at all. There'd be no call for me to be at the funeral." He frowned again as if that weren't quite right, but he didn't know why. Then his face cleared, and he looked at Annie. "And I don't want you over there. Do you understand?"

Annie nodded.

"I don't want you anywhere near the place. Just in case the Pierce brothers decide to cause trouble. Is that a promise?"

Annie nodded. She had known that Rose would not let them go, but it seemed strange to hear her father making such direct orders. She tried to remember another time when he had, and she couldn't. In a way it felt sort of nice. Meekly she nodded one more time to show that she understood. The thought of the two men in church no longer worried her.

Her father cleared his throat. "Well, then," he said, pushing back his chair, "I guess I better get back to the store."

* * *

That evening, like most Saturday evenings, Two-Time, Lilly, Otis, and Rose sat on the porch discussing the day while Annie, Cookie, and B.C. eavesdropped from the steps. Two-Time sat with his elbows on his knees, still dressed in his town clothes. The coat to the brown pinstriped suit that Lilly had made to special order extra-large hung over the back of his chair, and black garters stretched to their limit around his biceps held his white sleeves off his wrists.

Every Saturday, Two-Time went to town in Mr. Petus's pickup truck to get spruced up: a shave and a haircut at the barber shop, a shoeshine at the pool hall, then three beers at the Hi-Lo Club. This Saturday had been no different, and now he sat hunched forward, gleaming splendidly, smelling like rose water, still but not relaxed. A panther, thought Annie.

"Anything happening downtown?" Otis wanted to know, tipping his chair back against the wall of the cabin.

Two-Time closed his eyes. "Same as usual. Thomas Benton cut up his wife Friday night. Caught her at the Hi-Lo Club with Danny Evers. Fifty-two stitches. Two of the fellows had a fight over Reverend Henton. Both of them got shiners for their trouble."

Otis shook his head. "You right. Same as usual."

Cookie stirred on the steps beside Annie. "Why are the men at the Hi-Lo Club always beating women up?" she blurted. "Mama always tells B.C. if she ever hears of him laying a hand on a woman she'll kill him herself."

The porch was silent except for the rustle of Lilly's dress.

"Why don't they throw them in jail?" Cookie demanded.

"A man can only be pushed so far," Two-Time said, addressing no one in particular. "Then if he can't hit back at what's hurting him without getting shot or hung, well then, he'll get drunk and hit anything that happens to be handy—anything at all. It's handy for white folks, too. Keeps them from getting beatings they deserve."

After a long moment Rose spoke. "What else is going on downtown?"

"Mostly everybody is talking about Esther Pierce and that funeral she's giving," Two-Time answered. "It's that damn Henton. He's convinced her she can make things different. They'll be different all right. She'll be dead, and the Lord knows what'll become of them kids of hers then."

Annie shuddered. Everyone on the porch was nodding sadly, as if Esther Pierce's death were already decided.

Then Two-Time spoke, and his voice had an edge to it that made even B.C. turn around on the steps where he had been playing mumblety-peg with an old kitchen knife.

"Nothing not ever gonna happen here that didn't happen before. It's like being strapped to a wheel. You keep hanging on until you get all the way around; then it breaks your back."

In the chair beside him, Otis agreed, nodding matter-of-factly.

Lilly couldn't seem to find a comfortable place for her hands. She kept patting her hair or tugging at her dress.

"Well, not me," Two-Time went on with sudden intensity. "I'm not waiting around here until I get drunk some Saturday night and beat up Lilly."

Lilly gave a small shriek.

"And I'm not waiting until my back's broken either."

A deep hush settled over the porch. Warily Otis opened his eyes, and everyone sat perfectly still, waiting.

Suddenly Two-Time seemed hesitant, almost embarrassed, but his voice when he spoke was still angry,

"I'm leaving, y'all. Me and Lilly are gonna pack up and go before it's too late."

Lilly became as still as a quail under cover. Rose drew in one sharp breath.

"Where you planning to go?" Otis asked. "Things are the same everywhere."

"Not up north, not in Detroit, they're not."

"Detroit!" Cookie, B.C., and Annie demanded in one breath.

"You can't," cried Annie. We thought of it first, she would have added if Cookie hadn't poked her hard in the ribs.

"Annie's right," Rose said, her voice thick with feeling. "Why, I'd never see Lilly again—my only kin I got left in this world!"

Lilly's hands fluttered out as if she would touch her sister, then settled into her lap again.

"Don't you think I haven't thought of all that? Lilly's been crying her eyes out this whole week," Two-Time said, almost shouting. "Y'all are the only kin I got in this world, too, as far as that goes." His voice dropped. "Otherwise, I'd have been gone a long time ago."

Silence fell again over the porch, as everyone tried privately to digest Two-Time's awesome news.

Two-Time was the first to break the silence, restlessly rubbing the palms of his huge hands on his knees.

"What you think, Otis?"

Otis cleared his throat, but he seemed unable to find the words he needed.

"Otis?" Lilly prodded.

"I guess I'm thinking of Teddy Oliver and . . . " Otis

looked away from Two-Time, ". . . Ellis Wood."

Two-Time clenched his fists. "Detroit won't lick me, Otis. You won't catch me coming home with my tail between my legs. You know I'm twice the man Ellis Wood was. Why, he wasn't no more than a boy!"

"Teddy Oliver wasn't no boy," Otis said softly. "I reckon Detroit can take just about any sized man and stomp him down. Teddy told me it was like living in a jungle where every creature ate his own kind."

"At least a man can try—can hit back when he's hit," Two-Time said, balling up a square knot of fist.

Rose shook her head. "How come you want to be at the top of a heap like that?"

Two-Time looked full in Rose's face and spoke, slowly but clearly, his last word on the subject. "I got to have me some room. I know it. Lilly knows it, too. Else I'm going to start breaking things . . . and I don't know what all. My head is screaming louder and louder all the time. I won't never get no peace until I at least try. And I'll make it, too. You wait and see." Two-Time's huge fist slashed sideways into a pillar, and the whole porch shook.

Annie turned to see consternation written all over Cookie's face, but B.C.'s eyes were fastened on Two-Time, shining as if he had heard some call from Heaven and with one more word could lift right up.

"I heard that if you are colored, the police shoot first and ask you questions later," B.C. said, talking fast. "I heard everybody colored has to live all squeezed together in houses with rats big as tomcats."

Lilly gave another soft shriek and pressed her hands tightly together in her lap.

Two-Time grinned down at B.C. "They better get me

with the first bullet," he said, with a broad wink. "As for those rats you heard about, black folks grow 'em that big on purpose. They use 'em for watchdogs."

"What you gonna do about a job, Two-Time?" Otis asked quietly.

"I don't have one of them diplomas! So, I reckon they'll have no use for my brain," said Two-Time, frowning, "but if Detroit is anything like they tell it, somebody is gonna have some use for my muscles."

Lilly looked as if she would leap from her chair.

"Now don't you worry, Mama," Two-Time said, patting her knee. "I'm not going up there and get killed. I don't mean that kind of muscle." His mouth twisted down a little. "Let's just say when we come back, me and Hank Ketchum will have a lot in common to talk about."

Rose exhaled a long, slow breath. "You won't never *come* back," she said. "From here to Detroit is a one-way trip—less you come back in pieces. If you make it, there won't be any room for you here."

Two-Time met Rose's eyes. "You may be right, Rose. But that don't mean we can't visit back and forth."

"Two-Time, you got a good job up at the Petuses! A house to live in, friends, and family to stand by you . . . "

"I'm going, Rose, going Monday." Two-Time answered, cutting her off. "If I don't make it, I won't be coming back down here in no little pieces. But I'll send you Lilly home. I promise you that."

Throwing up her hands, Lilly burst into tears. She and Rose moved into the cabin, holding onto each other as they went.

"I'm going on home, Otis, and start packing," Two-Time said. "The sooner we leave now, the better."

Both men rose to their feet.

"Two-Time," said Otis, "I reckon coming home again can't be worse than never starting out." The two men, one head and shoulders taller than the other, shook hands, then awkwardly embraced.

Two-Time stepped right over Cookie's head onto the steps below her and was gone, crossing the pasture in great purposeful strides.

At the fence, he turned briefly. "Better tell Lilly to get on home soon. I'll be needing her," he called back. Then he held down the top strand of the barbed wire on the fence and was gone into the Petuses' pasture.

The screen door clicked behind Otis as he went into the house where Lilly could still be heard hiccupping softly.

"Did you hear that? Did you hear that?" B.C. cried in hushed tones, still gazing after Two-Time.

"The question is, did *you* hear that?" snapped Cookie. "Two-Time said *Detroit*. He's wrecked all our lovely plans."

B.C. waved a hand, still looking toward the fence. "We'll just go someplace else. New York City, maybe."

"We don't know but one train, and that train goes to Fayetteville and Detroit. At least that's all we know," Cookie pointed out.

Annie squeezed her eyes shut. No one talked. "Wait," Annie said, opening her eyes. "Who says we can't still go to Detroit like we planned? William won't be home for a whole week. Two-Time and Lilly are going Monday."

Cookie shook her head. "Soon as we get there, Lilly will just put us on the train and send us right back home. Besides, they're gonna have enough trouble in Detroit without three extra."

"That's right," Annie said, "but Lilly won't even have to lay eyes on us. Detroit's not like Fayetteville, where the minute you step into the station everybody in town knows you're there."

"I know," sighed Cookie.

"Maybe when B.C. gets his job and we are all settled, we could call them up," Annie suggested.

Cookie brightened at once. "Then we'd even have some family right up there in Detroit."

"Detroit," B.C. echoed. "I can't hardly wait. I wish I was going tomorrow."

CHAPTER 14

BECAUSE THE ACCIDENT happened Saturday evening after everyone had gone home for the day, even her father didn't know about it until just before church the next morning, when Otis came with the news. It was later still when Annie realized that it must have happened just about the time Two-Time was telling them he was leaving. Somehow it seemed like an omen, and Two-Time was right to go. But he wasn't right about Esther Pierce; she. was just fine. All these thoughts raced through her mind as she listened to her father tell her mother about the three little girls and Reverend Henton. There had been a terrible explosion at the Emanuel Methodist Church. Maybe the hot water heater, her father said. It was right beside the baptismal pool. The little girls and Reverend Henton were there to practice a song for the funeral the next day, and now they were dead.

"What were their names?" Annie whispered.

Startled, her father turned toward her. "I don't know. All I could think of when I heard was that it could have been you and Cookie."

Too late he realized his mistake. Her mother's eyes widened. "What on earth do you mean, Laurence? How could it have been Annie or Cookie? What is going on?"

Laurence Trammell lifted his hand in a soothing

gesture. "It's nothing, Louise. It's only that Annie and Cookie had—well, been over that way and they're the same age, and . . . " His voice trailed away.

"It's not nothing that I'm never told anything." She stared at Annie a little wildly. "Where do you go? What do you do? You never seem to do anything I ever heard of little girls doing."

Annie felt her face flame.

"That's enough, Louise," Laurence said, and his tone was more like the one he ordinarily used for Annie.

Her mother pressed her hands to her lips, then dropped them to her lap. Twisting her napkin, she stared straight ahead of her. "Sometimes I have the feeling that no one in this family really sees or hears anything I say or do. Well, I'm not dead, do you hear? I'm not dead."

Annie saw the familiar look of pain settle across her father's face. "What do you want, Louise? For God's sake, what do you want? I can't read your mind."

Her mother gave a cry and, flinging her napkin aside, rushed from the room. Her father slumped in his chair. To Annie the movement was more alien and frightening than if he had cried aloud or run from the room like her mother. He seemed unaware that she was even there.

"Daddy?"

"Yes, Annie?"

"Nothing, I . . . "

Her father straightened in his chair. "It's all right, Annie. Don't worry. I'll take care of it," he said, and his voice had a harsh edge to it. He had told her the very same thing about the men at the church. There seemed no connection, but three girls and Reverend Henton were dead now.

Her father seemed to read her mind. "Don't say anything about the men you saw at the church Saturday morning. Is that clear?"

He folded his napkin and laid his knife and fork across his plate.

Annie waited.

"Don't you understand? Those little girls are dead already. You and Cookie are what is important." His voice sounded strained, but still Annie could not fit the men and the church and the little girls together with herself and Cookie. Something terrible seemed to lurk just around a corner in her mind.

"I don't understand," she ventured.

"That's good. Maybe there is nothing to understand. But don't talk about anything you saw or heard. All right?"

Annie nodded. Awkwardly her father put out his hand and touched her hair. "I can count on you, can't I, Aunty?" he said.

Annie nodded, more confused than ever, but her father put his finger to his lips. "We'll talk about it later. I have to go."

"To the store? On Sunday?"

Laurence hesitated. "No, I've got to talk to Rose."

Annie stared after her father as the kitchen door swished. She remembered the touch of his hand on her hair. It was as if after twelve years, he had suddenly turned and seen her sitting there. His voice had sounded troubled, but his touch had been warm.

At that moment a pan clattered loudly in the kitchen.

Guiltily Annie rose, lest she be caught eavesdropping.

"Oh, Lord, Mr. Laurence. Oh, Lord help us," she heard Rose saying as she tiptoed away.

When her father came into her room, she searched his face, but it seemed deliberately still.

"Is everything all right?" she asked.

"Right? Maybe right has nothing to do with anything, Annie. It's funny," he said, "I always thought it had everything to do with everything. Now I just don't know."

For the first time Annie could remember, no one mentioned church or even brought in the Sunday paper. It was as if everyone agreed without speaking to set the day aside to be alone with their own thoughts.

That afternoon Two-Time told Mr. Petus and Miss Florence he and Lilly were leaving. At first, they were unbelieving, then appalled. Miss Florence cried, and Mr. Petus threatened to call in a doctor to see if Two-Time had had some kind of nervous breakdown. But Two-Time's stolid, unshakable silence finally wore them down. In the end, Mr. Petus told him to take the truck, so that the family and all the baggage could go to the station together. "And when you've had enough of Detroit," he added confidently, "well then, just come on back down where you belong."

* * *

Monday morning, with carefully suspended belief in the inevitable, Annie watched Lilly packing, moving silently back and forth in her cabin.

As she and Cookie pushed slowly back and forth on the porch swing, Cookie told Annie that her mother had asked all about what they saw at Reverend Henton's church. "And she wasn't even mad at us," she added, drawing her brows together quizzically. "But she told me not to tell a soul."

"I know," said Annie. "So did my daddy."

"Not even Two-Time and Lilly," Cookie said. "She said she didn't want Two-Time all riled up."

"Can we tell B.C.?"

Cookie's forehead wrinkled. "I guess not."

Two-Time and the others talked about the tragedy off and on most of the morning.

"Willy Reese told me that the sheriff was poking around mighty suspicious-like the whole morning," Two-Time said.

"Willy Reese always did talk more than was good for anybody," Rose said abruptly.

"Still," said Two-Time, "if I thought that anybody had deliberately . . . well, I wouldn't leave. I swear I'd stay right here until I'd torn somebody limb from limb."

"Don't these young'uns hear enough violence and meanness without hearing it from you?" Rose demanded.

Two-Time scowled. "You right. Look at Reverend Henton. He started with a funeral and no body, and now he's gonna have no funeral and four bodies—one his own. All on account of he wanted to fight back like a man."

Lilly straightened to pat his arm. "Hush now," she said, "it was a terrible accident, that's all."

Annie and Cookie kept uneasily still, wondering what secret it was that they really knew. It's nothing, Daddy said so, Annie reassured herself, only to turn and see Rose press one hand to her throat as if she might be ill. Annie opened her mouth to cry out, but Rose shook her head fiercely. Cookie must have been watching her mother, too, for at that moment she gripped Annie's hand tightly.

"Go on out and play till train time, you two," Rose said, and meekly they obeyed, grateful to escape the oppressive uncertainty of Lilly's cabin.

On the platform at the train station everyone seemed to vacillate between laughter and tears as they waited for the four o'clock Sky Chief to come. Laughing, Rose pushed a big box of cold chicken and biscuits into Lilly's arms, then grabbed her neck and squeezed and cried until the box of chicken fell unnoticed onto the platform. Moment by moment, Annie's feelings mirrored whomever she watched. She felt like this was her farewell too, for no one would be there next week to see Cookie and B.C. and her off.

"Rose, you take care of yourself, you hear me?" Lilly said, searching her older sister's face. "You not as young as you used to be. Let those chillun help you. Do them good."

Rose grinned and shook her head. "You the fretter, not me."

Lilly did not smile back. "You the one with the high blood, not me. Just this once, you listen to somebody else."

For an instant Rose sobered. "I'm listening. I'll take care." She glanced at Two-Time striding the length of the platform, scowling in the direction the train would come from. "Maybe it's the Lord's will, but it don't seem right. Families ought not to split up. Without family, you got nothing."

Lilly nodded. "He can't stay no more, Rose. Some can, some can't." She followed Rose's glance as it turned from Two-Time toward B.C., who stood at the edge of the platform, his eyes a blaze of excitement.

"It won't be long now, Two-Time," he said, his fists jammed into his pockets. "What is the first thing you reckon you'll see when you get off the train?"

Two-Time paused and focused his attention on B.C. "Another hundred tomfool black men getting off trains. Another hundred black men who have given up their homes and their families to come live in a jungle just so they don't have to say 'Yassuh' one more time."

B.C. frowned. "It's gonna be wonderful."

"You just mind your Mama and stay out of trouble and keep your mind off'n Detroit. If it was wonderful, we'd of heard before now."

Though Two-Time frowned when the Petuses' car came to a gravel-spraying halt beside the platform, no one was really surprised by their arrival.

Miss Florence led the way onto the platform, her face flushed, her hair flying this way and that. She stopped before Two-Time, squinting up into the sunlight. "Are you still determined on this foolishness?" Her voice seemed thin in the bright sunlight.

Two-Time nodded.

"After all we've done for you and Lilly, this is the thanks we get."

"Now, Florence," Laurence Trammell said, rising.

Two-Time's face darkened, and Annie marveled at Miss Florence's reckless courage.

"We appreciate everything . . . " Lilly began.

"Well, that's something. I guess I'll just have to wait until Two-Time comes to his senses and then mail you ticket money back home," Miss Florence snapped. With a frown, she turned to stare at the mound of baggage at the far edge of the platform.

Two-Time's fists clenched, and Annie took two nervous steps backward.

"Just up and go off. I still can't get over it," Miss Florence began.

Two-Time turned and crossed the platform to look down on Mr. Petus, who still hovered by the door of the car. "I think maybe Miss Florence shouldn't be out in this heat," he said, his voice flat and hard.

Mr. Petus's legs looked as if they would give way under Two-Time's glare. "Florence," he pleaded, looking toward his wife, "we've done all we can."

"We thank you," Lilly said.

"Shut up, Lilly," Two-Time snapped, in a voice that made Annie's scalp tingle.

Miss Florence blushed and whirled to walk back down the steps to the car.

"Here, Two-Time," Mr. Petus said, holding out a crumpled fifty-dollar bill, "to help out." But Two-Time only turned his back.

"Good-bye, then, and good luck." Mr. Petus turned and, with a nod to Laurence Trammell, was gone.

Like a fat brown robin, Lilly began fussing over the mound of luggage, and in the distance the long, low train whistle came.

"Hurrah!" cried B.C.

The Sky Chief braked at the last minute, as if reluctant to take on such a strange group of passengers.

Two-Time lifted a large trunk and handed it up to the baggage man. Then, bending down to Lilly, who was still gathering up scattered bits of clothing, he took her by the elbow and pulled her up.

A last whistle sent everyone scrambling for baggage, and the idea of departure finally became real. Lilly looked around at the town behind them and then into each of the faces, memorizing everything she could rake in with her eyes. Two-Time stood stiffly, squeezing her hand. "Come on, Lilly," he said.

"Good luck, good luck," everyone called, until the train had vanished around the curve and its whistle was just one long, low wail.

"Let's all go home now," Annie heard her father say into the silence. "It's been a long day."

Slowly Rose turned and walked across the platform, her feet dragging wearily. "Rose, you all right?" her father asked.

Rose nodded. "I'm fine. It's just like you said. It's been a long day."

"Well, you and Otis go on home in the Petuses' truck. We won't need anything at the house this evening. And you two girls," he said, turning toward Annie and Cookie, "you stick to the house, too. I've had quite enough excitement for one day."

To Annie, it seemed as if his eyes searched out Rose's and they gazed at each other with some sort of secret worry that seemed to have nothing to do with Two-Time and Lilly.

CHAPTER 15

IF MISS EMMA had not inquired about the lessons, they might have slid peacefully into oblivion, for, with Two-Time and Lilly's departure, the fabric of their daily lives seemed to have unraveled into unrecognizable threads.

Even Rose seemed to spend much of the day sitting at the kitchen table, her hands idle in her lap. But Miss Emma reported she felt Annie had been making rapid progress until this recent lapse, and midweek found Annie trudging up the back steps at Dr. Matt's.

Through the screen door, she could see Miss Lessie standing on a chair with both arms held awkwardly above her head. She was relieved, when she pushed open the door, to see Miss Emma crouched in just as strange a position under Miss Lessie's right arm.

Both jumped when the screen door squeaked, and Miss Lessie dropped her elbow, dead weight, on Miss Emma's head so that Miss Emma, the teacher, looked as if she were curtsying clumsily to her pupil.

"Stand still, Lessie," she snapped, straightening her tight curls under their hair net. "I declare, this is like fitting a hoe handle."

At least that's what Annie thought she said. Her lips were tight bands from which half a dozen straight pins protruded.

She spat the pins noisily into a saucer and turned toward the hall. Annie followed silently, giving Miss Lessie a swift curtsy as she went by. Miss Lessie only looked more strained than ever. Halfway down the dark hall, her voice stopped them.

"Emma? Emma?" she called softly.

"What is it now, Lessie?"

"I can't seem to get down."

Miss Emma kept her face toward the study. "Just take hold of the back of the chair, Lessie."

"That's just it, Emma," Miss Lessie answered, so softly Annie had to strain to hear. "I can't move my arms."

Miss Emma gave a strange snort, like an impatient horse makes on cold mornings. "Coming, Lessie. I do declare! You'll be the death of me yet."

When the offending pins were all removed and the dress with them, Miss Lessie stood primly before them in her cotton slip and white, open-toed shoes. Before Miss Lessie lowered her arms, Annie had seen a row of angry red dots which ran down the back of both her arms. The same neat row of crimson dots continued down each side of her petticoat, and the ones on the petticoat had grown until now some were half the size of a dime.

Miss Emma pushed Miss Lessie lightly on the shoulder. "Well, don't just stand there with no clothes on, Lessie."

A dark red stain crept unevenly up Miss Lessie's neck, working its way around the mole on her neck and leaving chalky white splotches here and there. Talcum powder lay in the hollows at the base of her neck. Grabbing the pinned dress from the back of the chair, she clutched it across her flat bodice and as she ran from the room, she

gave a small cry as if she had been wounded by yet another
pin.

Miss Emma turned on her heel, and she and Annie
marched, single file, back down the hall toward Dr.
Matt's study. As she listened to Miss Emma's sharp heels
on the wooden floor, Annie thought she heard her mutter
something about a heaven with no children.

Outside the open windows, the bees droned, hovering
motionless above honeysuckle bushes. While Miss Emma
talked on about something, Annie concentrated on
keeping her chin up, her eyes having long since glazed
over, so that nothing was clear except the dark shapes of
Dr. Matt's dumb cane and his old shotgun, which hung to
one side, keeping a bead on the threatening-looking plant.
How strange, thought Annie, Two-Time, B.C., even my
father doesn't exist here.

In the quiet, Annie found herself asking, "Miss Emma,
why does everything always seem to go wrong?"

Miss Emma pushed around in her oversized swivel
chair and peered over the top of her glasses. "Now that's a
pretty broad statement. Name three things."

Annie thought. She mustn't mention that she was
practically being forced to run away.

"Oh, I don't know. Like Two-Time and Lilly having to
go to Detroit, and William not liking B.C. anymore, and
the three little girls and Reverend Henton getting killed
and . . . "

Miss Emma held up her hand; her brow was creased in
long vertical wrinkles.

"It's violence, child. Pure-T violence."

Annie started, but Miss Emma seemed not to notice.

"Violence is where the South gets its strength and its pride. Papa used to say, 'Doesn't anything leave leftover violence like losing a war.' "

Annie was silent. She knew from past experience not to ask which war. As far as Miss Emma was concerned there had been only one war.

"Papa used to say that the South only seemed like the gentlest place to live, with all our flowers and warm breezes and easy way of living. It's all fed by an underground stream of anger that's as dark and turgid as swamp water."

"I never saw any violence my whole life," Annie protested, only half-sure she even understood the word.

Miss Emma smiled and nodded. "The worst kind of anger is always pent-up, seeping out a little here and there until one day—bang."

"But what's that got to do with everything going wrong?" asked Annie, her misery making her willing to question even Dr. Matt's theories.

"Why, it makes the reasons for things like you're talking about always different from what they appear to be. Two-Time may say he wants to go North for freedom. If you ask me, he's running from his own quaking violence, Lilly, too. The Reverend Henton and Esther and Burt and Jeb Pierce, all just full to the brim with violence—all trying not to let their own show while calling out the other's. Why, the walls of that old church just couldn't take the strain. But don't think they fell on three innocents. They were there to practice a song for that infernal funeral of Reverend Henton's, weren't they? Oh, I tell you, Annie, it's everywhere."

Annie shook her head. "I'm not sure. Maybe it's something else."

Miss Emma leaned forward and peered into Annie's eyes, and Annie peered miserably back.

"Yes, you are. You're growing right on up, Annie Trammell. Well, if you don't want to grow up blind, then listen to me. Next time things go wrong, mark my words, if you look for it, you'll find it's some of that violence stirred up."

Annie had a sudden vision of the two men who had crouched laughing against the wall of Reverend Henton's church as they worked with a jerky haste. One by one, other faces seemed to float before her. Wadine and B.C. in the canebrake, both their faces twisted with resentment; Two-Time, with his fists clenched; her own mother. Did violence explain her father's look of pain? Somehow she didn't think so. At the marshaling of so much evidence, she sniffed vigorously, her eyes threatening to betray her.

"Now don't start sniveling. I never said being grown up was easy, but you're getting a good toehold. Just because we don't like something we find to be true isn't necessarily any reason to fret over it, I've found."

Just then Annie heard someone screaming her name, and the screen door cracked like a shot. Miss Lessie's high, thin voice began, "No, no, no," higher and higher it rose, a piercing litany, then, almost pleading, "No men allowed."

A kitchen chair hit the floor. Then, before Miss Emma could rise from her swivel chair, there was a cry and footsteps were echoing in the hall. Clearly, over all the confusion of sound, Annie heard her own name being called over and over again.

The door burst open, and Miss Lessie, dressed now in a dark housedress, ran into the room. Her eyes swung wildly right and left.

"Papa," she cried, "help me."

"Lessie, stop that this instant," Miss Emma began, stepping toward her sister, but Miss Lessie was too quick for her. With a single movement, she eluded Miss Emma and reached for the gun above Dr. Matt's narrow bed.

There was a noise at the door, and Annie and Miss Emma both turned to see B.C. standing there, a hand out to balance while he tried to catch his breath.

"What's going on here?" demanded Miss Emma. "Don't you know better than to burst in here like that?" She stabbed a fat finger toward B.C.'s chest, and at the same instant the shotgun's noise tore the room asunder.

B.C. leaned one shoulder against the door jamb, an incredulous expression on his face. Then he sank slowly to his knees before he pitched forward across the faded rose carpet.

Vaguely Annie knew Miss Emma was slapping Miss Lessie hard on one side of her face, and Miss Lessie's mouth was twisted open. The muscles on each side of her neck were rigid with her screams, but the gun's roar had left a silent vacuum that stopped Annie's ears. Trembling, she knelt to touch B.C.'s cheek.

Miss Lessie was the first to leave. Miss Emma pushed her through an open window and took her to her room, walking around by the side porch. A key turning in a rusty lock was the first sound Annie heard. Then the bees took back the still air.

Without thinking, Annie knew there should be no more

hysteria, no screaming. Gently she lifted B.C.'s warm fuzzy head into her lap. A warm, dark-red stain spread slowly across the knees of her jeans, and still she thought only that she should be very still and hold B.C. as long as he would let her, because every moment that passed she expected him to open his eyes and push her aside with a harsh, "Do you want to get me hung, Annie?"

A black ambulance driver lifted B.C. swiftly onto a low stretcher.

"Don't tie his hands," Annie told the old man at B.C.'s head. "He would hate that." The old man, permanently stooped from sitting in the back of too many ambulances, looked up quickly, then nodded. He eased B.C.'s arms gently from beneath the restraints and laid them across the blood-stained sheet.

Laurence Trammell brushed past the old man and B.C.'s low bed. He swung Annie into his arms, pressing her face tightly into his shoulder. "He can still pick me up and carry me," Annie thought, surprised.

The ground was familiar, even in the dark, even under her father's long strides: the hard-baked dirt under Miss Lessie's pin oaks; two curbs; a brief scent of magnolia; the front walk; steps two at a time; then home. At the front door, her father set her down. As she squinted in the sudden light, her father knelt beside her.

"Are you all right?" he asked, as if she had been hurt instead of B.C.

Annie nodded, but it seemed more that she could feel nothing at all. Even her lips and tongue were so stiff and numb she could not speak.

"Don't worry, Annie," her father said. "B.C. is going to be fine."

Again she nodded, but for the first time in her life she wondered if there were things her father should not promise.

Annie turned toward the door when she heard her mother calling. Louise's voice, untouched by the morning's grief, seemed off-key and harsh, and Annie saw her father's face flush.

"I can't imagine where Rose has gotten to. Sometimes I could just brain her. The kitchen's empty, and your lunch is ruined, Laurence."

"That phone call I got . . . Miss Lessie shot B.C.," her father said flatly.

Her mother drew in a quick breath. "How terrible. Poor Rose. Is he . . .? I mean, will he . . .?" She stumbled over the distasteful word.

Annie's head suddenly snapped up. "Rose. B.C. came for me. It was about Rose."

"What are you saying, Annie?" her father said, dropping to his knees again and taking her by the shoulders.

Pulling free, she called as she ran. "Rose, I'm coming, Rose." And now the tears came, filling her eyes, wetting her cheeks. Sunlight splashed through the heavy foliage of the pecan tree and washed over her arms and legs like rainwater. Groping for the latch, she pulled open the heavy barn door and stepped into the cool darkness. She laid her hand against a plank worn smooth by hands and haunches. I would like to just stop here, she thought, without going forward or backward.

Chewing Tobacco shied into the side of his stall at the sudden noise and watched her approach, his lips drawn back to show long, yellow teeth. He's going to bite me if I go in, Annie thought, hastily wiping her eyes with the back of her hand.

"I hate you, too," she cried, "but you're worse. You hate everybody."

Flinging the gate back against the wall, she ran straight toward Chewing Tobacco and the small door behind him opening into the pasture. His fat sides heaved. As he reared on two feet above Annie, she drove her arm out blindly, striking him across his tender muzzle. He seemed to hang in midair, his small hooves thrashing just above her head. Then, wrenching his fat body, he fell heavily against his feed box and bolted for the open gate behind Annie.

At the gate to the pasture, Annie squinted and shaded her eyes against the sun. After a moment, she could see the scrub brush of the pasture's rocky slopes falling away from her toward the creek, where broomstraw crested gently in the hot sluggish noontime breeze. The plaintive, falling cry of the twelve o'clock whistle cut the day in half, telling Annie she could only go forward. The path was empty all the way down the hill. Only a single hawk hunted lazily, sliding gracefully down his own invisible path.

"Rose," Annie called, cupping her hands, "Rose." A pool of shadow at the cabin steps seemed to spread, long and thin, then widen, like spilled gravy on a tablecloth.

Where the path flattened, the straw on either side was crushed and twisted, as if a heavy weight had been dragged toward the cabin. In front of the cabin steps, Cookie sat without moving, without even breathing, it seemed to Annie. Rose's head rested on her knees, and the rest of Cookie's body—her back, her shoulders, her neck, all formed a protective arc over her mother. Rose lay on her back, her head and chest only slightly elevated by Cookie's knees. Her chest rose and fell rapidly, and her mouth gulped for air. When Annie dropped to her knees beside Rose, Cookie spoke without lifting her head.

"She fell—we drug her to here, then I sent B.C. to Dr. Matt's for you." Cookie laid one hand against her mother's cheek, but Rose's eyes did not move; they seemed to be watching the hawk as he climbed higher and higher until he was only a speck far above them.

"Does she know about our going to Detroit?" Cookie asked.

Annie covered her eyes and nodded. "It was me then. I talked to her like we planned. But I didn't think she guessed. Honest, I didn't."

Still Cookie didn't move. "So that's it, I reckon. We broke her heart."

A long shudder passed through Rose's body, and Annie drew back. "Why in hell isn't there a bell down here?" she hissed at Cookie.

"I guess Rose Holloway didn't have much call to ring for Louise Trammell," Cookie snapped back.

"Stop talking like Rose is dead. You're just talking her to death!" Annie cried. "We got to get a doctor."

Just as Annie directed Cookie to get blankets and pillows from the cabin while she ran for Dr. Mason, the long slow wail of an ambulance split the air for the second time that day, and this time from beyond the Petuses' house.

"Oh, Jesus, what I'd give for an ambulance," Cookie cried.

"Get those blankets," Annie ordered, already racing for the path.

Just before she reached the barn, the sound of splitting timbers and the screech of metal against metal stopped her in spite of her frantic haste. Looking back, Annie saw a long white car crashing backward through the barbed-wire fence that separated the Petus pasture from the Trammell pasture. It rammed a post once, twice, then careened on in drunken haste, weaving wildly toward the cabin.

Annie wiped an arm hastily across her eyes. It wasn't a car—it was the ambulance Cookie had prayed to Jesus for. On the far side of the ambulance, the stooped old colored man who had taken B.C. away such a long, long time ago stood on the running board, clinging desperately to the door with one hand and waving frantic directions with the other. On the near side of the car, at the wheel, sat Laurence Trammell. His head and shoulders were leaning far out of the open door, twisted toward the rear of the ambulance, but he seemed motionless in the blur of motion, the eye of the hurricane.

Cookie came bursting through the cabin door, both arms full of quilts, old blankets, and pillows. At the sight of the gleaming white ambulance, weaving backward toward her through the waist-high broomstraw, she dropped them at her feet and stumbled over them, waving her arms and calling toward the ambulance, "Thank you, Jesus. Thank you, Jesus."

Laurence Trammell, a dazed ambulance attendant, the regular driver, and the two girls were all needed to help lift Rose's heavy body onto the low bed and into the ambulance—a long dark room with all the curtains drawn against peering eyes. Laurence Trammell ran ahead of the ambulance to stand on the broken strands of barbed wire; the regular driver leaped behind the wheel. Some place past the Petuses', probably the Five Points intersection, the siren's long protest began again, and Annie shivered as a sudden gust of hot air touched her sweaty arms and face.

Neither Annie nor Cookie moved until Laurence Trammell returned to take them by the hand. "Come on, girls. We'll follow in the car," he said gently.

CHAPTER 16

THE COLORED "WING" of the hospital was actually the basement, half above ground, half below, and the usual antiseptic smells of a hospital were always mixed with the smell of damp cement blocks here. The furniture in the waiting room was hard, overstuffed mohair, the cushions rounded against the visitor as if to say, "Hurry now. Leave. There's suffering to be done."

Cookie could sit hour after hour on the unyielding chairs, waiting for visiting hours, waiting for Dr. Mason to come around, waiting for B.C.'s latest X-ray, or for Rose's new medication to take effect. She sat very straight in her chair, her face motionless as she stared down at an open movie magazine on her lap.

Annie glanced down at the picture on Cookie's knees as she paced by her again. "You can bet Joan Crawford wouldn't just *sit* there."

As happened so often these past three days, Cookie didn't answer. B.C. at least was fighting back with some sort of consuming anger. You could see it in his feverish eyes and clenched fists, hear its overtones in his garbled words. Sometimes Cookie seemed more likely to just slip away from her than B.C.

Annie sank down on the chair next to Cookie's. "Cookie," she pleaded, touching her on the arm, "this is a fight. We got to all fight together."

"Fightin's for winners."

"But how do you know who's a winner until the end of the fight?"

Cookie looked at Annie, weighing something, measuring, then with one side of her face, she smiled faintly. "I thought you was Presbyterian?"

"What's that got to do with anything?" Annie asked sharply enough to make a short, bustling nurse frown at them from her desk in the corner.

"Presbyterians are supposed to know everything's all decided, that's all," Cookie answered, dropping her eyes back to Joan Crawford and abruptly turning the page.

"What's decided?" Annie cried, wringing her hands.

Cookie's voice dropped so that Annie had to lean forward to hear. "I was always glad I didn't live on Northside. It made me and B.C. and Mama and Daddy seem different." Her face twisted like a drying lemon peel. "I thought that we were safe."

With both hands, Annie grabbed Cookie's arm. "You are safe. Everything's just gotten all twisted. My daddy can . . ."

"Your daddy can't fix the world any better'n mine can," whispered Cookie vehemently. "You hear? No better." Large tears made tracks down her cheeks. "I wish it was me Miss Lessie shot."

Annie dropped her chin onto her hands, her elbows braced on her knees. The top of her head felt swollen. She looked in the mirror on the candy machine, half expecting to find her head the size of a honeydew melon. It throbbed day and night. Cookie was right. How could her father fix anything when he didn't know what started it? Didn't

know it was all her fault. If she hadn't decided to run
away. If she hadn't tried to hint to Rose about their
leaving, she wouldn't have discovered their plan and
collapsed and B.C. wouldn't have had to come looking for
her. It was as if the violence Miss Emma had talked about
had burst like a bomb, ripping her world apart.

* * *

When B.C. began thrashing wildly in his bed, a thin line
of perspiration forming on his forehead below the huge
white bandage, Cookie's eyes across the bed turned to ask
mutely that she do something, as if she, too, realized
Annie was responsible. So, day after endless day, Annie
tried to reassure B.C. with foolish words and a stiff
smiling face. Then suddenly his raving stopped. In its
place came an awful silence, more fearful it seemed to
Annie than his ravings had ever been. Hour after hour,
B.C. lay staring at nothing, speaking only rarely, praying,
it seemed, for death. Rose, in the room next door, could
understand but had great difficulty making herself
understood. Some anchor in her mind that held her words
and the things they belonged to together seemed to have
pulled loose, and now her words drifted aimlessly,
catching meaning only occasionally. So Annie needed to
tell Rose in great detail about B.C. and the bad cold that
kept him from visiting, for Dr. Mason had declared that,
until her heart was stronger, Rose must not be upset. She
looked from Annie's face to Cookie's and on to where the
third face should have been, her eyes clouded with worry.
And Annie was almost grateful for Rose's jumbled words,
to which she could choose her own answers.

"Should we go to my house or yours?" Annie asked Cookie on the long walk home along the railroad tracks. "I reckon."

Annie thought the heat was going to make her ill, her neck and head ached so. "You reckon, what?" she said angrily.

Cookie only shook her head and lowered her gaze to the tracks.

Annie's thoughts seemed to shimmer elusively in front of her like the summer heat off the rails. She watched the distorted reflection of her arm swing over the track. "They won't die. I won't let them," she argued with the silent Cookie. "If you won't fight, I don't need you. You're so smart—go on to Detroit by yourself, and *you* be a Presbyterian." Her throat squeezed shut. If Rose and B.C. died, she'd just start bleeding on the inside, like Cookie said all women did every once in a while. Only her bleeding would just go on until she was as empty and dry as an old summer gourd.

Squinting her eyes against the rail's glare, Annie kicked viciously at the gravel spilling out between the ties. A piece ricocheted against the steel rail and sliced back across her shin. She shut her eyes against the sting.

"Your leg's bleeding all over your sock," Cookie's voice came, cool and faraway.

"I know, I know," mumbled Annie.

"If you don't speed up, your mama's going to know you spent another afternoon at the hospital, and that won't set well at all."

Annie sped up, watching her feet so that she wouldn't miss a tie and break her stride on the gravel.

It disturbed her to hear Cookie speak directly about her

mother. She had never done it, as far back as Annie could
remember, until B.C. and Rose were in the hospital. Now
she frequently seemed to pluck ideas they used to share
silently and lay them carefully between them. If Annie
denied it, she felt ashamed and foolish at denying what
they both knew to be true. If she agreed, she felt guilty of
betrayal, uncertain of what or whom she had betrayed.
So, often, in her confusion, she did both; she denied with
her lips and agreed with her actions and felt foolish and
guilty.

"You eating supper at the house tonight?" Annie said
into the silence, feeling a need to make some sort of
conversation to hide her racing thoughts.

Cookie cut across the tracks and scrambled up the steep
clay bank beside Hank Ketchum's shack, standing open
and empty now to flies and the afternoon heat. "Reckon
I'll fix supper for me and Otis at the house."

"At least you don't have to eat whatever Lavinia will be
calling supper tonight. Her cornbread alone could wipe
out the whole family."

"Lavinia?"

"I told you. Lavinia Parsons. She's Mabel Parsons'
oldest girl. Calls herself seventeen. She's just helping until
Rose is well," Annie finished awkwardly.

Cookie shrugged her shoulders and turned back
toward the path home.

"I already told you about her two days ago," Annie
protested, but Cookie only kept trudging toward home.

At the back porch, Annie paused. The air was full of
summer noises, the tiny hum of crickets and mosquitoes
and the chirp of tree frogs—so loud and persistent, yet
never there until you stopped and listened for them.

She hung there for a long time, until the sound of her father's voice pulled her toward the kitchen, in spite of the smell of burning cornbread.

CHAPTER 17

AT THE SOUND of Dr. Mason's familiar footsteps in the hospital's dark windowless hall, Annie rose and was beside him before he stopped in front of the nurse's desk.

"How are they today, Dr. Mason?"

He finished scooping up charts haphazardly off the nurse's desk and turned slowly toward Annie with a grin. "Think you could wait until I've taken a look first, or should I just improvise?"

He dropped a broad hand under her chin and lifted it gently. "I can tell you something about how another young friend of mine is doing. She's very tired, not sleeping too well, I imagine. She's pale, not getting enough sunshine and fresh air, I would guess. And she's too thin, probably from missing meals." He glanced toward the sack lunches beside Cookie on the bench. He nodded toward Cookie and added, "And she's got a friend who looks just about the same."

Annie moved restlessly under the firm fingers, and she kept her eyes on the buttons of Dr. Mason's wrinkled white shirt until he released her chin.

"Now if you two can wait a second, I'll see how the rest of my patients are doing."

When Dr. Mason came out of Rose's room, he gave them a wink and a nod and went next door to see B.C.

After a few minutes, he emerged, and Annie thought she saw him shaking his head as he rolled down his shirt sleeves. But looking up at Annie and Cookie, he gave them his familiar wide grin.

"Looks like you girls can relax. In fact, I prescribe a strawberry milk shake for you both," he said, fishing in his pockets for change.

"You're sure?" Cookie asked softly, gripping the edge of her chair. "Mama and B.C. are going to be fine? Good as new?"

"Well, Cookie, your Mama's heart won't ever be good as new again, but, yes, I think she'll be all right if she slows down a little bit."

"B.C.?" prodded Annie, remembering his face as he came from B.C.'s room.

"B.C." Dr. Mason repeated slowly, his eyes narrowing. "I got out the bullet and sewed him up. But it might take a little while for him to get over the shock. You know it does something to a person to be shot. I'm going to let him go home tomorrow—but even then, give him time." The doctor's face cleared, and he jiggled the coins in his pockets again.

"Thank you just the same, Dr. Mason," Annie said. "We better stick around a while longer."

The bandage on B.C.'s head only partially hid the nakedness of his shaved skull. One eye was still bruised and swollen where he had fallen on Miss Emma's faded carpet, but he did not make the effort to turn his good eye toward Cookie and Annie when they entered his room. He seemed to be watching something just above their heads.

"B.C.?" Cookie began. "Brother? Dr. Mason says you can go home tomorrow."

No answer.

"You're doing fine."

"That's all he knows," B.C. spat out.

"Being shot does something to you; it just takes time. Dr. Mason says so."

"How many times has he been shot?"

"Not any," Cookie answered slowly, "but he's a doctor. He knows things."

"Does he know that anybody that wants can shoot you, call you a thief or anything else they want if you're a black man? What you reckon I should give up—being black or being a man?" Now B.C. turned toward them, and his mouth was a dark twisted slit pulled across his teeth. His hands plucked nervously at the edge of the sheet, his eyes turned back to the white wall above their heads.

"B.C., please," Annie whispered, her eyes on the twisting fingers, "Miss Lessie didn't want to hurt you. She only wanted to stay safe in her house—and be a lady."

"I don't care," B.C. shouted, "she shot me. She knew it was me that raked her yard, carried her groceries, and ate oatmeal cookies at her table. And she shot me."

Annie grabbed one of B.C.'s hands, willing his smoldering eyes to look at her. "It's my fault, can't you see it's all my fault? Please don't hate Miss Lessie." B.C.'s taut form pulled even tighter.

"She doesn't hate you, B.C. She doesn't." A strange quaking seemed to be pulling her chest all out of shape.

"Then I reckon it's just as dangerous to have somebody be scared of you as to have somebody hate you. Leave me be. I'm tired," B.C. said, not taking back his hand, but turning his head to the window. "Either way, it looks like I lose."

"Is that you, honey? Is someone there?" Annie heard Rose's voice call as she came out into the hall. But she ran past Rose's open door toward the small square of sunlight at the end of the long dark hall. The antiseptic smells and clinking of dinner trays seemed to clog her ears and nose so that she could not hear, could not breathe. The small square of light seemed to recede slowly ahead of her and then was snuffed out altogether as strong arms stopped her flight.

"Calm down, Annie, calm down." Her father led her to the grass under a spreading oak just outside the hospital's entrance for colored people. "Now sit down and tell me why you were racing through the corridor that way." Annie still held a damp handkerchief of her father's balled in her fist.

"I thought if B.C. knew that everything was all right, and he and Rose both got well, everything would be the same."

A crow cried above them.

"Dr. Mason said they were going to be fine. Good as new. But B.C.'s not good as new," Annie said, fighting a quiver in her voice. "He's all old on the inside, bent and twisted like the junk he brings home, and he can't forgive Miss Lessie, and it's not even her fault. It's my fault he's hurt and Miss Lessie is locked up in her room all day so she can't even sweep, and maybe they'll even put her in jail."

Her father assured her she was not to blame for anything, that life sometimes just took strange twists. He talked about the law and the difference between commitment and being put in jail, and about forgetting, about time, but nothing about Rose or B.C. or Miss Lessie or anything that mattered. Still, there was comfort just in the rhythm of his voice, and Annie and her father, held between the knotted roots of the oak, leaned back, partially supported by the rough trunk, partially by the mutual pressure of a large back against a small one. Her father talked about how men sometimes have to choose not between right and wrong, which was plenty hard enough, but between maybe hurting somebody you loved and doing wrong by them or doing something that was wrong on general principles.

The crow cried again, much nearer now, as if he, too, had needed to understand such things. "One thing I know, nothing ever stays the same, Annie, not even dreams," her father said into the stillness. Rising stiffly, he held out his hand.

* * *

Dr. Mason decided to send B.C. home Saturday morning and Rose that same afternoon—partially so Rose wouldn't have to go home to the shock of finding that B.C. had entered the hospital the very hour she had, almost two weeks ago now; and partially, as Annie heard him say, because he seemed more in need of sunshine, fresh air, and activity for his hands than anything Dr. Mason had to offer.

To Annie, the world seemed a vast lemon chiffon pie, a cloud of clean freshness; the earth had finished some dark revolution and things were coming around right at last.

She spun, skipped, and hopped through the morning until her mother rubbed her temples every time Annie passed, and her father shouted after her to slow down. Annie laughed aloud picturing Rose fussing and fuming over all the things Lavinia had moved in her kitchen and B.C. turning over and over in the palm of his hand the real sculptor's knife she had ordered for him as a homecoming present.

Sometimes, for a moment, it seemed the world hadn't come all the way round yet. Cookie was still grieving for something, as if all along she hadn't been worried for B.C. and Rose but something else. The pale pink scar over B.C.'s right ear was fast disappearing under a light covering of black fuzz, but still a terrible poison seemed locked inside, intensifying his silent agitation. Miss Lessie still had to go before Judge Adams on Tuesday. And there was Annie's father; no matter what his body was doing, his mind was off somewhere else. But whenever she glimpsed one of these last shadows, clinging like a silver of rain cloud to the horizon, Annie just whirled faster, until it faded into only a thin gray line separating endless blue sky from endless green grass.

She and Cookie worked all day Friday on a welcome-home party for Rose and B.C. The biggest watermelon in the garden was hauled down the hill in Ruth-baby's wagon and put in the creek to cool. Lavinia was finally cajoled into making a sheet cake, her first, and Cookie and Annie made pink lemonade at the cabin. Laurence Trammell contributed crepe-paper streamers and balloons which Otis helped them drape across the front porch and the mantel and B.C. and Rose's pillows. For

B.C., there was the sculptor's knife, a set of wrenches from Otis and Cookie, and a baseball and glove from Annie's parents. For Rose, there was Blue Waltz talcum powder from Annie and Cookie, a Peace rosebush from Otis, and a new gown and slippers from Laurence and Louise. B.C. came home first, across the barbed-wire fence in the ambulance, just like his mother had left. Annie and Cookie insisted he wait for Rose to open his presents. Otis hung about nervously shooing chickens and sweeping the yard until noon, then left in search of Mr. Laurence, saying he would return before three o'clock, when Rose was due home.

The three friends sat on the steps, squinting in the hot sun. Annie and Cookie tried to get B.C. to lie down, but he only sat silently staring at the tangled barbed wire as if his mother might be there, snared by the vicious barbs, hidden by the soft waving straw.

Finally the ambulance appeared, traveling backward as before, but now reversing all the fear and terror of the past two weeks, like an old movie being run backward.

The ambulance men had to move Rose through a crowd of weeping, clinging children. Finally they got her into her bed, spread a large quilt over her still-swollen legs, then they drove away.

The next half hour was a blur of crescendos. B.C.'s sudden screams at Rose's prone figure, "Mama, they shot me," his hands gripping both sides of his shaved head as if he would rip it off and hurl it away; Cookie's quiet, "Mama, Mama, Mama," over and over, a chant of despair; and finally Annie's agonized confession to them all that it was her hints of farewell to Rose that had precipitated the whole nightmare. Each child cried his own grief, pleading for his own lost world, each uncomprehending, deaf to the others' agony.

When they quieted, Rose spoke for the first time. "Now, I want to see B.C. alone." She seemed as oblivious of the crepe paper, the cake, and the presents as the children were.

Cookie and Annie sat mutely on the steps. Once, Cookie looked bleakly at Annie and Annie pulled Cookie's arm through hers. Occasionally there was a hoarse scream from inside the cabin like Chewing Tobacco the time he got caught in barbed wire, Annie thought, her eyes flickering across the pasture.

When B.C. came to the door, he only said, "Mama wants you, Cookie," and left, jumping off one end of the porch, keeping his face averted and heading for the wooded back reaches of the pasture.

"Even Rose can't make it all right again," Annie thought, closing her eyes and slumping against the porch pillar. The racket in her head subsided, as if her brain were too weary to sustain its frantic circlings any longer, and an awareness of her body floated to the surface of her mind. Drops of sweat trickled from the nape of her neck down her spine until they were absorbed by her sticky blouse. Her arms and legs felt deboned, flaccid, and useless to her body. A heavy tiredness pinned her unresisting body to the warm rough boards of the porch. The sun, shining through her eyelids, danced in multicolored circles. Insects droned steadily, and chickens scratched at her feet as if she were no longer there. Maybe my body has dissolved, she thought. The sun could do that—bake me slowly back into warm weightless dust. The sun could bake B.C.'s roaring anger, if he would allow it, into no more than the scratching of hens and Cookie's grief into no more than the drone of bees and crickets—if they'd let the sun work, the searing heat would heal as it burned away their pain.

The screen door slammed lightly behind her. When she slit her eyes against the sudden assault of light, Cookie's silhouette, directly above her, wavered erratically as if she might topple off the porch any moment.

"What'd she say?" Annie asked.

"I don't know. She seems . . . she seems to be someplace else a long way away from here." Cookie paused, shaking her head. "I don't even think she knew we were fixing to leave for Detroit. She wants you now."

Annie rose slowly, the porch suddenly hard and unyielding under her stiff legs and feet.

The neck of Rose's white long-sleeved gown had pulled open under the pressure of her heavy, unsupported breasts, and her dark skin gleamed in the oblique light slanting through windows shuttered against the noon heat. The quilt had been taken from her legs and folded neatly behind her head to help her sit straighter on the low-backed sofa bed that, open now, filled half the room.

Annie pulled up the same cane-bottomed chair B.C. and Cookie had obviously used, until her bare knees rubbed against the edge of the bed. Rose's left hand lay palm down, fingers spread, across her worn black copy of the New Testament, as if she were touching base. As Annie's knees brushed the bed, her eyes flickered open only for a moment, then closed again. Annie picked up Rose's right hand and intertwined the broad brown fingers with hers.

Silence, thick as April pollen, covered everything, and in it a tiny seed of hope germinated: perhaps Rose really hadn't understood; perhaps she had not known they had planned to leave.

Rose's calloused hand lay still and open in hers, and her breath whistled softly through her parted lips.

"Rose?" Annie whispered and felt Rose's hand stir, but her eyes remained shut. She does know after all. She can't bear to lay eyes on me, Annie thought, and felt her heart beating erratically. Maybe she won't ever speak to me again. Her fingers closed tightly over Rose's. "I'm sorry, Rose. I'm sorry."

Rose sighed. "He'll get over it. He has to unless he wants to end up really dead. Lord willing, someday he'll even know it was only crazy old Miss Lessie what shot him."

"Please, Rose, it wasn't Miss Lessie's fault. It was mine. But it'll be different now. You wait. I'll do everything just right. I'll even be nice to Mary Ellen Parker."

Rose's next words seemed spoken in her sleep—slow and flat. "Different or dead."

"You mean B.C.? He's fine. Dr. Mason said so. Soon as his hair grows back he'll be just the same as always."

"Into Egypt will I send my son," Rose mumbled, her eyes still closed, her full lips drawn down. "Money is the root of all evil."

Annie wiped the back of her free hand across her damp forehead. "Money, is that it, Rose? Don't worry. There's plenty of money. Two goldfish bowls full. All your friends brought it to the hospital and won't take it back."

Rose sank further back into her pillows. Though Annie was still holding her hand, the motion was one of leave-

taking, and Annie groped desperately for something to
bridge the widening gulf between them.

"Wait, Rose, there's more. There's our money for
Detroit. It's buried under the pot of geraniums on the
back porch. We'll bring it to you. Then we *can't* go. You'll
see." She rose from her chair, still holding Rose's hand,
willing Rose to look at her just once, but she did not. At
the door Annie paused once more. "I'm going now. To get
the money, Rose, the money we saved for Detroit."

As if she had just awakened, Rose turned her head
toward Annie and opened her eyes, "You see it, too,
then?" she whispered softly. Tears stood in her eyes.
"Detroit."

"No, no, Rose. I promise. I'm bringing you the money.
Just rest, Rose. I'll be right back—and you mustn't be sad.
Everything will be fine."

Rose seemed to be looking past her now through the
screen door. "Jesus wept," she rebuked Annie softly.

The next morning, Rose had Annie bring both the jar
and the goldfish bowls full of money from the mantel
where she had placed them the afternoon before and set
them on the bed by her Bible, and now her left hand
always rested lightly against the largest jar the way it had
lain earlier on the only book she owned.

*   *   *

Day after day, Rose did not stir from her bed, though
Dr.Mason urged her repeatedly to walk a little every day.
Annie's father came every afternoon and sat by Rose's
bed for a minute or so, but some unspoken pact bound
them to silence. If Annie or Cookie or B.C., especially

B.C., were not sitting beside the bed, touching her arm, she seemed restless and turned constantly under the twisted sheet. She never really slept, only napped until the hand resting on her arm involuntarily twitched from tiredness. Then she was awake immediately, moving her arm to stroke Annie's knee or to finger the hem of Cookie's dress. Her eyes followed their every movement around the room, as if she were measuring something and there was no room for error.

Otis came in for lunch and was back by sundown, but he seemed always just beyond some circle Rose drew with her eyes. Rose herself was at the center of the circle, then came B.C. and further out Cookie, and near the outer rim, Annie herself.

Annie had become aware of the circle suddenly, while she was walking slowly uphill toward home one evening. Watching a small rope of cloud tug at a full moon, she knew she could put her finger on that moon to show her exact place on the circle, and Cookie's, and B.C.'s. But remembering Rose's dark face and eyes as she watched B.C. move around the cabin, she shuddered in relief that she was no nearer the center of the circle. It was not partiality, but something else, something frightening, that held them all in their places.

CHAPTER 18

ON WEDNESDAY MORNING Annie's legs were already sticking to the sheets when the faint crow of a rooster woke her. Quietly, she picked up the jeans and shirt still lying on the floor beside the bed, put them on, and crept toward the door, walking next to the wall so a creaking board wouldn't waken Ruth-baby. At the door, she paused to look back curiously.

It seemed years since she had seen anyone except Rose, Cookie, and B.C. Maybe Ruth-baby had grown some, or maybe she had long silky hair now like Mary Ellen Parker. If she had changed, she hid it well under her usual twisted nest of blankets.

In the kitchen, she hurriedly spread three pieces of bread with butter and molasses and stacked them together. Lavinia would get to the house by seven, her arrival would awaken Annie's father, and Annie would have to eat a huge bowl of cream of wheat, with lumps big as marbles that weighted down her stomach the rest of the day, and toast hard enough to break a tooth.

Licking the sides of her sandwich, she hurried around the side of the house to bring in the morning paper. As long as it was laid neatly beside her father's plate, it seemed to indicate to him that the world was turning smoothly, everything and everyone fulfilling their prescribed responsibilities.

As Annie picked up the dew-damp paper, she thought she saw a small square of white disappear behind a big double-trunked oak across the street. She smiled. Miss Lessie was sweeping again, for the first time since her shot had cracked all their worlds apart.

"Morning, Miss Lessie," Annie called, walking toward the curb. No one answered.

"It's only me, Miss Lessie," Annie called loudly. An old cane yard rake clattered noisily against the packed bare dirt and the tree's gnarled roots. Annie's glance automatically followed its arching fall, until the flash of white apron hurrying toward the back steps caught her eye.

"Miss Lessie," Annie called again, but too softly. Miss Lessie couldn't have heard.

A shrill "Yoo-hoo" from the corner told Annie that Lavinia would have breakfast ready in no time, and she turned reluctantly back toward the kitchen with her father's paper.

Later, pausing in the barn's thick silence on the way to Rose's, Annie realized that Miss Lessie's court appearance must have come and gone. The thought of her world, careening on past dangers toward some unknown end without her, was disturbing; and she hurried out of the barn's shadows into the sun-streaked pasture. Everything must have worked out all right, she reassured herself. With her own eyes she had seen Miss Lessie sweeping the yard this morning. She thought almost eagerly of her deportment lessons—perhaps next week.

The morning was full to bursting with Rose's restless watching, measuring, and remeasuring.

B.C. sat beside his mother, and Annie and Cookie lay curled up in two overstuffed chairs. Annie read and reread the Kerry Drake strip just above the back of her chair. Then, after a long while, it seemed that Rose slept, then Cookie.

When the noon whistle blew, it sliced through Annie's own dream of early morning sausage, eggs, and grits. She groaned as the bell at the house joined the whistle, summoning her to another of Lavinia's noontime disasters.

She stretched to poke Cookie's drooping head with a finger. "You want I should bring lunch back for everybody?"

"Not 'less you mean to bring a coal chisel, too," Cookie answered grimly.

Little puffs of dust sent up tiny smoke signals between her toes as Annie climbed the hill. Chewing Tobacco gave an almost friendly whinny as he heard her familiar footsteps. In the yard, the bell still swung lazily, just short of ringing. As she neared the porch, she even thought she smelled fried chicken. Suddenly, she wondered if Miss Lessie had come out again to sweep. She paused. It was more important than that. Her budding optimism demanded one more sign.

The strange car at the curb in front of Miss Emma's and Miss Lessie's looked like it had been made of leftover bits and pieces of all the old cars in town. No two fenders were even the same color and in the front windshield was a small round hole with countless radiating frosted lines, made by a piece of ricocheting gravel—or maybe even a bullet. "I bet he runs moonshine," Annie mused. The main body of the car, once apparently dark green, was now much faded and speckled with spots of rust. Leaning against the front fender nearest the curb was a short, fleshy man in a dirty Panama hat. He kept thumping the hood impatiently, staring toward Dr. Matt's front door.

Curious, yet strangely repelled by the man and his bizarre automobile, Annie walked slowly across the front yard and stopped in the shadow of the large magnolia.

Miss Emma stepped out on the porch, carrying a small suitcase tied securely with a piece of green twine. The man watched her struggle awkwardly with the suitcase as she came slowly down the steps, but he made no move to help. Automatically, Annie waved and ran toward Miss Emma to help her. Why, she thought, they're taking a trip, maybe the first one they've ever taken. It seemed an incredibly gay thing to do. Dragging the bag toward the car, Annie asked a dozen questions, too excited to wait for Miss Emma's answers.

Finally, at the door of the car, the man reached out a short arm for the bag and threw it offhandedly through the back window. Not a vacation, Annie suddenly knew. The car, the man, throwing Miss Emma's bag—all wrong for a vacation.

As she turned back to Miss Emma, she heard her saying quickly, as if anxious to get the distasteful words out of her mouth: "Freck Barnes, our second cousin . . . he's offered to help Lessie . . . too far for me . . . only relative we have who could do this sort of thing . . . grateful really . . . "

The screen door made a soft clapping sound behind them, and she stopped talking abruptly and stared at her feet.

Miss Lessie looked different from any way Annie had ever seen her. She had on a pale-blue voile dress. Soft ruffles covered the backs of her rough hands and the brown mole at the base of her neck. Where her white apron usually hung, she clutched a white linen bag that bulged with invisible objects.

"Better get a move on," the man said abruptly. "Tuscaloosa is four hours, and I don't want to be pulling into no nuthouse after dark."

"Please," Miss Emma protested hoarsely.

Miss Lessie moved slowly down the steps, glancing about her with a little frown. A moment later, she stepped deliberately from the walk toward the rake she had dropped that morning. Annie knew she meant to put it in its proper place on the back porch.

"No, no, Lessie, there's no time for raking now," Miss Emma said impatiently, hurrying her words. She moved to take Miss Lessie by the arm.

For a moment Annie thought Miss Lessie would resist, but she did not pull away, and sank so pitifully into herself that her gay summer dress was a cruel mockery.

Miss Lessie shuffled slowly past, so close her skirt brushed Annie's hand.

Annie whirled and grabbed Miss Emma's arm.

"Wait," she cried.

"I ain't got all day, you know," a rough voice behind her said.

"Just one minute. Please. Just one minute."

"Oh, all right," Miss Emma said. "But hurry, Annie. It's best for us all to be quick."

Annie raced toward the back door and took the steps two at a time. Kneeling on the spotlessly clean, cracked brown linoleum, she pulled open one drawer after another, scrambling the contents of each and spilling things heedlessly on the floor around her. In the last drawer she found what she wanted and raced back toward the front walk.

"Annie," Miss Emma cried, stamping her foot when she saw what Annie had, "you know as well as I do, Lessie doesn't read. Even if she did, she won't be able to do any . . ." Her voice trailed away uncertainly as she glanced toward her sister.

Annie took one of Miss Lessie's hands and pressed the heavy cookbook into it. Then she held out her other hand.

"Have a nice trip, Miss Carter," she said in as full a voice as she could manage.

Miss Lessie stared at Annie's hand. Annie stood straight, her chin lifted, her outstretched fingers almost touching Miss Lessie's bag.

After a moment, Miss Lessie began fumbling awkwardly with the book and her purse.

"Here, Lessie, here," Miss Emma said. "I'll take that. You hold on to that purse. Heaven knows what all you've got in there. I'll just take the cookbook back in the kitchen." She reached for the book, but Miss Lessie took a small step backward. Shifting the book and the heavy purse clumsily to one arm, she held out the other hand to Annie.

"Thank you so much. I'm sure I shall," she said in her soft dove's voice. Then she turned toward the car. For the first time she seemed to realize she was to be driven by a man, and her eyes widened in fear. He still stood leaning over the front fender, waiting for Miss Lessie to get into the car.

Miss Emma quickly grabbed her sister's elbow. "Lessie," she said in a pleading voice, "this is our cousin.

He's kin to us—like Papa. He's Papa's own nephew."

Miss Lessie looked around to find Annie again, and Miss Emma nervously jerked open the front door of the car.

"The finest ladies usually ride in the back seat," Annie suggested softly to Miss Lessie.

Miss Lessie nodded, lifted her chin, and stepped up to the back door. Turning to her astonished cousin with her warmest smile, she spoke. "If you please?"

As if compelled against his will, the cousin slowly moved to open the back door for Miss Lessie, and something in her "Thank you so much," as she slid gracefully into the strange car, made him close the door gently behind her.

As the car neared the corner, Annie saw a small lace handkerchief waving gaily from the open back window.

"Well, I do declare, my best Belgium lace handkerchief," Miss Emma cried, "Lord, I wonder what else is gone." She glanced anxiously back toward the house, but she did not move. Instead she dabbed at her eyes with her sleeve, then said, "Did you ever hear that blood is thicker than water?"

Annie nodded, having heard the expression from her mother as long as she could remember.

"Well," said Miss Emma, "I'll tell you this. It is true, but you won't know how true until too late." Reaching out, she put a finger lightly against Annie's chest. "Be good to Ruth-baby, child. Will you remember that, always?"

The admonition eased the ache Annie had felt in her chest ever since she realized Miss Lessie was going away. Here was something she could do for Miss Emma and Miss Lessie. Solemnly she nodded, and Miss Emma nodded in return. The bargain sealed, the scepter passed, Miss Emma turned and walked up the walk toward her silent house.

*   *   *

Annie's mother clapped her hands together softly, delighted with all the puzzled faces that surrounded her. "You *are* surprised! It's perfect. I knew it would be. Lavinia was such a dear to help. She came at six o'clock. Imagine! A birthday breakfast."

Annie saw her father smile weakly at the gay place cards and beribboned packages piled in the center of the table. Balloons hung from the light over the table. In the packages, there were three new hair ribbons, patent leather shoes with no straps (just like Mary Ellen Parker wore), and a new jump rope from Ruth-baby.

Annie looked from face to face. The room was so quiet, she could hear the grandfather clock in the living room ticking, but she could not think of any two words that belonged together.

Her mother began nervously gathering the wrappings and crushing them in her lap. "Hampton's had the cutest china birthday cups," she said brightly, "one for each day of the week. I almost got you one of those but yours said 'Thursday's child is full of woe.' Isn't that the silliest thing you ever heard? How they expect to sell any Thursdays is beyond me."

Laurence smiled at his wife. "Everything's lovely, Louise."

Annie, her mind still a wordless blank, leaned toward her mother, who had smoothed the used paper until it

looked almost as fresh and new as it had on the packages.
"Might as well be breakfast and just family for a
change, I said—though I loved your party last year. I
mean, with William not back from camp until tomorrow
and Rose and B.C. sick and Two-Time and Lilly gone..."
She paused as an expectant swimmer does at the edge of
the water when he notices how swift the current is.
"Sometimes I feel as if the whole world has gone off and
left me behind."

Sometimes people don't move from one place to
another. They are just suddenly there. Now Annie was
unexpectedly in the circle of her mother's arms. She
lowered her head to her shoulder, grateful for her pristine
cleanliness and the smell of lilacs. Her mother gave her a
delicate squeeze and Annie realized that, at thirteen, she
was already bigger and stronger than her mother.

"Maybe if somebody warned us. Maybe if they just let
us know that the world is always and forever falling apart
and rebuilding, it wouldn't come as such a shock," her
mother whispered, her lips against Annie's hair.

Annie tried on the shiny patent pumps. They were too
small, but would never be exchanged. Her mother
laughed gaily and tied two ribbons, a soft lavender and a
bright yellow one, in her hair. Standing back to admire
her work, she gave one of her frequent little sighs that
could mean anything. Annie saw her shake her head as if
to rouse herself.

"My baby. A year from now you won't know yourself."

Laurence pushed back his chair. "Now, Louise, don't
rush things. She's only twelve."

"Thirteen today," her mother said.

"Rush what things?" asked Annie.

Her mother gave her a conspiratorial wink. "Fathers are always the last to know."

"What things?" Annie repeated.

"Well, if your mother is already seeing a future full of orange blossoms and wedding bells, I better get to the store and start calling in all the old debts." He patted Annie on the head. "It's a hard world, Annie."

"I have to go, too," Annie said, her heart pounding. Where had the time gone? William was going to be back tomorrow, and her mother was as good as planning the wedding already.

"To Rose's, I suppose," her mother called after her, her voice high and thin.

In the darkness of the hall her father paused. "You seem to be walking on your toes."

"These shoes are a little tight."

There was a long silence. "So were my Christmas pajamas."

Annie giggled, thinking of the apricot silk pajamas. "I know, I saw you tiptoeing, too."

"I didn't know about the birthday breakfast, but I do have something in my room I have been planning to give you today. It isn't wrapped."

The small book lay comfortably in the palm of Annie's hand. Its leather binding was still a rich caramel color, though the bottom edges of its spine were frayed.

Her father cleared his throat, and it sounded loud in the silent hall. "It's probably all wrong, since you're a girl, or maybe it's just too late. Anyway, it was my favorite book."

Unable to read the tiny faded gold lettering of the title in the dim light, Annie turned the book over and over in her hands, feeling its warm smoothness.

"It won't matter. I always love books."

"Laurence," her mother called, "are you still there?"

"Yes, Louise."

"Don't you think a birthday breakfast is something Jeanne Thornton might want to put in the *Winton Bugle*?"

The leather book thudded softly as it hit the hall runner. Her father stooped to pick it up, straightened, gave Annie the book and a light pat on her cheek.

"Better not, Louise. Some of your friends might be offended that they weren't invited."

Annie heard her mother's sigh, then the clink of a coffee cup set down on its saucer. "I suppose you're right."

"Have a good day, Annie," her father said. Half-turned toward the front door, he hesitated again.

"Annie, you know the two men you and Cookie saw at Reverend Henton's church?"

Annie nodded.

"Are you sure they were there?"

Puzzled, Annie nodded.

"Would you know them again if you were to see them?"

"The smaller one, I would for sure."

Her father sighed. "Don't speak to anybody about them, all right?"

Solemnly Annie nodded again. She could not make anything of her father's words, but instinctively she knew that if anybody needed watching, it was the short man she had seen at the Emanuel Methodist Church.

"Don't forget to thank your mother for the surprise breakfast."

"I won't."

"You are getting grown, aren't you?" her father said as he pushed open the front door.

* * *

Annie left the new shoes under the nearest yellowbell bush and walked barefoot through the barn and down the pasture path toward the cabin. Her ribbons fluttered against her cheeks, lavender and yellow commas just at the edge of her vision.

The cabin, still partially shaded by the hill, flaunted the same wispy flutters of color, as ribbons stirred in the breeze all along the edge of the porch—crepe-paper remnants of the welcome-home party. "Ribbons make the saddest rags," Annie chanted softly. Pleased with the words, she wondered if they were poetry.

As soon as Annie had passed into the cool no-man's-land of the barn, the birthday breakfast, the too-tight shoes, even the book from her father were forgotten—no, not forgotten, they just didn't exist. On the other side of this buffer zone, time was so disjointed as not to exist in any ordinary way. There were still one or two familiar phrases about time: "It's time to feed the chickens." "Day in and day out." Such fragile threads seemed to Annie the only things that held the cabin anchored on its gentle broomstraw sea.

If you sat on your haunches in front of the cabin, as she had done, watching B.C. idly run his hands over the rusty hulk of his racer, the illusion that the cabin was floating, tugging gently against its four stone anchors, was very real. The house seemed to rest lightly on the new summer tips of broomstraw. The straw gave only glimpses of the steps and the rock pillars and no view at all of scratching hens and bare earth. Yet it bowed occasionally—or perhaps the house rolled a little on its flat bottom—to give you a glimpse of the straw sea beyond.

Inside the cabin, there was no day or night, only naps and short flurries of activity when chairs were exchanged or someone came in or went out. There was no breakfast, no lunch, no supper time. Instead, someone was always scrambling eggs or making a peanut-butter-and-banana sandwich at the oil-cloth-covered table in the corner, or standing at the open refrigerator door taking pinches of this or that.

*   *   *

That first Sunday after Rose and B.C. were back home, when Annie had come down to the cabin after church as usual, her arms full of the Sunday paper, Rose hadn't even known what day it was. Annie had spread the funnies on the table, but they lay untouched, accusing them all, until Annie rolled them up and placed them in an empty grocery sack. In a few minutes, B.C. had taken them out to the incinerator behind the cabin.

Always before, the four of them, even Otis if he were there, read and reread favorite ones aloud. Afterward, a place was carefully chosen for each sheet on the wall. The choice was difficult, because each time a new page went up, an old favorite was covered.

Their freedom from time's demands and penalties had become so complete that Annie was startled when she saw the cake in the middle of the kitchen table. It stood half-submerged in runny white icing, its bare brown shoulders exposed and listing sharply to one side.

"Happy birthday, honey," Rose called, almost full-voice.

B.C. nodded his head toward the table. "How you like your cake?" His ever-present anger made the question hard and ugly.

Cookie rotated the platter slowly, then licked her fingers. "It's a marble cake."

"You can say that again," B.C. said.

"Marble's her favorite kind. Mama said so. Besides, I baked it by the very same recipe Mama always uses."

"The very same," Rose affirmed. Her top lip seemed to be giving her trouble, she kept tugging at it.

"Part of it must have been torn off," B.C. said sourly.

Annie hung awkwardly in the door, one hand still holding the screen door open, the other gripping the door frame. One hand seemed determined to pull her into the room, the other to keep her out.

Rose pushed up from her bed, leaning heavily on an elbow that sank out of sight under her weight.

"If you'd rather this wasn't your birthday, just say so," said B.C. "We'll just cancel it. It don't make no nevermind to me."

Rose shuddered and pulled at her worn wedding-ring quilt as if B.C. had just done something awful, like dragging a carcass across her clean floor. He had actually done that once—drug in by the tail the carcass of a stinking, bloated cat that Annie and Cookie had called Trash Can. After carefully scrubbing his hands and both arms to the elbows as he had seen the doctors do in the movies, he had performed an autopsy on the kitchen table. Gagging, but unwilling to leave, Annie had watched as B.C.'s hands, pulling and turning an old kitchen knife, had found heart, lungs, stomach, intestines, and, finally, a fishbone stuck sideways across the esophagus.

"Never mind him, honey," Rose said. "I didn't shine at birthday parties either. Come on in before the flies beat you to your cake."

Cookie slapped her thigh. "Whoo-ee, would you look at those fancy ribbons."

Annie reached quickly for the ribbons, then let her hand drop again, empty. "They're from my mother. I had a surprise birthday breakfast this morning."

Cookie's face sagged with disappointment, and suddenly Annie was laughing. B.C. and Rose looked from Annie to Cookie and back again, puzzled.

"If you'd just tilt your head a little and put a dab of icing on each ear, you'd look just like your cake, Cookie."

Cookie's mouth pulled down further.

For a silent minute, Rose and B.C. examined the evidence, as if Cookie were Exhibit A and the cake Exhibit B.

B.C.'s harsh giggle behind his hand seemed to hurt him. Rose fell back, and her pillows gave a loud whoosh of protest. "Better laugh, Cookie. You're going to keep right on looking like that chocolate marble cake until you do," she said between her own chuckles.

"Never mind, I'll eat it all myself, then y'all won't have anything to compare me to." But she carefully straightened her face as she moved behind the cake and picked up a knife. With a tight grin she asked, "How does marble cake go with a birthday breakfast?"

"After Lavinia's birthday breakfast, anything goes,"

Annie assured her.

It was only after Cookie had cut four big pieces that they realized B.C. had left, silently as a cat, somehow, through the usually squeaky screen door.

Rose made Cookie go to each of the windows and the door to look for him, but he seemed to have evaporated into the still air.

"He's only gone out to sulk in the back pasture," Cookie said.

Rose absently tugged at a short wiry braid of hair the color of cold ashes. Her other hand wandered over the coverlet until it came to rest on and gripped the mouth of the large jar full of coins and tightly folded paper money.

Cookie pushed back from the table. "Let's eat our cake on the porch," she said, nodding at Annie.

Annie hesitated, waiting to see if Rose minded being left alone. Absently Rose nodded, her eyes still on the jar of coins beside her.

The sun's heat was as precise as it was all-encompassing, so that Annie's knees were hotter than her feet, and her head felt so hot after a few minutes that she imagined heat waves must be shimmering off her hair like off a blacktop road in August. B.C.'s dismembered bike lay on its side in the yard, covered with rust.

Cookie stabbed her fork into her cake once, twice, three times without taking a bite. "Mama has got B.C. on the brain."

"Is he still having those headaches?"

"All I know is that he's as mean and ornery as a cornered cottonmouth."

Annie looked toward the dark green line that marked the edge of the back pasture. "Dr. Mason said—"

"Dr. Mason said Mama would be up and working by now, and she sinks further into that bed every day—and it's B.C. keeps her there, if you ask me." Cookie spat the words out as if they were scorching her mouth.

"But he told us—"

Cookie tossed her head angrily. "Dr. Mason said he'd done everything he could for B.C. He was right about that one. He sits out in the cool woods all day throwing rocks at toads while we sit here steaming, watching Mama breaking her heart over his tough hide. Maybe he is just a no-good nigger. One of those bad ones they talk about."

"Don't you ever say that again. Not ever," Annie almost shouted.

Cookie turned to look at her inquisitively. "Sometimes I almost think you love B.C. better than me."

"That's not true. It's just that B.C. . ." Annie flushed. ". . . Well, he needs loving more. But me and you, we're sisters."

Cookie nodded. "I know. I just wish I knew what was eating on him so."

Annie nodded. "I reckon it's just everything. William turning out not to be his best friend, Miss Lessie shooting him." A picture of B.C. and Wadine Pratt flashed before her.

Cookie shook her head doubtfully. "I think it's more that he can't fight back about any of it. B.C.'s a fighter, like Two-Time."

"Time—" Annie began.

Cookie squeezed her eyes shut. "That's the ugliest word I ever heard of. Don't ever say that word to me again. Nothing's ever going to be right around here again."

Annie pushed herself to her feet. "I better go back for lunch."

At the edge of the yard she paused and turned back. "You're wrong, Cookie. Everything's gonna be all right. I'm gonna make it be."

Halfway up the path, she heard the bell ringing, just once, as if the ringer didn't care whether she came or not. Then from behind her, fainter than the bell, came Cookie's voice, "Happy Birthday, Sister Annie."

* * *

Ruth-baby was actually blowing tiny bubbles in her sleep, a tiny strand of crystal beads that dangled from one corner of her lips. Each deep breath added a new bead just as another down the chain burst. Annie watched in tired fascination. The hall clock had already struck ten. The house and everyone in it had been still and silent for hours, it seemed.

Annie swung her feet restlessly over the edge of the bed and kicked irritably at an upside-down sneaker. Birthdays never know when to quit, she thought. They should stop at noon. Then there would be time to go on to other things, or back to whatever you were doing the day before. To hang on and on like this only meant you had to eventually lie in bed with nothing left to do but think about the present you didn't get, the person who didn't come to your party, or a party that left the taste of sour lemonade still in your mouth and you feeling old and tired.

The clock downstairs struck the half hour, and Annie

remembered that she still didn't know what book her father had given her. She knew from its old leather binding that it had once been his father's before him. Could one book tell the same story to three different people from three different worlds? Her father had once told her that Grandfather Trammell had loved beautiful books, the way some men love beautiful women. Beautifully bound leather books had lined one long wall of the living room from floor to ceiling. Just before he died, he had called all five of his children together and coughed and grumbled until they divided the books among themselves. Her father had laughed then, saying his brothers and sisters had gotten furious with him for going so slowly. He had been only fifteen, and the burden and importance of each choice seemed to mount until he thought he could not go on. Grandfather Trammell had seated himself on the living-room sofa and steadfastly refused to let the others hurry him. The empty wall of shelves had long since been removed, and Laurence Trammell kept his books in his bedroom. Now he had given one of them to Annie for her thirteenth birthday. Suddenly eager, she rushed down the steps into the inky darkness of the hall.

Running her fingers along the polished surface of the hall table, she felt the book where she had left it that morning and hugged it to her chest as she turned to grope her way back upstairs. Through her thin nightgown, the book felt smooth and almost warm.

Since the least little light made Ruth-baby toss and turn and occasionally call out for her mother, Annie got her flashlight and pulled the covers over her head as she always did after her father had called up, "Lights out and that is final." Her father rubbed his books' leather covers with lemon oil, and, covered by the close warmth of her sheets, the faint smell of lemon made her feel as if she could throw back a flap of her tent and walk through a sighing lemon grove to a tropical beach.

In the flashlight's small yellow circle, she read *The Adventures of Robinson Crusoe.* In disappointment, Annie pushed the book toward the edge of the bed. "Darn," she thought, "I've already read that."

She switched off the light and lay in bed, still under the covers, then restlessly switched on the light again and began to read.

Just as the sunlight in the room pierced her tent enough to wash away the edge of the flashlight's yellow glow, Annie threw back the sheet. Her lungs ached for fresh air, her eyes burned from her long night's reading. The house was still silent, and so she opened the book to the place which she held with her finger and finished the last few pages. Below the last printed words were two words written in pencil in irregular letters: "Poor Friday." The pencil had been pushed so hard that there was a small hole in the heavy paper at the bottom of the "y" in "Friday."

Troubled, Annie lay back on her pillow, slowly stretching her cramped legs. Poor Friday. Poor Friday. Her father must have written those words. What had made her father so sad, or maybe angry was the right word. He had pushed a hole in the page of one of his cherished books. She tried to think what the words meant. But her body ached, and she was ravenously hungry. Her eyes kept drifting toward the door, and her ears kept listening for her father's shower or the rattle of a kitchen pot. The two small words were forgotten. The small book slithered silently from her open hand. "I can't possibly eat until I sleep," she mumbled, "and I can't possibly sleep until I eat."

CHAPTER 19

THE SECOND SUNDAY morning Rose was home, just before church, B.C. came to the back door and called. Since Lavinia wasn't there on Sunday mornings, no one heard B.C. until he began kicking the bottom of the screen door with his foot. Then everyone started for the back door to see what was causing all the racket.

First Laurence, then Louise, then Ruth-baby and Annie burst out onto the small back porch. But no one called to B.C. or tried to open the door.

Somewhere between his first unanswered summons and their belated response, something frightening had happened to B.C. Now he stood staring blindly at them through the screen. His face, even through the dusty screen, seemed dark and enlarged, as though all his blood had been pumped to his head and held there by the repeated pounding of his foot against the trembling door. His glistening eyes looked as if they were ready to burst from their sockets.

"B.C., B.C., what's all this commotion about?" Her father's voice was full of authority, but B.C. heard nothing.

Annie turned and ran toward the side door. At B.C.'s side, she tried to pull him away from the door. She screamed at him as if he were deaf, "It's not like before.

This is my house, not Miss Lessie's. There's no gun, B.C. No gun."

With a long tearing screech, the lower panel of the screen door gave way. B.C.'s foot kept smashing at the splintered edges.

Then her father's voice cracked over them like a rifle shot, "That's enough, B.C.!"

B.C.'s foot seemed to catch on air. He raised a hand to the scar barely visible over his right ear. His left arm dragged against Annie's grip and he dragged and tipped forward in the same small bow he had made toward Miss Lessie and Miss Emma.

"He's only fainted," Annie heard her father say. "Pull him back from the door a little, Annie, so we can bring him inside."

Louise Trammell gave a small cry. "Laurence!"

"On second thought, he'd be better off at home."

"Daddy," Annie cried, "do you think something's happened to Rose . . . like before?"

Her father's eyes narrowed. "I don't know why he came. But I want all of you to stay right here until I come back."

"Daddy!"

"I'll come back as quickly as I can, Annie. Now you go in with your mother and sister." He stooped and put his arms under B.C., then he stood up slowly, readjusted his almost man-sized burden, and walked toward the pasture gate.

"Wait a minute, Daddy. I'll help you with the gate."

"Stay with your mother, Annie. I'll manage," her father called back sharply.

Her mother sat at the breakfast-room table, which was

still littered with dishes, bread crumbs, and half-filled cups of coffee. Absently she took a sip of cold coffee. "Stop jerking at your sash, Annie, that dress is supposed to last the summer," she said.

Silence thick as molasses settled over the breakfast-room table.

"Morning everybody," Cookie said, sticking her head through the open kitchen door.

Louise's cup clattered against her saucer. "Don't you know not to scare people like that, Cookie?"

Cookie frowned. "Mr. Laurence told me to light out like a scalded cat and tell you folks that everything was all right and to go on to church without him."

"Church! That was hours ago," Annie protested.

Cookie glanced at the clock behind Annie. "It only seems like hours when you're fooling with B.C. If you hurry, you'll be there way this side of the first scripture lesson." Cookie's head disappeared.

"Cookie Holloway, come back here." Annie called. "What did B.C. want?"

Cookie's head reappeared. "Mama only sent him to tell your daddy she needed to talk with him about something. Don't ask me what."

"But it's Sunday morning," Louise protested.

"Not down that hill," said Cookie. She paused and looked around the room swiftly. "Through with the funnies yet?"

Annie shook her head. "I'll bring them after church, like always."

"Okay, okay. Better get back." She waved and gave a small nod toward Annie's mother. "See you after church," she said to Annie and was gone.

Her mother had already gathered her hat and purse and gloves, muttering under her breath as she moved about the room. "Well, I never. Just sent for him. Bold as brass. Sunday morning." Louder she said, "And you fetching Cookie the Sunday papers."

Annie moved quickly toward the hall door. Her mother had forgotten Annie and Ruth-baby's hats—straw sailors with long navy grosgrain streamers. They made the girls look as if they might flap their wings and take off. "Just tell me why she doesn't come get them herself?" her mother was saying.

Pulling Ruth-baby by the hand, Annie paused, then remembered one of her mother's favorite words. "It's a tradition."

Her mother sighed, and Annie inched nearer the door, hoping her mother would follow without remembering the hats. "It's getting late," she urged, glancing at the clock.

"So it is," her mother said, following Annie's glance to the clock with an eager smile. She loved church. It was the only place she still went regularly. "You two girls run along and jump in the car. I'll get your hats for you and be right there."

Annie opened her mouth to protest, then her eyes widened. "Are you going to drive us?"

"Goodness! I forgot! Run next door and catch Claude Spears and tell him we want to ride as far as the Presbyterian Church with them." She snapped her fingers. "And hurry, missing them won't help you any. If necessary, you'll have to walk to church and send Florence Petus back for me."

All the way to the Spears and back again, Annie

listened for sounds from the pasture, longing to follow her father, but she heard nothing, and she dared not disobey. She had seen that in his eyes.

* * *

At the foot of the hill Laurence Trammell realized that B.C. had come to and cautiously set him on his feet.

"Mama wants you," the boy said, his eyes averted. Before Laurence could respond, he had taken long strides toward the woods. For a moment Laurence watched him, frowning, then he turned back toward Rose's.

The small cabin was surrounded by broomstraw that quivered in the early morning breeze. When had it turned such a velvety gray? Laurence wondered. And why hadn't Otis mentioned that the porch sagged dangerously at one end?

Rose shifted her weight on the pillows behind her as he pushed open the creaking screen door.

"Morning, Rose. You're looking better every day." He glanced around the room. "Where's Otis?"

A shadow seemed to pass across Rose's face. "Mr. Laurence, I got to talk to you before I talk to Otis. All Otis knows is who he loves. He can't see the black trouble I see." She sighed. "We'll let him be as long as we can."

Laurence started to protest as he pulled a chair up beside the bed, but Rose held up her hand to silence him. For the first time he noticed that she was thinner, thinner even than when she had come home from the hospital.

"You're getting downright slim. Dr. Mason's going to be pleased."

"Dr. Mason is wasting his time."

"Now, Rose."

"Mr. Laurence, we don't need to be talking about me. You know what we need to be talking about as well as I do."

Laurence looked down at his hands folded in his lap. "I know, Rose. But we can wait until you're stronger. We have to."

Rose shook her head. "I know you been trying to wait for me, Mr. Laurence, and I thank you. But we can't wait no more. B.C.'s not a bit better. Either hate and fear are gonna eat him up, or he's gonna blow up."

Laurence looked up quickly, remembering B.C.'s blind attack on the screen door.

"And Cookie and Annie. What's to become of them? As if they weren't gonna have trouble enough, loving each other the way they do. The world's not like it was when you and Otis were boys."

Laurence put his hands to his knees and stood up, not wanting to hear Rose's blunt words. Behind him he heard the bed creak under Rose's weight.

"Mr. Laurence, did somebody blow up that church— for sure?"

Without turning, Laurence Trammell nodded.

"What kind of monster could kill three innocent little girls and a preacher?"

Laurence turned again to take his seat by the bed. "Rose, I'm awake most of every night thinking about it. Whoever it was, I don't believe that they meant to kill anybody. The girls and Reverend Henton had come to practice a song for Esther Pierce's . . . memorial service. Nobody knew they would be there. Those men probably just wanted to prevent that service from taking place."

Rose's eyes widened. "And Annie and Cookie? What exactly did they see?"

Laurence reached to take Rose's hand in his. "From the way they describe it to me, they saw the two men laying wire and hiding the dynamite behind a flower box that sits on the railing of the baptismal pool. The baptismal pool is right beside the choir loft."

Only the pressure of Rose's fingers disclosed her alarm. "Do they know who . . . ?"

Laurence shook his head. "Not by name, but their descriptions were accurate enough so I think I do. Burt and Jeb Pierce, Amos's brothers, own a farm outside town. They come to town every Saturday drunk and spoiling for a fight."

The pressure of Rose's hand increased. "Mr. Laurence, if they ever find out Annie and Cookie saw them . . . The Pierces have always been mean as snakes, every last one of them."

Reluctantly Laurence nodded. It seemed as if a bomb were again ticking away, this time inside his head. "But Rose," he said finally, "you can't just let people like that go scot-free. You got to fight back."

"Can you guarantee me it won't just end up two more chillun to put to rest—our own chillun—before that trial's over?"

Laurence stared straight ahead. "I'd protect them. Nobody would dare."

Rose shook her head. "Maybe—only maybe, I say. But there would be no room in Winton ever again for Cookie, and that would mean B.C. too, 'cause he wouldn't just stand back. They'd be branded uppity niggers for life."

"No, Rose. They could always stay here, with us."

"Like prisoners?"

The ominous ticking in Laurence's head seemed to fill the room. "Rose," he said, forcing the words out. "We can't just look the other way. People like that have to be stopped."

"And afterward? After the trial, with umpteen other Pierces still loose, and Burt and Jeb probably out in six months for good behavior? What then?"

Laurence shook his head. "There are so many things that must be changed. And this . . . atrocity . . . If we don't see that this act is exposed for exactly what it was, we give the lie to every decent thing we've tried to teach B.C. and Annie and Cookie."

Rose's eyes filled. "I am a mother, Mr. Laurence. Nothing is worth my babies being hurt or killed. I just want them alive."

Laurence turned away from Rose's pleading eyes. "Like B.C.?" he said softly. Then, to soften the blow, he went on quickly. "Rose, we'll hire extra help. Someone just to stay with the girls night and day."

Impatiently Rose tugged at her covers. "You a good man, Laurence Trammell. As good a one as I know. But Cookie and B.C. gonna have to leave—go to Detroit to Lilly and Two-Time. I've known B.C. had to leave for a long time. I just couldn't bear saying it out loud. So now Cookie needs to go, too. The only difference that bomb makes is that they can't come home again no time soon."

Laurence averted his eyes. "You could all go. Just for a little while, until everything quiets down."

"I'm too tired. So is Otis."

"Rose . . . "

"It ain't your fault. Maybe if it hadn't happened this

year, it would of next. B.C. especially. He's just not made
to take the world like it is." Rose's head lifted. "He's too
full of dreams and hope and brains."

"Yes. He'll make a fine man," Laurence agreed.

"In Detroit."

Laurence turned in his chair to look out the window
toward the woods where B.C. had disappeared.

"When you gonna tell them?"

"I'll have to talk to the sheriff," Laurence said, and the
words felt heavy as lead, "but I hear they plan on the
investigation and the trial being pretty much routine. You
know Sheriff Coggins; his goal in life is avoiding
trouble."

"Mr. Laurence, lots of people gonna hate you, and
maybe worse, your family after this, even though folks
know as well as I do that those Pierces are no-good trash.
Annie, she'll have to live with jibes and ridicule from
some people the rest of her life."

"I know."

For a moment silence filled the cabin. "About the
leaving. Let's not tell them about leaving until after the
trial. One thing at a time."

Laurence felt this throat tighten. "Rose, don't say it like
it was something that was going to last forever."

Rose leaned forward and touched his arm lightly. "Like
I said, you're a good man, Laurence Trammell. But you're
like Otis, powerful slow to admit the bad in this world."
Pressing the heel of her hand beneath her breast, she
rubbed. "It seems like only yesterday they was knee-
babies."

*   *   *

The Trammell pew was down near the front on the right-hand side of the church. It was a good one, for it gave a clear side view of Miss Adelia Cotton, whose eyes, nose, tongue—her entire face—moved with every note she played on the organ. It was also directly under one of the four tall stained-glass windows that lined each of the side walls.

The windows were like revolving doors, except that they swung out at the bottom and in at the top. On hot summer Sundays, ushers with long poles pulled the latches at the top and bottom of each window and canted them open to let east-west breezes cross the church.

There usually wasn't much breeze, but with the window open, you could see all the old reprobates sitting on the courthouse steps, talking and spitting tobacco juice at the curb. It was obvious that some pretty hard things had to happen to you for a pretty long time before you were excused from church. If the benches were by any chance empty or all the old men were nodding in the sun, you could watch squirrels playing chase in the bottom branches of the oaks in the yard outside, and sometimes hear faintly the fast, foot-tapping music of the Baptists on the other side of the courthouse.

When the sun got high enough, it came slanting through the top half of the window, which leaned into the dark, still air of the church and laid a rainbow across your lap.

Today the rainbow was a mockery. Directly in front of Annie, William Petus's red head, still wet from combing, bobbed up and down, tilting now right, now left. He was drawing pictures of fighter planes in death duels, guns blazing, streams of black smoke pouring through the loser's fuselage. Miss Florence always held her hymn book open and standing straight up on her lap so whoever sat on the other side of her couldn't see his drawings.

When they stood for "Blessed Be the Tie," Annie cupped her hands and leaned toward her mother. "Where's Mary Ellen?"

A little line creased her mother's forehead. "Gone."

"Gone where?"

"Not now, Annie."

"But where?"

"Home, of course."

"You mean . . . ?" Annie's voice had lifted to a high squeak, and William turned around and gave a noisy, "Sssh."

Miss Florence thumped William hard on the ear, and Annie smiled as she watched it slowly turn a deep red.

Miss Adelia Cotton pushed her tongue over her lower lip, opened all the stops, and the soaring notes of the last hymn lifted the wilted, grateful congregation to their feet.

Annie sidled to the very edge of the pew as the anticipated taste of freedom and Sunday lunch made her saliva flow.

"Annie!" her mother whispered, grabbing for her sash.

"I'd rather walk home," Annie whispered back as she stepped into the aisle. She walked up the aisle so close behind Reverend Askew that she could have stepped on his robe.

"Enjoyed your sermon, Reverend."

"Which part, Annie?" Reverend Askew asked, smiling.

Annie screwed up her eyes at the unexpected question. "The fifth part. That was very . . . "

Reverend Askew still held her hand, pumping it slowly

up and down. "I only recall four points."

Annie glanced nervously back over her shoulder; maybe her mother could help. William Petus pushed right past without shaking hands. "Hi, Shorty," he said, casually as you please, "you and B.C. still going to race that wreck Wednesday?"

At first, Annie couldn't believe her ears. She stared blankly at William's disappearing back, her hand still pumping up, down, up, down. Then she believed. She bit her lip, but it was too late. Her laugh, through pressed lips, was high and excited, stopping all the idlers around her in their tracks. Retrieving her hand from a startled Reverend Askew, she brushed past several ushers, still juggling stacks of collection plates.

As she heard the pelting clatter of coins scattering across polished pine floors, she cleared the bottom step. She had darted between the courthouse benches, now empty as the various old men shuffled to the curb to see what the ruckus was about over at the Presbyterian Church, and was on the other side of the courthouse, heading for home, before they had decided *she* was the ruckus and began their slow pivoting turns with shuffling feet and tap-tapping canes to follow her with their watery eyes.

Some place back of Jack "Shorty" Tate's filling station, she lost both her new patent leather shoes without any straps, but not before they'd rubbed blisters the size of quarters on the backs of both heels.

At the corner, one house down from the Petuses' house, her side hurt so she had to stop twice and spit under a rock. Then she ran on toward home bent over at the waist.

She staggered up the steps at Rose's, bent over, a hand

on each knee to steady herself, gasping noisily for air. The screen door squeaked, and her father stepped out onto the porch.

"Annie! What are you doing here? I'm having a talk . . ."

Oblivious to her father's words, Annie caught the handle of the door as it bounced back toward her. She ran across the room, still canted forward like the church windows, and dropped on her knees beside Rose's bed.

"Where's Cookie? Where's B.C.?" she said, above the roar in her ears.

Rose placed one hand on her forehead, the other across her damp hand, which clung to the edge of the bed.

"Sssh, they still at church—with their daddy. You run along now 'til they come. And sit in the shade; you're hot as a ginger mill."

Annie threw back her head. "Hah!" she cried. "Cookie was all wrong about everything! There's not going to be any wedding at all!"

"Whose wedding was you two planning on?"

"Why mine, mine and that loudmouth's, William Petus. Cookie said it was all arranged. Everything would be ready soon as William went to camp one last time."

Annie was surprised and, in some way she didn't quite understand, hurt when Rose suddenly threw back her head and laughed.

"Child, you only twelve!"

"Thirteen. And Mama can't do a thing with me. You've said that yourself a hundred times."

"Well, never mind that. Your mother would see you a nun before she'd see you married to William Petus." Rose laughed again so hard she had to wipe away tears with the back of her hand. "Hadn't you never noticed all the red hair that runs in the Petus and Trammell families?"

The screen door opened, and Annie heard her father cough.

Rose glanced over Annie's shoulder. "Well?" she asked.

Annie turned toward her father, but he was looking out the window toward the woods where B.C. liked to hide.

Rose watched Laurence Trammell's back. Without turning, he gave a small nod of his head.

"Well, what?" Annie urged.

"Well, don't you think it's strange how your father and your Uncle Clovis and Uncle Tommy and Mr. Petus all turn their feet out when they walk and cock their heads whenever they're listening hard?"

Annie had a fleeting memory of running to the corner to meet her father coming home from work, only to find that it was Mr. Petus who had decided to walk home from his big office at the mill, but it didn't seem to have any connection with her problem with William Petus.

"What of it?" she asked.

Her father nodded again, as if to tell Rose to continue.

Rose cleared her throat and tried again.

"I guess you might say you and William Petus are kissing cousins, once removed, or some such thing—if what they say about your great-grandfather and Amy Petus is true."

Annie looked from Rose to her father. "What does she mean? The Petuses are no kin to us."

Her father shuffled uneasily, and Rose traced her quilt's faded design with her finger.

"I guess you could say it's a rather unofficial relationship," Laurence Trammell said, a faint blush on his pale cheeks.

Annie's eyes widened. She still was uncertain about her relationship to William Petus, but the results were becoming clearer.

"You mean it's like a tradition?"

"What is?"

"That Petuses don't ever marry Trammells?"

"Hrum, well, maybe you could say that—at least not for another generation or so."

Annie looked first toward her father, then Rose, tears of relief in her eyes blurring their familiar forms.

Rose's hands drifted slowly to the jar of money still lying on the bed by the wall. "You were really worried," she murmured softly. "Detroit, you kept on about Detroit . . . " Then she sighed and gave Annie one of her warm, watchful smiles. "Good then, one of my babies is settled for sure."

"Cookie and B.C. were going to come with me," Annie said, relieved that she could talk about it at last. "But don't you worry, Rose, none of us won't ever even think of leaving you again."

"Baby, baby," Rose moaned, as if that were the saddest news she had ever heard.

"Don't be sad, Rose. Nobody's leaving. Really. Everything will be just the same. We never did want to go."

"Life is full of leavings, child. Don't make promises you can't help breaking." Rose put her arms around Annie, and together they rocked back and forth, Annie still kneeling beside the bed, her head cradled against Rose's stomach.

Her father's hand dropped on one of her shoulders. "Leaving is hard, but staying can be harder yet to bear,

Annie. There's strength and bravery in staying, too."

"Ain't that the truth," Rose sighed. "Ain't that the Lord's truth."

Annie moved uneasily under her father's and Rose's touches. Their sad words seemed all wrong. Didn't they understand that it had all been a big mistake?

Just then the front steps gave an angry protest under B.C.'s stomping assault. "B.C., Cookie, there's not going to be any wedding!" Annie called out.

Cookie opened the door slowly, almost as if the news were disappointing. "How come?" she demanded.

Annie searched through her father's and Rose's confusing explanations. "We already got too much red hair in the family as it is."

Cookie shook her head at Annie's father. "That ain't going to stop Miss Louise or Miss Florence Petus," she warned.

Her confidence shaken by Cookie's assurance, Annie silently weighed the importance of toeing-in versus toeing-out, or whether or not the bridegroom cocked his head at you when you talked to him. A picture rose in her mind of a smiling Miss Florence and her mother sitting arm in arm on a church pew and in front of them row after row of red-haired children, all sizes and all ages, all sitting with their heads cocked to the left as if to hear the preacher better.

Her father's voice broke the stillness, "Cookie, Annie, there will be no wedding. Because I say so. Because you're only thirteen. Because you have a whole world to see before you worry about such things. Because when you do get married it should be to someone you love and who loves you." He paused and looked at the four faces turned toward him, and his face was touched with the look of pain Annie had seen so often. "Love should be a freeing thing, not a binding one."

He rose and held out his hand. "Let's go home, Annie. Lord, what do you think Lavinia's done to Sunday dinner by now?"

He turned toward Rose. "Rose, hurry up and get well. Can't you see how much we all need you?" Then, as if finishing the talk he and Rose had had earlier, he said, "Everything will work out. You'll see."

Rose's voice stopped him. "Mr. Laurence. You said that love was supposed to be a freeing thing. I'm counting on you to see that that's so." It was not a plea, but a simple statement of fact.

"Now, Rose . . . "

Rose pushed up from her pillows, never taking her eyes from Laurence Trammell's face.

"Mama?" B.C. said, looking from face to face.

To Annie it seemed that her father's face paled.

"I'll talk to Otis this evening," Rose said.

"What about, Mama?" B.C. asked.

But Laurence Trammell only shook his head and turned to look down into the upturned faces before him. He spoke softly, almost as if talking to himself. "Sometimes doing right seems like the most foolish, thankless thing on this earth. Sometimes, doing right even seems wrong—but I guess it never is."

B.C. rubbed a hand over his close-cropped head, his brows drawn in puzzlement. He turned toward his mother, but she had turned to look across the room out the narrow window.

Laurence paused, his eyes still on the young faces

around him. "Let's all sit down. I have something to tell you. I guess it might as well be now.

"Several weeks ago, just before Rose got sick and B.C. got . . . hurt, before Esther Pierce had her memorial service, Annie and Cookie went to the Emanuel Church to see what was going on. Accidentally they witnessed what I believe was part of a crime."

"A crime?" cried Cookie. "We didn't see nothing at all."

Laurence chose his words carefully. "It seems as if the explosion that happened later that day was not caused by a hot-water heater blowing up, as they thought at first, but by a bomb. The two men you saw in the church that morning may have set the bomb. You girls may have to testify as to exactly what you saw and identify those two men." He paused. "Do you think you could do that?"

Cookie and Annie stared silently at each other as the weight of what Annie's father said settled in them.

"My God," B.C. suddenly whispered, "that means that Reverend Henton and those little girls were . . . " His eyes widened in shock and disbelief, and Rose struggled to lean far enough over to place a soothing hand on his arm.

"Not exactly," Laurence said hurriedly. "The men had no way of knowing that the four of them would come early to practice. But a crime was committed just the same, and they should be punished."

B.C. twisted back to his mother. "Do you believe that, Mama? If Annie and Cookie stand up there and say what they saw, those men will go to jail?"

Rose's hand stayed on B.C.'s arm, but her eyes met Laurence Trammell's across the room. "Maybe. Maybe not."

"Rose!"

"The law plays funny tricks with black folks," she answered quietly, then she turned toward B.C. "But Mr. Laurence is right, B.C. It's worth doing right, even if it seems the most foolish thing in the world." Her voice fell to a whisper. "As I live and breathe, I believe that, B.C."

B.C. stirred uneasily under his mother's hand. "I'd sooner get Two-Time down here to bust some heads."

"Ah," Rose murmured, "you'd have Two-Time just like them, then?"

Biting his lips, B.C. turned again to Laurence Trammell. "They're white. They'll let them loose for sure. Have you thought about what will become of Cookie and Annie?"

"I have," he said softly. "I believe I can protect both Cookie and Annie," he added, turning to Rose. "Both girls will have to sign a statement, but only Annie need testify."

B.C.'s harsh laughter made goose bumps rise on Annie's arms.

"What would you do in my place, then?" Laurence asked B.C.

Silence filled the cabin. No one moved. B.C.'s face twisted. "Tell on them—if they skinned me alive for it."

"B.C.," Laurence said, "it may be that why we do this is more important than what we do. If revenge was all we cared about, we'd just need to blow them up. But there's more to it. Much more. The hardest thing I know is to fight hatred and violence without using hatred and violence, but I believe it's important." Laurence Trammell's eyes turned toward Annie. With difficulty, he spoke again. "Important enough to risk all you possess or hold dear."

So, Annie thought, Dr. Matt was only partially right. The violence he had known existed was here, but perhaps not inevitable. They could fight back another way, she and Cookie and her father. As she and her father walked up the hill, Annie reached to take his hand.

CHAPTER 20

COOKIE WOKE Monday at daybreak. Her mother had gotten up from her bed sometime during the night, for the first time since she came home from the hospital. Now she sat in her favorite armchair facing the window, her back to her sleeping family, her mending basket drawn up close to her chair.

"Mama," Cookie whispered, proud and yet worried that her mother should have tried so much alone. She swung both feet swiftly to the still-cool floor and tiptoed across the room to sit on the arm of her mother's chair. Halfway across the room, Cookie paused. It seemed as if her mother had thrown up her hand, a familiar gesture to signal her that her movements would frighten some small creature she was watching from the window.

Cookie held her breath and strained to hear the flutter of wings, or the quarrel of chipmunks. Then, in the silence, she knew Rose had not raised her hand. She was not listening to anything nor watching anything from the window. Her invisible salute had been for Cookie—not stop, but good-bye.

Quietly Cookie pulled a small straight-backed chair up beside her mother's big one. Laying her hand on the sleeve of her mother's gown, she sat quietly beside her. The sun came up from behind them, chasing the deep pine shadows back into the tangle of vines, trees, and underbrush across the creek. Then the gentle gray mourning doves that Rose loved did walk past the window in dignified pairs, softly calling to each other in their low, silvery voices. And the chipmunks left their fallen log and chased each other, furious over some unshared crumb.

B.C. opened his eyes and knew. Cookie heard his breathing change and turned toward his bed, frightened, yet needing him to know, too. He never turned his head, just lay stretched taut beneath the sheet, his face staring at the rain-stained ceiling.

Softly Cookie spoke his name. Still staring at the ceiling, he shouted so loud the blood vessels jumped on the side of his neck, "There will be no wedding—because I said so!"

Otis rolled over in the sofa bed he had shared with Rose since she got sick. He rubbed his eyes with the backs of both hands and stared at them and around the room, looking for the wild sound he had heard in his dream, still not certain of where he was.

"Daddy . . ." Cookie began.

For a long, long time, Otis lay on his side as still as B.C., his head on Rose's pillow, his knees pulled in to his chest.

Then he spoke in a voice as low and gentle and dignified as Rose's mourning doves, "B.C., you will not say one more word to upset your mother." Pushing stiffly against the bed, he rose and took the chipped enamel bowl that held his shaving things and walked into his and Rose's small bedroom at the rear of the cabin to shave. The familiar sound of splashing water and the smell of shaving lotion meant that someone should be at the sink cracking eggs and laying bacon in the pan. In the past two weeks, this had become Cookie's job, and now life's pull toward the ordinary, the necessary, made her turn away from her brother with an aching heart.

Otis stepped back through the curtains that hung across the door. He was dressed in his Sunday trousers and a starched white shirt. His suspenders dangled below his fingertips.

"I'll fix breakfast," he said firmly. "You two children dress."

Following her father's cue, Cookie pulled her white Sunday dress with the blue sash from the wardrobe in the corner. She paused, then got out B.C.'s best pants and shirt and laid them carefully at the foot of his bed, wanting to help, yet fearful that even this might shake his trembling, tenuous self-control. He did not seem to see her, but he gathered his clothes as soon as she dropped them and moved slowly, like an arthritic with early-morning stiffness, toward the curtained door.

"Should we go up the hill and tell somebody, Daddy?"

"No, let them sleep. Let's just have our breakfast together and do our chores now."

At breakfast, life began its first changing, and Cookie knew what loneliness meant. Otis said grace instead of Rose, a grace Cookie had never heard before.

Cookie cleared the table of the uneaten breakfast, and B.C. and Otis moved Rose back to the sofa bed and spread her best quilt with the flower-garden pattern over her, though heat already drew beads of sweat from B.C. and Otis, as they struggled to carry their burden.

Cookie could not look at her mother weighted down by the hot, heavy quilt. She longed for Annie. Something in her, she knew, would wait, would feel nothing, would believe nothing until Annie came.

"Should I go for Mr. Laurence now?" she asked her father.

Otis looked quickly at Cookie, then away, as if her question had hurt him. "No." He looked absently around the room. "Make the beds first. Didn't your mother have you make your beds?"

Cookie nodded and began tugging at B.C.'s bed covers—the tangled, sometimes even torn remains of terrible battles he fought in the dark.

The noontime sun, a poisonous yellow, had silenced even the rap-rap-rap of B.C.'s heels kicking against the porch before Otis let Cookie go.

"It's all right now, Cookie. Go get Mr. Laurence. Tell him your mother is gone." Before he let her go, he smoothed her hair with his hands, and Cookie felt the hard calluses and enlarged knuckles tap and stroke her head with a blind man's gentle, remembering touch. "Don't be long," he admonished, as if he was now anxious that the terrible wheels of events might turn too slowly because he had spent the morning holding them back.

Lavinia frowned when Cookie stepped inside the back door. She thinks this is her kitchen, Cookie thought, painfully holding her face still.

"What you want?"

Cookie marched silently past her and pushed through the swinging door into the breakfast room. Laurence Trammell stood at the other door—on his way back to work. He and Cookie stood, each guarding a door. Cookie's silence held them all still. Cookie watched Annie, her eyes pleading, yet dreading the moment she would make everything true, when neither she nor Mr. Laurence nor anybody else could guard the doors any longer.

Please hurry, Annie, she thought, suddenly so tired it was difficult to stand, yet vaguely aware of the treacherous swinging door behind her.

Annie rose. "Cookie?" she said wonderingly. Then, "Mama," she cried, slow and dying, like a talking doll tossed on its back. Although it was not her mother she looked at when she cried out, but Cookie.

"Laurence, *do* something," Cookie heard Louise Trammell say.

"Not now, Louise, for God's sake, not now," he answered.

Louise Trammell folded her napkin, creasing it hard between her fingers. Then she rose and left the room— pushing past her husband, as if contemptuous of his belief that he had been guarding the door for *or* against them.

*   *   *

Annie leaned over the half-door of Chewing Tobacco's stall, straining forward, squinting her eyes to bring the details of the cabin into focus. Her mother's anger floated between her and the fall of land below her like a morning fog clinging to low places.

"And I say she will not set one foot inside that cabin," her mother's voice had come from her bedroom, as high and biting as the vertical saw at the lumber yard when it ripped off the last inch of pine plank and was silent. There was a long pause. Her father must have answered—but too softly for Annie to hear.

"She's not your son, Laurence. Haven't you noticed? She's my daughter!" The words, the claim, the voice were shrill and vibrant—the saw showering blue sparks about the room. Listening, Annie had drawn a deep breath and held it—protection against the sparks, which might clear the charged air or fall among tinder-dry, forgotten layers of sawdust and blow them all to pieces. Dust to dust, ashes to ashes . . . was that in the Bible?

Her father left—angrily, from the sound of the side door. Annie's breath came out in a long stale whoosh. Drawers slammed, the bathroom faucet was turned on full force, then off again. The air was still charged, danger everywhere, postponed.

Now Annie felt a threatening wave of nausea. Her throat was hot and dry, and her lower ribs burned from the weight of her body across the barn door. Still she could only catch glimpses of the path, a chimney, the porch of the cabin. Was the dark shadow the rusty remains of B.C.'s racer? Why hadn't she known before now that he was much too old for racers?

Behind her, her own yard, her house, her world would be as starkly exposed as the pasture was shrouded. Her mother's anger, which Annie had never seen naked before, brought a shudder, even now in the dark warmth of the barn. The strength of it kept her there, with not one foot inside the pasture.

Below, a long white ambulance floated under the spreading green of the pecan trees toward the cabin. Many people seemed to cluster briefly on the sagging porch, leaning out over the undulating waves of straw, then they dispersed quickly as if fearful their craft might list, throwing them all into the fog-shrouded waters.

The familiar sight of the wavering, backing ambulance convinced Annie of nothing; she had seen it too many times before. Even the well-known feelings of terror, grief, and guilt she questioned. Hadn't everything always come right again? Wasn't everything finally the same?

CHAPTER 21

HER MOTHER had been put out, but there was no help for it. Annie had to have a new Sunday dress for the funeral. Her father called and had them send out a dozen from Campbell's Department Store and told Annie and Cookie both to pick one. She and Cookie had spent the last evening trying them on. Tissue paper, ribbons, and a rainbow of dresses had lain all over Annie's room mocking their sober, uneasy faces.

Cookie puckered her lips and peered into the mirror standing in the corner of the room. She and Annie both stood stiffly at attention in their cotton slips, the crinoline standing out from their long thin legs, their shoulders exactly even.

"Pitiful," she declared.

Annie nodded, relieved by Cookie's honest appraisal.

"Too skinny," Cookie added.

Annie narrowed her eyes like Cookie's. "Too tall."

"The Lord just went too far in every direction on us. You're too white, and I'm too black."

Annie stared at her pale face that would never tan, only freckle lightly across the bridge of her nose. Beside her, Cookie's blackness seemed absolute. Annie shook her head fiercely.

"No! Not far enough. Once he'd come this far he

should have had the gumption to go the rest of the way. Then I would have been silver, and you would have been purple."

"Purple?" said Cookie indignantly. "How come purple?"

Annie kept her eyes on the mirror. "Can't you see it? Dark, dark purple. Like kings and queens wear."

"I reckon," said Cookie, somewhat mollified as she turned her arm slowly to catch the light from the lamp.

Annie glanced uneasily toward the pile of dresses and felt her lips quiver. "Let's go down to your house."

"What about picking dresses?"

"Lavinia can do that. Come on, let's go."

Cookie shook her head. "Uh-uh. B.C."

Since Rose's death, B.C.'s seething anger had become transmuted into brooding despair. He did not shout at Cookie or Annie over trivial transgressions, did not tear at his food, or storm out of the cabin leaving the air charged behind him. He rarely moved from a chair beside the fireplace. He had stared at the ashes and charred remains of last winter's cheerful fires until Otis had silently swept out the ashes and charred bits of logs and laid a new fire. But B.C. kept staring blankly as if he still saw only ashes. B.C.'s anger had seemed private—his own thing that they could accept or ignore. But now his brooding, frowning silence seemed to pull them all down, to muffle speech, and to push them back out the door. And Cookie and Annie avoided him whenever they could.

Annie flapped her hand helplessly against her thighs. "All right, we'll get on our jeans and go down to the barn."

From the vantage point of the loft, Annie and Cookie watched the afternoon stretch across both their homes, and for once there was no traffic on the steep, hard-packed path between them.

* * *

No crowing rooster, no wafting smell of frying bacon issued in the triumphant morning. Night simply ebbed, drained by those who would not rest in it, and a pale wash of color seeped into night's abandoned berth. Annie swung her feet to the floor and stood beside the bed, uncertain how to begin such a day. Then Lavinia called for her to hurry up for breakfast. Annie pulled on her jeans, and the day began to take care of itself.

Two-Time and Lilly arrived in the middle of the morning on the train. Two-Time wore a new black suit, and Lilly had on a pearl-gray dress with a huge artificial rose pinned deep in the center of her bosom. She was wearing shiny patent leather shoes with tall narrow heels, but she walked like her feet hurt. Her eyes were red and puffy, as if she hadn't slept well on the train or had been crying. B.C. allowed Lilly to hug him close. For a minute he seemed to go limp against her, drowning in the familiar scent of her body, her remembered warmth and strength. Then he pulled back stiffly, shook Two-Time's hand, turned suddenly, and left the platform, walking down the railroad bed toward Hank Ketchum's and the shortcut home.

Lilly watched him go with worried eyes, but shook her head when Two-Time moved after him. They rode home in the delivery van from the furniture store, Lilly and Annie and Cookie in the back, Two-Time and Otis in the cab.

In the van, Lilly settled herself comfortably on a brand-new, quilt-wrapped, rope-tied sofa and held out both her arms for Cookie and Annie. Otis drove home slowly, the long way down by the Firestone store to give them plenty of time.

When they felt the van pull into the driveway, Lilly wiped their eyes and blew her nose loudly on a pink handkerchief the same color as the rose now hanging damply on her dress. "There now, that's better," she said almost cheerfully. "You can't get new growth off old griefs." She looked down at Cookie and Annie and tenderly stroked each of their cheeks. The van stopped. "Now, where will B.C. go?" she asked as she rose and adjusted her dress around her heavy thighs. "Do you think he'll be all right if I just leave him be 'til after the funeral?"

Annie and Cookie looked hesitantly at each other.

"It's that bad, is it?" Lilly nodded. "Well, I'll tell Two-Time to keep his eye on him and after the funeral . . . well, I'll talk to B.C. then." She held out her hands gracefully toward Otis and Two-Time, who had come around to help her from the back of the van, and Annie and Cookie followed.

At one o'clock, Otis looked down at his old-fashioned gold pocket watch, and a hush fell in the cabin. Lilly folded her hands in her lap, and Two-Time's fork hung in the air over the piece of coconut cake someone had brought.

Otis stooped awkwardly in front of Annie, touching one shoulder lightly with his rough hand.

"You better get home, change your clothes now, Annie."

Suddenly the last two days began to come into focus, to be real. Her head pounded, something rose in her throat. "I think I'm going to be sick."

Lilly studied the backs of her strong brown hands. "Annie, life is a test. The good Lord gives everybody all they can bear—never more—so if you fail, He knows it's 'cause you wasn't trying your best." Tears clung to her lower lashes. "Always remember, whatever you love the most, want the most, is in mortal danger. Hold something back, don't never give your whole heart to anything. That way you'll have something left of yourself to survive on—whatever happens." After a long shudder, her eyes seemed pulled against her will toward Two-Time.

Two-Time banged his fork so angrily down on the table his coffee cup rattled. "That's not nothing in this world but poor nigger talk, nothing but an excuse for sleeping on the road 'cause the pavement's nice and warm, never mind cars and trucks bound to use the same road to get somewhere."

B.C. gave an abrupt bitter laugh that startled them all. "Guess we better get reconciled to sleeping in the cold, then."

Two-Time shook a huge fist angrily at B.C. "Guess you better get used to doing without sleep. A road is to go places on. This world was never meant to be just the waiting room for Heaven."

Like the Colossus in Annie's Greek mythology book, Two-Time stood spread-legged in the middle of the room, both arms above his head, his fists two tight balls. "You want something in this world, you go get it, then hang on to it with your hands, your feet, your fingernails, your teeth. Don't hold nothing back."

"Life ain't that way," Lilly said in a soft, tired voice, as if she had said this many times before. "The stiffer your back, the easier it is to bust."

"Rose didn't think so," Two-Time thundered.

B.C. gasped and looked from Lilly to Two-Time. Lilly shook her head in protest.

"No, I won't shush. Your own sister knew what I am saying was true, else I wouldn't be here."

"Shut your big mouth, Two-Time," Lilly snapped, sure again of her territory. "We'll all talk later. You children go wash your face and hands. It's time."

Instinctively, Annie reached for the heavy bureau to steady her shaking legs. "Come on, Sister Annie," Cookie whispered in her ear, "I'll walk you halfway."

*   *   *

The car had been parked at the curb since early morning, and the heat inside was stifling. Her mother carried a stiff cardboard fan with a wooden handle that said, "First Presbyterian Church, Winton, Alabama," on the back and had a picture of the Last Supper on the front. Jesus and the twelve apostles, dressed in cool white robes, made polite curtsies, then retreated as her mother snapped the fan back and forth.

Otis, Cookie, B.C., Lilly, and Two-Time left right before them from the front yard of the big house, riding in a long black Cadillac from the funeral parlor. Her father had stood stiffly, holding the door for them, his summer Panama held across his chest as they clambered awkwardly into the huge car. Just before he ducked inside the door, Otis touched the brim of his own hat lightly with one finger, and Annie saw her father nod.

At the Elijah Baptist Church, her father pulled his car up to the curb, and their doors were immediately opened by men in dark suits, gleaming white shirts, and narrow ties with large jeweled stickpins. Each wore a white carnation in his lapel.

As her mother stood beside the car smoothing her gloves, the Petuses' car pulled up behind theirs. "Isn't that sweet, Laurence? The Petuses have come too." Her father nodded and spoke solemnly to the dark, dignified men on either side of him.

Inside the sanctuary of the church, they were led to a section of the pews on the right side specially marked with large white bows for the white mourners. The Trammell family was given the place of honor on the front row of the side pews. Both side sections faced the center section of pews so that Annie sat directly opposite Cookie but at right angles to her.

The church was full and, though the congregation sat silently, full of sounds. Overhead, ancient ceiling fans clacked softly, each in its own irregular rhythm. Wooden pews creaked under shifting weight, and shoes moving on bare wooden floors made the scratchy, hesitant sounds of a soft-shoe dance. Just behind Cookie, a hungry baby fussed as he tugged at the buttons of his mother's blouse. A determined fly made Annie flick her arm once, twice, again before he left to find his way to an open window. Outside, the gears of a large truck clashed as the driver impatiently made the long back-road detour around the town.

The sleepy peace was broken suddenly, as ushers moved to open metal folding chairs across the back of the church for latecomers. As though this were a signal, a heavy silence fell over the room. Feet and hands were still; even children sat motionless, holding their breath. Two or three women in short white dresses, like nurses or maids at a party wear, moved down each aisle. Each one had a large corsage of carnations and lilies of the valley pinned on her shoulder. A low hum seemed to vibrate from them, just at the threshold of Annie's hearing.

Reluctantly Annie followed them with her eyes as they moved to the front of the church and passed in front of the casket that Annie had carefully avoided looking at. The long, silver-gray casket lay just below the podium, its lid covered with a blanket of red carnations. On each side of the casket were half-a-dozen or so beribboned wreaths and sprays of flowers that filled the air with their heavy sweetness.

On the podium, in an outsized, ornately carved chair, just under the plaque giving the Sunday school attendance figures, sat the Reverend Titus Williams. His close-shaved head was tipped slightly forward, and his eyes were closed behind his gold-rimmed spectacles—an attitude not quite of prayer, but of listening all the same. He wore a crimson fez with a long golden tassel which swung lightly against his sunken cheek in the breeze of the ceiling fans. His suit was powder blue, and the coat appeared to be cut like an old-fashioned frock coat, except much longer. It hung down over his knees like a skirt when he was seated.

The humming ladies in white nodded solemnly to Reverend Williams as they passed him to take their places in the first two rows in the choir loft behind him. When they were all in their places, Reverend Williams, without raising his head or opening his eyes, lifted his arms dramatically and called for the Mockingbirds to help him in his hour of grief. Slowly their hum became a sigh, then a low moan of sliding notes; shoulder touching shoulder, they leaned slowly left then right, like tall pines resisting the sad song the wind would have them sing.

Whole rows in the center section of pews began to moan softly and sway back and forth, following the Mockingbirds with upturned eyes.

Tears had streamed silently down the gentle Lilly's face from the moment she stepped into the church, and now even B.C. yielded to the steady pressure on either side and swayed back and forth, his eyes closed, his face looking smooth and young.

Annie's eyes stayed on the Mockingbirds as they beckoned and cajoled grief upon grief into the heavy air. Only her mother's tense body and her hand placed firmly on Annie's knee kept her body still and her loneliness pinned tightly inside her.

Reverend Williams stood and lifted his arms high over his head. The moaning and swaying stopped, but the Mockingbirds continued their low, vibrant hum.

One of Reverend Williams's arms dropped heavily toward the casket at his feet. "And there, Lord, lies one who knew what suffering meant!"

Laurence Trammell stirred uneasily in his seat.

"And what woman here today doesn't?" Reverend Williams cried, nodding so vigorously that even Louise Trammell was moved to nod along with all the other women in the congregation.

After each phrase, the Mockingbirds' hum became a short cry, a muted crescendo of pain, then subsided once again.

"She tended the sick, fed the hungry, clothed the naked, cheered the sorrowing, and now she's gone to her just reward."

"Amen, amen," came from a deep voice in the center section.

"Streets of gold! Robes of silk!"

"Amen," said a different voice.

"Ambrosia! Heavenly music!"

"Amen, amen!"

Then Reverend Williams's glowing face frowned. He stabbed a long, thin finger at his narrow chest.

"But what about us, Lord? We needed Rose Holloway. There was much work left for her to do."

"Aah," sighed the Mockingbirds angrily.

Annie watched, grateful but frightened for this tall, cadaverous man who dared to shake his finger at the Lord.

Reverend Williams cocked his head solemnly as if waiting. "Behold," he said, a smile breaking across his face, "we are not left empty-handed. No, no. Rose, our beloved friend, planted four seeds, watered and tended them before she was called to her heavenly rest."

"Aah."

"Brothers and sisters, the fruit is ours! Praise the Lord!"

Here the Reverend Williams leaned over his podium and crooked one finger at B.C. and Cookie and the other at Annie. Ruth-baby had long since fallen asleep across her mother's lap.

As she stood, her knees shaking, her fingers gripping the pew in front of her, Annie felt every eye in the church upon her. What seemed like a brown rainbow of faces solemnly examined the fruit Rose had left them. She felt her mother straighten indignantly and heard Ruth-baby's soft even breath. "Sit down, Annie," her mother whispered from behind her fan.

"Where there were two hands, there are eight; where there was one sweet voice, there are four; where there was one true believer, there are four, Lord," cried the Reverend Williams, with a flourish of his wrist. "You are plenteous in your mercy!"

A sea of happy eyes turned back toward Reverend Williams. Annie still stood awkwardly in her place, as did Cookie and B.C. Reverend Williams seemed to have forgotten them completely. His voice dropped to a whisper.

"Now, friends, it is time to say good-bye. To send our beloved flower, Rose, lighthearted on her way. Give a Hallelujah, if you please."

"Hallelujah," sighed the congregation softly.

"Lighthearted on her way." Reverend Williams admonished them again.

"Hallelujah," came the exultant cry, and Annie felt a shiver of joy sweep through her body.

Two of the dark-suited ushers moved silently to remove the blanket of flowers and to open the upper half of the casket. Row after row, smiling or weeping, the congregation filed past Rose's body. Many squeezed her hand or placed a small flower or ribbon in her folded arms. Then the family stood, and Two-Time helped a weeping Lilly and stunned B.C. into the aisle. Otis, his arm around Cookie, moved shakily behind them.

Then Reverend Williams held out his arms to invite the side pews to come forward. Annie turned to look down at her mother. Louise Trammell gripped the sleeping Ruth-baby and shook her head. Then she lifted her small face toward Annie. Bitter loneliness lay like a black pool in her eyes.

Laurence Trammell stood slowly, his eyes rimmed with tears, and held out his hand to Annie. Together they walked behind Otis and Cookie to the front of the church.

The Mockingbirds were singing now, about Beulah Land. Rose had on her best dress, the pink linen one with a white lace collar that she had used for weddings and when she presented the secretary's report in church once a quarter. She seemed thinner to Annie and not quite happy in her sleep. Her father paused a moment in front of the casket and Annie saw his tears fall on the brim of the hat he clutched in his hand. Annie kept her eyes on Rose's soft dimpled hands. She grieved, but remembering her mother's eyes, she could not weep.

Then the casket was closed, and the congregation followed it into the bright sunshine of the cemetery beside the church. The silver-gray casket was lowered on creaking leather straps into the red earth. The Reverend Williams said something Annie didn't hear, then a buzz broke out among the crowd, and Annie felt herself being swept away by a gentle tide, back among the tombstones to the front of the church and into her father's waiting car.

The ride home was a silent one. Her father, from where Annie sat beside the sleeping Ruth-baby in the back seat, looked as if his thoughts were far away. Her mother sat stiffly beside him, in rigid protest against some unseen foe.

When they pulled into the driveway, her father cut the engine and slumped tiredly over the wheel.

"For heaven's sake, Laurence," Louise began, but Laurence did not move, and her voice trailed away. Slowly she raised trembling hands to her hat. Carefully she removed two hat pins and replaced them in the crown of the hat and put the hat in her lap.

"I'm going down to Rose's," Annie said quickly into the silence and reached for the door handle.

Louise watched Annie hurry with long, loose strides toward the pasture gate. "Look at that walk," she said quietly. "It's impossible."

Laurence did not lift his head. "Louise, it doesn't matter how she walks."

Louise stared bitterly at her husband's back. "Just like that! It doesn't matter, Louise! For twenty-six years my papa trained me, scolded me, lectured me on being a Fairbault, a real lady: how to walk, how to talk, how to think, how to feel. Why, I was supposed to be the backbone of the South, the key to our whole way of living. I was Papa's only child, and I loved him, so I set myself to fulfill his dreams.

"For twenty-six years I waited for someone who 'measured-up,' according to Papa's lights, that is, but no one ever did." Louise Trammell twisted in her seat, her face flushed with her agitation. "By the time I finally realized Papa's world didn't exist, I didn't know how to belong to any other. Then he just turned his face to the wall and died." Her lips pulled back showing narrow white teeth. "I'll never forgive Papa."

"Your Papa couldn't very well help dying, Louise," Laurence stated softly.

Something like hatred flared in his wife's usually fathomless lilac eyes. "Not his dying. I could have stood that. It was the rest. It was all the lies. The jewelry of Mama's that was sent off to be reset for me and never came back. Tales of anxious suitors who whispered to Papa in town but never came to the house, for fear of rushing me. Drinking his sherry all the afternoon, while he filled my head with a world that wasn't there." She dropped her head into her hands. "Uncle Jake, not even kin, except by marriage, gave Papa money every month to tide him over—Uncle Jake, one of the 'merchant class' Papa was always poking fun at."

Louise lifted her eyes and, with a shudder, faced her husband. "Oh, gradually I knew, but I didn't know what to do or where to turn. At the end, Papa would do nothing at all except spin daydreams. I was so terrified of what would become of me, I would have married a sharecropper."

Laurence turned to gaze unseeing across the backyard. He had dreaded this conversation for so long that, now it was actually happening, it seemed almost over-rehearsed. The pain was there, but duller than he had expected, more bearable than he had expected.

He had always known that there had been no money at the end. When your wife's father dies, you learn those things. But he had not known that she knew. He had always wondered why she had chosen him, and the answer was perversely comforting. He had not fooled her with his charm and good looks. Laurence turned his head further away and resisted the mocking laughter he felt rising in his throat. All these years they had suffered. He, because he thought he had rushed a young woman into marriage, carefully hiding his unloveableness in one supreme burst of subterfuge that failed him as soon as the marriage was accomplished. And Louise, had she suffered any less? Her pride and terror had made her just as anxious to deceive him as he had been to deceive her. Her voice broke the stillness.

"The idea of sewing and cooking and having babies and . . . loving a man other than Papa terrified me. I would actually get faint. But instead of getting impatient or angry with me, you seemed anxious to pay some kind of homage." She drew a deep breath. "It seemed such an easy role to play. And whenever I was tempted to shatter my glass cage, the terror returned. You would hate me. Worse yet, you would leave me."

Laurence felt her turn toward him, but he kept his gaze on the yard, thinking only that it would soon be all over.

"You're too good for your own good, Laurence Trammell. You know that, don't you? Goodness sticks out on you like a bad case of warts."

"Louise, that's not true, I . . . "

Her voice hardened. "You almost force people to take advantage of you." A small sigh made Laurence turn at last toward her.

"No, that's not true. That's just another excuse I've used all these years. The truth is that I knew you'd never desert a wife who was sickly and helpless. And never demand anything of her either. The truth is that I'm not good like you, Laurence. I don't even want to be." She sighed again. "I am, after all, my father's daughter."

Tiredness tugged at Laurence's neck and shoulders. Only with a concentrated effort did he remain erect against the seat. "Louise," he said, "that's all in the past now—all dead, and you're alive."

Louise gave a short mocking laugh. "Am I? I never wanted your life, Laurence, and I was too frightened to make my own. For almost thirteen years, I have watched Rose Holloway live the best parts of my life for me." She leaned back against the seat.

"Well, Laurence, I'm too tired to be frightened any more. I would gladly trade my glass cage for Rose's casket."

Laurence's lips parted slowly, and he leaned forward, his whole face drawn in an effort to find the right words.

Watching him, Louise drew herself erect. "Laurence, I know everything you've tried to keep from me. I know about the bombing, and that Annie and Cookie were witnesses. I know they've made statements and that is one reason you want Cookie and B.C. to leave town today before the trial starts." She paused, her face paling. "I know that Annie is going to testify in two days."

Laurence said nothing, waiting, disbelieving. This could not be the Louise he knew.

"Will the men be let off?"

Without looking at his wife, Laurence shook his head. "There's no way I can predict that, Louise. They could be." For a long moment he was silent. "Sheriff Coggins thinks that the most they will get will be six months."

Louise gasped, but she did not cry out. "Does it have to be done?" she asked.

"I believe so, Louise. There comes a time when you have to do right because it's right to do right, no matter if what you do doesn't fix everything, even if that one act won't change much at all."

"Even if it means your daughter will bear the brunt of it?"

Silence as thick as an evening fog filled the car, and part of a long forgotten line came to Laurence. "The sins of the fathers . . . But doesn't the cycle have to be stopped somewhere, Louise?"

"I am going with you to the trial," said Louise, only to have a sudden spasm of coughing leave her breathless.

Anxiously Laurence reached for her hand, but Louise pulled away. Her eyes narrowed, and a dark flush spread across her cheeks. "If you say, 'Now, Louise,' Laurence Trammell, I'll never speak to you again as long as I live."

Laurence exhaled as if she had hit him in the stomach. He threw back his head and laughed. The sound inside the closeness of the car was deafening. Louise's mouth trembled, her flush deepened, then drained into angry splotches. She stretched out an arm that trembled as if she were a bird whose flight had been disrupted by a sudden crosscurrent of air. Then, dropping her hand lightly on her husband's shoulder, she smiled. Hesitantly. In a moment, her light clear laughter joined Laurence's.

With tears streaming down both cheeks, Laurence turned to look at the sleeping Ruth-baby. "Did you hear that, Baby? Did you hear that?" he cried.

*   *   *

Two-Time studied the large watermelon carefully. It was unusually long and slender. Darker green stripes with crenelated edges ran lengthwise, like the tight plaits on Cookie's head. Cold creek water still ran in tiny rivulets down the sides. Picking up a long, sharp kitchen knife, Two-Time made a neat incision just to the left of the deep navel at one end. He pushed both thumbs deep into the incision and, with a satisfied grunt, ripped the watermelon into two oblong halves.

"Did you see that?" cried B.C.

"Life ain't all ripping watermelons," Lilly cautioned mildly.

Two-Time only snorted and handed each of them a big piece of dripping melon. Lilly took hers and sat on the edge of the porch, kicking her feet like any girl, and leaning out sideways as far as she dared, to keep the sweet juice off her dress. She caught the seeds daintily between her teeth and dropped them onto the baked clay soil below her. B.C. carried his to the far end of the porch. He tore off large chunks of the red meat with his teeth and spit the seeds like bullets at the bantam hens as they pecked lazily in the dust below him.

Annie struggled shyly with the question she'd been turning in her mind all afternoon. Finally the words seemed to take shape on their own. "Lilly, please stay. You and Two-Time don't need to go back to Detroit. Mrs. Petus still needs you very much. Every day she calls Mama and cries and says she just can't get any decent help since you're gone."

Two-Time threw back his head as if to laugh, but Lilly waved a hand, and he bent again over the watermelon, slicing the second half into long, fat pieces.

Encouraged, Annie went on quickly, "And Cookie, and B.C., and me, we need you, Lilly." She glanced along the porch that seemed empty and still, a beached boat that wouldn't sail again until the tide had turned.

Lilly glanced anxiously toward Two-Time. He heaved a piece of rind that smashed wetly against a sapling. The bantams were flapping toward it before it hit the dust.

"That's a good idea, honey," Lilly began.

"Tell her, Lilly," Two-Time broke in, his voice a low growl. "In a hundred years, haven't you learned nothing about killing folks with kindness."

Annie looked from Lilly's face to Two-Time's and wanted to cover her ears. "Never mind," she said softly, "it was a dumb idea."

Lilly shook her head. "You are right, you know. Cookie and B.C. do need somebody. I been thinking that myself."

The cabin seemed to shudder a little and dip in a freshening breeze. She left me out, thought Annie, more hurt than surprised at the omission. "Reverend Askew said the sins of omission are the worst kind," she heard herself saying stiffly to no one in particular.

"Annie, you have your mama and daddy and Ruth-baby."

Annie concentrated fiercely on an anger that seemed to burn in her stomach. Like a piece of pine kindling, it glowed hotter and hotter. She stared out over the pasture. What does Lilly know? It's Lilly and Two-Time's extra weight holding us here. This boat isn't beached.

"Go back to Detroit—please, go back," she said aloud, her voice an awful croak.

Lilly smiled in relief. "Why, honey, that's what I been trying to . . . been afraid of telling you all day. We leaving for Detroit on the four-o'clock Sky Chief today. Cookie and B.C., too. It's all been decided."

"Cookie can't. She's got to be in the trial with me."

Cookie nodded. "I want to stay. Me and Otis can live here."

Lilly turned sorrowful eyes on Cookie and Annie. "I guess Sheriff Coggins thinks he just needs one of you to say what you saw. Besides, honey, girls need a mama. Otis don't know nothing 'bout raising young girls, and he's at the store all day long."

The cabin shuddered but still held. The tide was rising fast now; they wouldn't need to jettison much weight after all—something small would do.

For the first time, Otis spoke. Rising from his cane-bottomed chair, he went to Annie and put an arm around her shoulders. "Rose decided it herself, Annie. Made me and Mr. Laurence promise if anything happened to her . . ." His shoulders sagged. "I reckon she was right, Annie, though I never would have seen it myself."

"You'd go, too, Otis?"

"No, honey, reckon I'm too old for Detroit. It just seems like a step down to me—that's how behind I am."

So, there was not much time. She and Otis must both be left behind, and before four, or the tide would recede again, and no one would ever know where this boat was bound. As Annie looked past the porch's warped, weather-beaten planks out over the pasture, no one spoke. The only sound was the sagging screen door tapping gently now in the breeze.

Had there ever been a cabin, a pasture, a bell on the hill, or only this impatient sea, and this tiny ship, waiting for a stronger wind or a lighter load, to finish its journey begun long ago on another dark, now-forgotten sea.

CHAPTER 22

AT FOUR TWENTY-TWO the Sky Chief still had not come. Twenty-two minutes full of feelings pulling them up and pushing them down.

B.C. stood a little apart, one foot resting lightly on the inside rail. As soon as they got to the station, he had gone and asked Peter Riggins, the toothless old stationmaster, which track the four-o'clock Sky Chief would come in on. Now he stood with his foot on the rail—waiting, Annie thought, for the first vibrations of a magic current that was going to bring him back to life. His back was toward Annie, straight and tense under his starched shirt. His eyes were pinned on the narrow cut in the bank where the tracks turned for their long curve around the back of the Petuses' and Trammells' pasture toward—Annie supposed—Detroit.

Two-Time paced restlessly, only four long strides taking him from one side of the platform to the brink of the other. His face and hair, his whole body, seemed bristling with energy, like a circus tiger pacing in his cage when he hears the band's fanfare and the metallic rattle of the chute gates between him and the arena.

Lilly moved quietly around the platform, crossing behind Two-Time to move a bag, refold a coat, or absently stop to pick up an old Lucky Strike package.

When Two-Time reached the far side of the platform and turned, bearing down again on their small group of belongings, she would pause until he passed and then cross quickly behind him like a piece of flotsam bobbing in the stern of a speed boat. For a while, Annie watched Lilly's face and took comfort from it. She seemed neither reluctant to leave nor anxious to go, but rather determined that where they were now should be comfortable and neat. Like a small brown bird who makes a new nest every day, she swept back and forth across the platform until the nest was as ready as she could manage. Then she opened her parasol and settled comfortably on a bench, her belongings all gathered at her feet. Only occasionally did she glance nervously up the track. Did she hear a faint whistle blow, or was it B.C., standing defiantly outside the circle of her nest, that her darting eyes fell upon?

Annie tried not to look at her father, but no matter where she sat on the small platform, the jerky movements of his hands and the long curve of his back seemed to fill the corner of her eye.

He held his heavy gold watch chain in one hand and fingered the small ivory-handled knife that hung from the middle of it with his other hand. Every few seconds he dropped the knife into his pocket, extracted his pocket watch with two long fingers, and stared at the familiar Roman numerals. When they had first gotten to the station, he had automatically chosen a seat facing the tracks and turned to see that there was room for Otis beside him. But now his small maddening movements seemed designed to keep him from seeing the tracks or Otis sitting beside him.

In all the movement—smooth, jerky, slow, fast, erratic—of all the people around him, Otis was an island of stillness. The sun glinted off his round, gold-rimmed spectacles, hiding his eyes, but from the tilt of his head, the slight turn of his shoulders, you could tell he was looking down the long stretch of track—not toward Detroit, but the other way. Hank Ketchum had told Annie it went south all the way through Georgia to Florida.

Cookie sat beside Annie, her feet swinging off the edge of the platform. When she saw her daddy looking steadily down the tracks, she had gotten on to him. "Detroit is the other way, Daddy," she had said, ashamed and angry at his ignorance.

Otis did not smile nor move his head, only answered softly. "I reckon I know which way Detroit is, miss."

"Well, what you staring backwards for, then?"

"Cookie—!" Laurence Trammell jerked his eyes forcefully from his watch, his eyes as angry as Cookie's.

Still Otis did not move. "I wasn't looking at where you and B.C. are fixing to go, but where I come from."

"Otis," said Annie, "you always lived right here, just like us."

Otis shook his head the least bit. "Nope. My daddy and mama walked me down that there railroad track. Don't know where we started from anymore. Daddy wasn't a talker. Met your granddaddy in a wagon, though, at the water tower. I was sick, and he fetched us to the house." He smiled the least bit at the corners of his mouth. "Your granddaddy was new to town, too. A stranger, like, and lonesome. That's when my daddy and your granddaddy began."

"Is that right, Daddy?" Annie asked.

Laurence Trammell wrapped both his long arms across his stomach as if wounded by the simple story.

Nervously, Annie caught Cookie's hand.

Laurence Trammell lifted his head and looked at them, his eyes avoiding their locked hands.

"That's right," he said flatly, ". . . if only he had kept going."

Otis shook his head. "He had a wife and child. They hadn't the strength."

Laurence Trammell squeezed his eyes shut. "My father was wrong to pick them up. Your father, at least, could have finished his trip."

"He did finish his trip, Mr. Laurence. He had already come far as could be expected. I was the one stayed, never going farther."

The two men faced each other now, curved toward each other with the sloped shoulders of old men.

"Because of me, only because of me, Otis."

Annie wanted to move away, but a heavy lump somewhere deep inside her kept her pinned to the platform like a sack of flour.

A finger, stiff, yellow-jointed, like an old piece of bamboo cane, poked at her shoulder.

" . . . thirty minutes more, at least," old Riggins, the stationmaster, said.

Cookie pulled one of her daddy's big white handkerchiefs from her pocket. "Jumping Jehoshaphat, it's hot enough to fry eggs out here now," she said. First wiping her wet forehead, she wrapped the handkerchief bandanna style around her neck and stood up. Lilly had pomaded Cookie's hair into a sleek, shining cap; the sun made it glisten like a wet duck's back. Now she glared angrily at Laurence and Otis. "I'm not sitting here one more second."

"Good idea," Laurence said, automatically searching his pockets for the right coin, but Otis had a quarter all ready in his outstretched hand.

Cookie looked uncertainly at the billboard on top of Carter's Drugs, just visible over the fire station, then back along the tracks toward Hank Ketchum's and shook her head unhappily.

Way down the track, a dark, shabby figure stooped and something glittered a moment in his hand and disappeared. A wide smile broke over Cookie's face.

"We'll just walk down the tracks a piece."

"Not in your patent leather shoes," came Lilly's voice from the end of the platform.

Cookie hesitated, and Annie bumped into her from behind.

"We didn't tell Hank Ketchum good-bye," Cookie said. She glanced back at Laurence and Otis, still leaning toward each other—parentheses around a void—and leaped off the platform, heedless of Lilly's plaintive protests behind her. When they passed B.C., he turned his head as if they spoiled his view.

Feet and knees high, like majorettes, Cookie and Annie scampered across the four gleaming ribbons of track and ran down the sliding gravel toward the moving, stooping figure who had almost reached the long curve in the track where it turned toward north.

"Hank, Hank Ketchum," both girls shouted until they were too winded to shout and run.

They were almost beside him before Hank raised his

eyes from the tracks and looked at them in that calm, deadpan way of his. His shaggy brows lifted quizzically, and he shook his head slowly, disapprovingly. "Don't you girls know it's one hundred and one degrees in the shade? That's no way to be moving on a day like today."

Annie and Cookie obediently walked the last few steps to draw even with Hank.

"What you found this afternoon?" Cookie asked to change the subject.

Hank's face brightened. Holding them up one by one, he showed them: a piece of rubber hose; one man's leather house shoe, almost new; some rusty six-penny nails; and a double-faced mirror with a metal rim and a missing handle. One side was just a mirror. The other side made your face jump out at you, huge and blurry.

"And where you going this fine day, Cookie?" he asked, leaving both girls openmouthed. He took a few steps, then turned back. "Stopped you in your tracks, didn't I?" He giggled loudly at his joke, one hand rubbing the stubble on his chin.

"Who told you?" demanded Cookie.

Hank chuckled again. "You did: grease on your hair, patent leather shoes, standing around on the platform just before the Sky Chief is due in." He squinted at the luminous, cloudless sky.

"Late, I imagine."

"But, Hank," Annie suddenly heard herself shouting, "you don't understand. "She's not coming back. She is just leaving, and I'm staying here!"

Cookie let out a sliding cry and tugged at the handkerchief around her neck.

Hank's face puckered.

"Let's us have a nice Coca-Cola," he said, and turned

off the tracks onto the path that led to his hut. Annie and
Cookie followed, sliding and stumbling behind him.

By the time Cookie and Annie sat down on the log in
front of Hank's hut, he had already brought three warm
cokes and opened them with an old, rusty church key and
sat down on the log between them.

The dark warm liquid burned Annie's throat and tears
started to her eyes.

She and Cookie threw themselves at Hank and each
other at the same moment, their cokes spilling unheeded
across the thirsty red clay.

Hank put an arm around one and leaned his head back
against a dusty chinaberry tree.

After a long while their steady sobs ebbed away into
two long sighs.

Then the smell of Hank—creosote and sweat—and the
sweet smell of coke filled Annie's nostrils, and the blood
surged into her neck and face. What a baby she was! Even
Ruth-baby wouldn't crawl up in smelly, dumb old Hank
Ketchum's lap and bawl like a new calf. She was afraid to
move for fear of shaking loose his high, roller-coaster
giggle.

She saw Cookie get just as still on Hank's other side,
her face pressed into his chest where a pocket used to be.
She stole a cautious look at Hank's face. A small fly had
landed on his face just beside his nose, but he seemed not
to know it was there. Beside the fly ran a stream of tears.
As the stream widened, the fly shook a dainty foot and
flew away.

Insect drones filled the air with sound as thick and hot
as the steam through the grate in the alley behind the
cleaners.

Hank shifted his weight, stretching his legs, though he

kept an arm lightly around Annie's and Cookie's waists. As if he had been talking to them for a long time and just paused for breath, he said in a singsong, faraway voice, ". . . Dora Mae wasn't a bit bigger than you girls in her shiny sort of blue dress with the white ribbon round the waist. I could put my hands around that waist and the thumbs would overlap all the way."

He shook his head slowly, and a hot tear splattered on Annie's arm. "She would of stayed if she could. She said so herself. But it wouldn't of done no good. Like putting bugs in a jar.

"I shouldn't call her Dora Mae. She hated that name. Said ever since she could toddle, boys and men been hollering 'Dora, May-I?' at her. She wanted Dora or Doreen." Hank paused, and his face turned the rusty red of the railroad banks behind him. "What do I know? When I was a little boy, I wanted to play May-I too, but I couldn't get it right, so they never let me."

" 'Hank, would you get my shoe?'

"Dora, May-I?

" 'Hank, would you comb my hair?'

"Dora, May-I?

"I wouldn't never have forgotten to say 'May-I?' to Dora Mae."

"Hank," said Cookie, sitting up straight, "was you engaged to Dora? I heard someone say. . ." she stopped, embarrassed at the memory of the jokes about Hank's mythical engagement.

But Hank smiled proudly. "We was. Official. Dora took my mama's ring to wear forever and gave me her locket."

He leaned his head back against the tree and stared

down at the tracks. "She jumped off the Sky Chief good as any man, in a blowing cloud of blue dress and yellow hair. Scared the wits out of me. I half broke my neck getting down there to see what poor girl done killed herself. She was laying full out on her back in the Johnson grass. Like one of them Coca-Cola girls. So clean and pink you'd hate to put a finger out, even to see was she real. Then she opens her eyes, and she laughs at the sight of me—said my hair looked like it was going for a walk." He shook his head, his no-color eyes shining. "What a tongue that girl had! Mama had just died and Sheriff Coggins had explained about me having to leave our house in town and all. That's when I came down here and fixed me this place to live. And that first day, when nothing felt like home, here comes Dora Mae, who never had no home at all, and made it a home before the sun set."

Hank nodded proudly toward the hut. "Dora Mae's own hands found every piece of furniture, every pot and pan, its own special place.

"One morning—Monday, she said it was—she squinted at me in that funny way she had and said she could tell I was on my feet again and she better catch the four-o'clock Sky Chief.

"I don't mind saying I cried like a baby. I begged that girl to marry me. Said I would throw myself in front of whichever train she left on."

Cookie slapped her hand over her mouth. "What did she say, Hank?"

The huge head slumped to his chest. "She said she would—would marry me—Hank Ketchum." He wagged his head in disbelief.

"But I saw her blue eyes follow the Sky Chief down the

tracks that afternoon and the next morning, and I know'd it wasn't no good for her."

He grinned and tears slid over an apple cheek, cutting a new path across the red dust that coated his face like fine powder. "So we got engaged instead. I thought of putting it in the paper, and went down there, but Miss Thornton down at the paper said it wasn't a good idea, 'cause I didn't have no picture of Dora Mae. She told me she'd tell a lot of folks around on her own though. That was right nice, wasn't it? But I wish I had had me a picture."

"Isn't she ever coming back?"

"I reckon so," Hank said, "if the Sky Chief ever comes full circle."

"Are you still engaged with her gone?"

Hank looked down. "Will you still be friends, even with Cookie gone?"

Cookie and Annie looked at each other and nodded.

"I can come back from Detroit, Lilly says, maybe Christmas," said Cookie.

"You're lucky all right," Hank answered. "I don't reckon Dora Mae was going no place with no definite name, so how's she to know when it's time to turn around and go back again?"

"Nobody told me about Christmas," said Annie.

"Well, Lilly only said 'Maybe,' and Christmas seems too far away to be cheerful about."

Annie studied Cookie's glistening face, puckered against the sun. Suddenly Annie remembered the story her father had often told her about catching lightning bugs to chase away the dark.

"Cookie, were you like a lightning bug I caught and put in a glass jar?"

Cookie screwed her eyes even tighter until her lashes disappeared. Annie thought of her father and Otis leaning toward each other, two uncertain question marks, each question answered only with its own mirror image. How heavy questions are, she thought: her father's question bending his back, pulling him down; Hank's making him long to throw himself in front of the Sky Chief.

Cookie opened her eyes, "I guess I am more like a bug that was born in a jar."

Annie bit her lip to still its sudden quiver. "People only catch lightning bugs because they're scared of being alone in the dark."

"I know."

A long, eerie whistle made both Cookie and Annie turn their heads toward the tracks.

Hank rose. "It's just hollering up Titusville. Plenty of time to mosey back to the station. Don't need no sunstrokes today." Cookie and Annie seemed unable to move, as if they had rooted into the hard, red clay.

"Y'all, come on," Hank urged, taking them by the hand. "I'll walk you halfway."

EPILOGUE

The town was more crowded than Annie had ever seen it, even on a Saturday. Cars and pickups lined the curb all the way around the courthouse, and the lawn was littered with bikes. The children, who weren't allowed inside the courtroom, were perched like birds on the low window-sills of the wide courthouse windows.

Uneasily, Annie moved on the hard bench. She had already given her testimony. Judge Hartman said just say what she and Cookie had seen, and she had. But he had not told her that Burt and Jeb Pierce would sit and glare at her across the room, nor that umpteen-dozen of their aunts and uncles and cousins would be lining the walls, also staring. Her mother and father, sitting on either side of her, appeared not to notice them at all.

Annie felt her father tense and looked up to see a juryman hand a small slip of paper to the judge. Judge Hartman scowled and cleared his throat. "This court," he said, "finds Burt and Jeb Pierce guilty of one count of accidental homicide. They are sentenced to two years in jail."

Behind Annie, Sheriff Coggins leaned forward to whisper in her father's ear. "That means six months—just like I said, Laurence."

Laurence Trammell nodded, and slowly and

deliberately rose, stepped into the aisle, and stood back to let Annie and her mother pass.

They were almost to the front door of the courthouse when a large, red-faced man in dirty overalls stepped in front of them.

"Young lady, you caused a lot of trouble for my friends today," he said, his voice a low growl.

A silent crowd gathered, carefully keeping a little distance from the man in the stained overalls.

"No, she didn't cause the trouble, I did," said Laurence. "What have you got to say about it? We were only telling the truth."

The angry man bellowed in disbelief. "The truth! You was only protecting a damn, black, troublemaking nigger, you mean!"

Laurence was silent, searching the man's face. "We cannot talk," he finally said. "We both know with absolute certainty that we are right. Nothing will convince either of us differently. And so we all lose; and we pass our defeat on to a new generation, crippling their minds with anger and hate, or forcing them to flee."

The man's red face turned a shade darker. "Damn it. You cut out that double talk."

Turning away, almost as if he had not heard the man, Laurence turned to Annie and Louise. Louise was holding Annie's hand tightly. She was so still and pale that, except for her red hair, she might have been one of the marble statues that flanked the courthouse doorway. Laurence held his elbow away from his side for Louise to take.

Behind him, towering above his head, the man in the overalls raised a fist over his head as if he meant to fell

Laurence with a single blow. Deftly Louise slipped her trembling arm into her husband's and turned him. Holding the man's eyes with her own, she walked between her husband and her daughter toward the door.

Outside, on the sidewalk, a small cluster of blacks suddenly got news of the verdict. A low murmer ran through the crowd. Then, without changing expressions, the people turned and began moving toward the far side of town, each person pausing for a moment to nod silently to Laurence Trammell. Only one man, small and slump-shouldered, remained behind.

When his eyes caught Laurence Trammell's, they filled with tears. "So," he said softly when Laurence stopped in front of him.

Laurence fell into step on the other side of his friend, and they moved again toward home, but Louise released her grip on her husband's arm.

Laurence turned back for a moment, but Louise shook her head and gripped Annie's hand even tighter. Laurence fell into step again with Otis and the two moved off, their heads bent together in old familiar silence.